"It's not a story of future heroism. It's not even, really, a story about robots. It's a story of live and failure and expectations. It is, perhaps, in its relentless examination of one woman's life, one of the most realistic science fiction stories ever told."
Michael Ann Dobbs for io9

"Cassandra Rose Clarke has proven she can write with the best of them in this one and I expect this was just a taste of what is to come from her."
The Troubled Scribe

"I absolutely adored this novel. It made me laugh. It made me cry. It made me think about the true meaning of love. True love, not something cut out of cardboard and taped together with lies."
Insomnia of Books

"I just absolutely loved this book. The characters are spot on, the writing is beautiful, the pacing is deliberate but still absolutely engaging."
Karissa's Book Reviews

"Its fluid prose, naturalistic dialogue and pace make *The Assassin's Curse* supremely readable. And in Ananna, the young offspring of pirate stock, we have a heroine both spirited and memorable."
Stan Nicholls, author of the Orcs: First Blood *trilogy*

D0111890

PRAISE FOR CASSANDRA ROSE CLARKE

"A kick-ass pirate heroine gets into and out of (mostly into) trouble in this invigorating fantasy."
Kirkus Reviews

"Unique, heart-wrenching, full of mysteries and twists!"
Tamora Pierce, author of Alanna: The First Adventure

"An exciting and original YA novel with magic, pirates, myth and adventure, *The Assassin's Curse* will hook you in and keep you tugging on the line for the next book in Clarke's series."
USA Today

"Ananna of Tanarau is a delightfully irascible heroine, inhabiting a fascinating and fresh new world that I would love to spend more time in. Pirate ships? Camels? Shadow dwelling assassins? Yes please! Can I have some more?"
Celine Kiernan, author of the Moorhawke trilogy

"Inventive and individual storytelling about engaging and intriguing characters."
Juliet E McKenna, author of The Tales of the Einarinn and The Chronicles of the Lescari Revolution

"An enjoying, compelling read with a strong and competent narrator ... a highly satisfying adventure."
SFX Magazine

"A fun, quite often snarky, action-adventure tale filled with sorcery and elemental magic, political intrigue, strange and sometimes ethereal places, and interesting creatures."
Popcorn Reads

"*The Assassin's Curse* has a sweet mix of all my favorite things in a rip-roaring YA adventure read."
The Diary of a Bookworm

"Ananna and Naji's world is rich with magic and bursting with the potential for adventure."
Violin in a Void

"Cassandra Rose Clarke has landed herself on my teeny tiny list of authors to auto-buy."
Small Review

"*The Assassin's Curse* is what I would shamelessly call 'masterful'."
The Authoress

"I can't remember the last time I had this much fun reading a book."
www.fantasyliterature.com

"A story that will draw you in with its rich setting filled with assassins, pirates, magic, and two lead characters that you can't help but root for. A highly recommended read!"
Fantasy's Ink

"This is a book like no other YA book I've ever read, and I'm really hoping that it'll start a new trend. Please bring more pirates into YA!"
One Page at a Time

"An inventive debut with a strong narrative voice, a glimpse of an intriguing new world."
Adrian Tchaikovsky, author of the Shadows of the Apt series

CASSANDRA ROSE CLARKE

The Wizard's Promise

STRANGE CHEMISTRY
An Angry Robot imprint
and a member of the Osprey Group

Lace Market House,
54-56 High Pavement,
Nottingham,
NG1 1HW,
UK

Angry Robot/Osprey Publishing,
PO Box 3985,
New York,
NY 10185-3985,
USA

www.strangechemistrybooks.com
Strange Chemistry #30

A Strange Chemistry paperback original 2014

Cover design by Sarah J Coleman.
Set in Sabon by Argh! Oxford.

Distributed in the United States by Random House, Inc., New York.

ISBN 978 1 90884 474 3
Ebook ISBN 978 1 90884 475 0

Printed in the United States of America

9 8 7 6 5 4 3 2 1

CHAPTER ONE

I was picking ice berries for Mama's start-of-spring cake when a spark of magic smacked me in the side of the head. My basket hit the ground and berries rolled out over the mud, and I scowled at the little trail of amber lights darting back and forth through the air.

"Larus!" I shouted. "What do you want?"

The light flickered and coiled in on itself. For a moment I thought it was going to extinguish, since Larus doesn't exactly have the most reliable magic in Kjora. But instead it just zipped off to tell him where I was.

I cursed under my breath and knelt down in the soft, cool earth to gather up the escaped berries. A trail of light from Larus meant one thing – somebody had a message for me. Larus, untalented wizard though he may be, was still the only person in the village who had trained at the academy in the southerly seas and officially been named a wizard by the capital, and thus the only one people ever hired to do tracking spells. He took that job seriously, too, the prig. Like carting weather reports around the village made him important. It wasn't as if he had even trained someplace renowned, like the Undim Citadels.

So someone was looking for me. I knew it wasn't Mama or Papa or my brother Henrik, since they all knew this little road leading away from the sea was the best place to pick late-season ice berries. My friend Bryn never hired Larus for anything after he ruined one of her best dresses with a love charm. And nobody else in the village had any reason to send for me.

Except Kolur, of course. I'd bet my entire basket of berries Kolur was the one looking for me.

I cursed again.

The wind, still sharp-edged with winter's cold, blew through the bushes. I stuck my hand in the brambles and pulled out another handful of berries. This would probably be the last time I'd get to harvest them before next winter, and I wanted to collect as many as I could before Kolur's message ruined my day. That you could still pick the berries this late in the season was why Mama used them in her start-of-spring cakes, since she always said spring was as much a goodbye to winter as it was a hello to summer. Mama liked winter, for some reason. Papa always said it's because she grew up in the south, where heat is dangerous. I could never imagine it.

Larus took a long time following his tracking spell back to me. I'd managed to clear out most of the remaining berries by the time I spotted his tall, gangly figure up on the road. He raised one hand in greeting, the embroidered sleeve of his red wizard's cloak billowing out behind him.

"Hanna Euli!" he called out, as formal as if he were a wizard from the capital. "I have a message for you."

"Yeah, I noticed." I sighed and hooked my basket in the crook of my arm and hiked through the mud to the edge of the road. Larus watched me, his eyes big and blue and round. He wasn't much older than me, although I was still expected to treat him like an adult, given that he was an official wizard. I didn't, though.

"Is it Kolur?" I said. "It's Kolur, isn't it? Couldn't he have let me have a few days of spring?"

Larus cleared his throat and made a big show of pulling a scroll out of the cavernous depths of his sleeves. I sighed and shifted the basket of berries to my other arm. Larus unwound the scroll. It was a short one.

"Get on with it," I muttered.

Larus drew back his shoulders and held his head high. Delivering messages was pretty much the only wizardly thing there was for him to do around the village, so he always took it too seriously. "Kolur Icebreak wishes you to meet him at the village dock at the start of longshadow. He wishes to set sail for the Bathest Chain, as he–"

"What?" I tossed my basket to the side and stalked up to Larus, reaching to grab his scroll. He jerked it away from me and sparks of magic flew out between us, stinging my hand.

"Don't touch the scrolls," he said.

I glared at him and rubbed at my knuckles. I called on the wind, too, stirring it up from the south, but Larus just rolled his eyes like it didn't impress him.

"Tell Kolur I'll sail with him next week," I said. "I've got to help Mama with chores today."

"Let me finish, Hanna." Larus struck his messenger pose again. "For the Bathest Chain, as he's thrown the fortune for the coming weeks and found that the fishing will be excellent for the next few days. He's already spoken with your mother and knows that she can spare you."

I glowered at Larus. He coughed and looked down at his feet. I made the south wind stir his robes, tangling them up around his legs.

"Stop that," Larus said. "You know some child's trick doesn't make you a real wizard."

"Is there anything else?"

"No." Larus pulled a quill out of his sleeve. "Would you like to send a reply?"

"Do I have to pay for it?"

"All messages cost one common coin." He glared at me. "You know that."

"No thanks, then." I picked up my basket. Sometimes you can wheedle a free message out of Larus if he's in the right mood, but I should have known better than to try after teasing him with the wind. He doesn't like being reminded that I'm a better wizard than him, even if I am a girl.

Not that I needed to send a message. Kolur knew I would show up whether I wanted to or not, because I was his apprentice and he was friends with Mama, and between the two of them there was no way I could ever slack off work. I mostly just wanted to send him something rude so it would annoy him.

"Has the message been received?" Larus asked, back to playing the village wizard.

"Yeah, yeah." I ran my fingers over the ice berries, relishing the feel of their cool, hard skins against my fingers. The last crop and I probably wouldn't even get a slice of Mama's cake, since Henrik would eat every crumb by the time I got back. It was always that way, fishing with Kolur. He didn't go out for just one day – no, he had to go out for three or four at a time. Only way he could get a decent haul.

"Well, if there's nothing else," Larus said.

"There's not. Thanks for nothing."

He made a face at me. I didn't bother trying to retaliate, just left him there, making my way down to the road, toward the little stone house where I lived with my family.

When I walked up the muddy path, Mama was out in the garden, tending to the early-season seedlings she'd finished putting in the ground a few days ago. She waved, her hands streaked with dirt. I figured she'd been out here waiting for me, seeing as how she received word from Kolur before I did.

"Did you get the message?" She sat back on her heels. Mama's accent was different from mine and Papa's and everyone else's in the village, since she'd grown up speaking Empire her whole life. Normally I liked it, because it gave her voice this pretty melody like a song, but today even that wasn't enough to sway my annoyance.

"You knew!" I tossed the basket at her and she caught it, one-handed, not spilling a single berry. "Why didn't you just come tell me yourself?"

She smiled. "Oh, I don't like stepping in between your arrangements."

"Larus said he checked with you first!"

"You know what I mean." She stood up and tried to shake the mud from her trousers, although it didn't do much good. "It looks like you have a good crop of berries here."

I scowled.

"Oh, don't be like that." She came over to me and draped one arm over my shoulder. "You know you'd be bored if he hadn't sent for you."

"It's only just starting to get warm! The sun's out–" I gestured up at the sky "–and the south wind's blowing. I was going to practice my magic."

Mama gave me one of her long sideways looks. "You can practice aboard the *Penelope*." She paused. "You know, when I served aboard the *Nadir*, there were no days off, warm sun or not."

I'd heard this story before, and a million like it besides. "That's because the *Nadir* was a pirate ship. Fishing boats have rules. He can't just run me like a slave driver."

"And he's not," Mama said sharply. She lifted up the berries. "Come, let's go make the start-of-spring cake so you can have a piece before you leave this evening."

She strode out of the garden, and I shuffled along behind her, my hands shoved in the big pockets sewn into my dress. It was nice to be back inside, since for all my protestations about the warmth, the spring cold had been starting to get to me, and our house was always warm and cozy from the fire Mama kept burning at all times. Henrik was sprawled out in front of the hearth, pushing his little wooden soldiers around. He ignored both of us, and Mama stepped right over him to get to the tall table where she did all her hearth work.

"Are you going to help me, or you going to sulk?" she asked over her shoulder.

I crossed my arms over my chest and didn't answer. Mama took that as a yes to helping her, the way she always did, and handed me the berries. "Clean those off for me while I mix up the batter."

The basket dangled between us, and she was already pulling the little ceramic jar of flour toward herself with her free hand. She'd hold the basket there all day if she had to. I knew I'd lost. No fisherman's ever gone up against a pirate and won, that's what Papa's always saying. Although in his case, she just looted his heart.

I sat down on the floor next to the fire and started separating the stems and leaves from the berries. Henrik kept on ignoring me, he was so involved in his toy soldiers. Mama hummed to herself as she worked, an old pirate song about stringing up the sails. She'd sailed under one of the greatest pirates of the Pirate's Confederation, Ananna of the *Nadir*, and when she was my age, she was living on board Ananna's ship and sailing to all ends of the earth, fighting monsters and stealing treasure and basically having a far more interesting life than I could ever hope for. Sometimes I tried to imagine what it would be like to sail the seas in search of adventure instead of fish. I wondered about the sort of people I'd meet outside of Kjora, if they'd be as strange and different as all the elders in the village claimed, with antlers growing from their foreheads and cloven feet tucked inside their boots. Mama told me once that was a silly northern story, but I wanted to see for myself.

Mama met Papa when the *Nadir* blew off course and wound up in the waters off Kjora, where she and some of her crew hijacked Papa's fishing boat. Apparently, Papa had been so handsome back then that she'd taken one look at him and decided to stay on the islands – at least, that's how she told it. Papa said the story was a bit more complicated than that, but he never gave me any details.

At any rate, when Mama decided to stay, part of the deal to convince Ananna to let her go was that Mama'd name her firstborn daughter after her. And that turned out to be me. Of course, no one in the village could say "Ananna" right, so the name got distorted to Hanna. I didn't mind. I liked having two names, a fisherman's name and a pirate's name. I took it as a sign that someday I'd do something more with my life than work for Kolur, that I'd sail beyond the waters of Kjora and see the rest of the world and all the excitement it held.

I finished stripping the berries and then carted the basket over to the ice melt we kept next to the stove so

I could rinse off the dirt. By the time I'd finished that, Mama had the cake batter all whipped together in a bowl, and she let me stir the berries in before dumping the whole thing in the long, low pan she used for start-of-spring cakes. Henrik was still occupying the space in front of the hearth, and Mama had to shoo him aside like a fly so she could stick the cake into the heat.

"Did I ever tell you about the time Ananna and I stole a cake from the Emperor's own bakery?" Mama asked me. She turned to Henrik. "Sweetling, why don't you dry off the bowls?" He sighed and tossed his soldiers aside and did as she asked. I was already stacking the mixing and measuring bowls for cleaning myself.

"Yeah, all the time," I said.

Mama smiled and went on like I hadn't answered. "It wasn't an ordinary cake, of course. It had been enchanted. Anyone who ate even single bite could be controlled by the person who had served it to him. A dangerous thing." She lugged over the bucket of ice melt and set it on the table, and together we set to cleaning. "And worth a fair price, too, on the black market, which is what Ananna wanted with it. Of course, as a cake, we only had a few days to steal and sell it – there was no use trying to go after the Emperor's magicians to try and learn the spell, they're too highly protected. So we had a few of the crew disguise themselves as guardsmen, and Ananna and I dressed up like noble ladies, and we walked right into the Emperor's palace." Mama laughed, plunging a mixing bowl into the ice melt. "We were able to get ahold of the cake easily enough – it was in the kitchen, and the kitchen crew ran scared when they realized we were pirates – but carrying it while being chased through the streets of Lisirra, that was no easy task. The cake wound up falling and melting in the sand." Mama and I lined up the mixing bowls to dry, and I waited for the usual final line. "I supposed it was all for the best. No good could come of magic like that existing in the world."

I nodded in agreement, my expected response. I thought it sounded fantastically exciting, running through Empire streets in a lady's dress, trying not to drop an enchanted cake, but I knew my life didn't have anything like that in store for me.

Mama settled down in her favorite chair to wait for the cake to be finished. "I remember learning how to make start-of-spring cake. Your grandmother had to teach me."

I'd heard this story, too, but I didn't say anything. I liked listening to her stories.

"I gave up on the second try and stomped out of the kitchen, cussing and shouting, just as your father was coming from his fishing. He hadn't caught much that day, either." She smiled again, and the hearth light made her brown skin glow, and I wondered if that was how Papa had seen her that day as he walked in from the gray, cold sea. She must have been a shard of Empire sunlight here in the north. "And he told me it didn't matter to him one whit if I could bake a cake or not, that he had married me for me, and if it was such a problem, then he'd bake all our cakes himself."

I gave the expected titter. Henrik wiped off the wet mixing bowl with a scowl.

"Would you ever make a cake for your wife?" I asked him.

"Wives are stupid." He set the bowl aside.

"Spoken like a man of the Confederation," Mama said gravely. "As it happened, your father was the one who finally taught me how to make a start-of-spring cake, the next year. It was quite the scandal for a few days, a man teaching a woman how to cook." She winked at me. "But I taught him some tricks myself."

I'd heard all those stories, too, about how Mama'd gone aboard Papa's fishing boat and showed his crew a better way to string up the sails so that they could move more quickly through the water. That had generated a scandal for more than a few days, from what I gathered.

We finished cleaning up the bowls. Henrik went back to his toy soldiers, Mama went back to her garden and I went into my bedroom to pack up my things for the fishing run with Kolur. The sweet berry scent of the start-of-spring cake filled the house, and I told myself it'd only be two or three days' time before I'd be back home, ready to practice calling down the wind and finally welcoming spring to Kjora.

I rushed down to the docks, my hair streaming out behind me, a couple of slices of start-of-spring cake dropped in my pockets. It was already past longshadow and the sky was turning the pale purple-blue of twilight. I figured I could give Kolur a slice of cake for waiting.

The *Penelope* was the only boat in the dock, its magic-cast lanterns throwing a pale bluish glow over the water. Kolur waited for me on land, his arms crossed over his chest, the lanterns carving his rugged face into sharp relief.

"You're late," he said.

I reached into my pocket and pulled out a piece of cake wrapped up in a scrap of old fabric. Kolur stared at it.

"I said longshadow," he told me. "Not the middle of the night."

"And it's not," I said. "The stars aren't even out yet. Are you going to eat the cake or not?"

Kolur's pale eyes glittered in the lantern light. Then he plucked the cake from my hand and dropped it in his satchel.

"Get on board," he said. "If we don't leave soon, we'll miss our window."

"I hate night fishing." I sighed. "I've been up since this morning, you know."

"You can sleep once we get to the islands." Kolur gestured at the gangplank. "Go on, then."

I squared my bag on my shoulder and walked aboard. The *Penelope* was small and sturdy, the sails knotted in the pirate style – Papa wasn't the only one Mama taught Confederation tricks. There was a narrow cabin down below where Kolur let me sleep, since he preferred to stay out on deck in case of emergencies. We had a storage room too, and a galley for preparing meals. I went down to the cabin and dropped my bag on the cot, then joined Kolur up on deck, where he was already plotting the navigation that would take us out to the open sea, toward the Bathest Chain.

"Unmoor us," he told me without looking up.

"Aye." I pulled up the gangplank and unlooped the rope tying the *Penelope* to the dock post. She floated free in the bay, the frozen twilight shimmering around us. I called on the wind before Kolur could cast one of the cheap charms he always bought in the capital – it was easy work, since the wind was already blowing from the south, pushing us where we needed to go.

The *Penelope* glided forward, her sails snapping into place. We drifted silently through the moonlit water as Kolur steered from the wheel and I tended to the sails and all our fishing equipment, ensuring that everything was in its place. It was dull work, but at least I got to practice a bit of my magic. Besides, there was something calming about the rhythm of moving through the boat, going step by step to make sure everything was perfect. Like arranging the parts for a spell or a charm. If I used my imagination, I could pretend I was apprenticing for a wizard and not Kolur.

We sailed on toward the northwestern corner of the sky. I dropped the fishing nets at Kolur's feet and then sank down in them, quite prepared to get in a nap before we started fishing. But Kolur was feeling unusually chatty. Just my luck.

"Saw a big school of skrei in the bones," he said, looking straight ahead out at the starry night. "Last of the season."

I pulled out my cake slice and nibbled at it while he droned on about throwing the old fish bones he kept in a pouch around his neck. "Odd to see them this time of year, you know. Usually we're just pulling up ling and lampreys. That's why I wanted to give it a go. Bones told me they'd be gone by next week."

I made a muffled *humph* sound, my mouth full of cake.

"You need to be learning this, if you want to take over your father's boat someday."

He paused, waiting for my answer. I took my time chewing.

"Henrik can take over Papa's boat," I finally said. "I've got other plans."

Kolur laughed. "Taking cues from that friend of yours? You'd be better served learning how to dance than learning how to fish, if you've got your eye on a husband."

He was talking about Bryn, who was quite beautiful and already had a handful of marriage prospects. Good ones, too. Elders' sons and even a wizard from Cusildra, two villages over. Most of the girls in the village planned on marrying, but Mama had pushed me into fishing with Kolur. She said I needed to make my own way. I didn't disagree with her, but fishing wasn't where my future lay, I knew that. I was going to be a witch.

"Nah," I said. "Not unless I can marry someone from outside the village. The boys here are dull." I didn't bother telling him my real plans. Kolur didn't talk about much, and I didn't think he'd understand. All he needed to know was that I didn't want to be a fisherman or a fisherman's wife. Ideally, my future would involve as few fish as possible.

Kolur laughed again. "Ain't that the truth? Glad to see you've inherited some of your mother's good sense." He tilted the wheel, and the *Penelope* turned in the water, splitting open the reflection of the moon. It was full and the stars were out, but the night still seemed too dark, like it was trying to keep secrets.

"Here, take over for a bit." Kolur jerked his chin at the wheel, and I hopped to my feet and gripped the smooth, worn wood while he knelt down on the deck a few paces away, rubbing the space with his hands.

"I just keep going straight?"

He nodded. I tightened my grip and steadied the wheel. Kolur took off his pouch, dumped the bones in his palm and muttered one of the old fisherman's incantations. As far as I knew, this was the only spell he'd ever attempted.

The bones leapt and rattled in his hand, a tinny, hollow sound, as they charged with enchantment.

He tossed them along the deck like dice. And then he gasped.

Now, I'd learned to read fish bones when I was a little girl, hanging around down at the docks while Papa tended to his own boat, the *Maia*. It's easy, easy magic. So I knew what I was looking at when the bones scattered into their preordained patterns. A twist of tail curving out from jawbone: times of strife. A tooth inside a chest cavity: stranger coming to town. And two skulls facing away from each other: romantic troubles.

Not a single thing about the state of the ocean. Not a single thing about skrei.

"What the hell?" I dropped the wheel. The *Penelope* swung out from under me, and Kolur cursed and I shrieked and realized my mistake and jerked us back into position. The bones scattered over the deck. Kolur slid with the boat and gathered them all up in one clean motion.

"Pay attention, girl!" He squeezed his hand into a fist and when he opened it, the bones were jumping again. "I didn't tell you to play fortuneer; I told you to take the wheel. You know what happens when sailors don't do their assigned job? Your mama ought to have made that clear."

"I'm not a sailor," I said.

Kolur threw the bones again. This time, they fell in more common patterns, twists and squiggles that gave us a direction, northwest, and the promise of a good catch.

"Told you," he said. "A school of skrei in the northwest." He pointed at a scatter of teeth that looked like islands in the Bathest Chain. "There's our destination. Getting all worked up over nothing."

"That is *not* what I saw the first time."

"Because the moonlight was paying tricks on you. It's what I saw the first time, until you tilted the damn boat."

"Then why'd you gasp like that?"

"I didn't gasp like nothing." He gathered up the bones again and dropped them back in his pouch. When he stood up, his face had a hardness to it I'd never seen before. A determination. I'd never seen Kolur look determined about anything except the ale down at Mrs Blom's inn.

"Let me take that." He grabbed the wheel away from me, and I knew enough to let go. I was still seething about what I'd seen in the bones. He was lying. Which he did often enough, but it still annoyed me.

"Where are we going?" I glared at him, my hands crossed over my chest.

"Told you, girl, the Bathest Chain. Now go set up the nets before we sail right over the damn things."

He wouldn't look at me. Kolur was already pretty old, older than Papa at any rate, but in the darkness he seemed ancient. Like the capital wizards who have cast so many spells that the magic keeps them from dying.

"Do it," he snapped, and this time I did, because I knew if I didn't, he'd tell Mama and I'd be washing out the outhouse for months. But I wasn't happy about it.

Kolur and I worked well into the night, the *Penelope* slipping through the water with the nets splayed out behind her, the fish glinting silver in the moonlight. The air turned colder, and I was lucky I had one of my old winter coats stashed down below so I wouldn't freeze. Trawling like that was dull work, but with the waters as smooth and calm as they were, it wasn't dangerous. Most of the night, I just sat around on the boat, waiting until Kolur decided it was time to heave the nets aboard and check the catch. We worked together to get the fish on the deck, then Kolur had me cast the charm to keep them fresh for the two or three days we'd be out at sea, sailing a wide circle around the Bathest Chain. When the *Penelope* couldn't hold any more fish, we'd sail back to Kjora, and I'd be free until the next time Kolur decided to drag me away from home.

I thought about home as we sailed through the cold, shivering night. Kolur didn't go in much for talking if he could help it, but he was unusually quiet tonight. Withdrawn. I didn't mind the silence; I'd gotten used to it since becoming his apprentice, but it could get tiresome, being alone with my own thoughts all the time. Bryn would probably have some news about her suitors when I got back – she liked to tell me all the details about their weird habits and conversational topics. Mama'd probably make me help in the garden, and we'd sing old pirate songs as we worked. Papa'd come home with stories about his own fishing trip – all of them dull compared to Mama's stories, even the ones I'd heard over and over. But still, he'd pick Henrik up from the floor and swing him around and then give Mama a big hello kiss. Maybe the sun would even dry up the mud by the time we made it home, and I could go out in the fields and practice my magic without anyone watching.

"Check the nets," Kolur told me from his perch up at the wheel. I pulled myself away from my thoughts and did as he asked.

"Everything's fine." My voice carried with the wind. It was definitely stronger now, the sails snapping and pulling tight on their ropes. I frowned up at them. There hadn't been anything in the fish bones about inclement weather in *either* of the castings, and generally I had an easier time controlling the winds than this.

I glanced up at Kolur. He held the wheel tightly and didn't look at me.

"You think a storm's coming?" I shouted. "You said the weather would be smooth."

Silence. The wind was howling now, cold and sharp as knives, the *Penelope* tilting back and forth in the water. I reached out for it, trying to call it back through me so I could work my magic, but it was as slippery as the ocean.

"Kolur!" I shouted.

This time, he glanced over at me, his dark hair flying into his eyes. "Yes," he said, in an odd, flat voice. "Yes, a storm is coming."

Storms had never scared me much, not even out here on the open sea – I've got my affinity with the wind, and I knew enough protection charms to keep the boat safe. But I didn't like Kolur's behavior at all. It wasn't like him. Normally, when a storm blew in, he'd be fussing and fretting over his precious *Penelope*.

"Do you want me to bring in the nets?" The wind zipped my question away as soon as I spoke it. Kolur looked at me again.

"Yes. The nets. Of course."

Fear gripped me hard and cold. Kolur wasn't much of a fisherman, but he never forgot the nets.

I didn't like this at all.

I pushed my alarm aside and grabbed the nets with both hands and hauled them aboard. If I stood around feeling scared, then that'd be the end of us for sure.

The nets were empty save for the glitter of old fish scales. Ice water splashed over the railing, slapping across the boards and leaving a pale froth in its wake. It was too dark to see anything but the confines of the boat, even with the magic-cast lanterns swaying back and forth. Kolur was still at the wheel. He might as well have been a statue.

I ran up to him and grabbed him by the arm, steadying myself against the podium. "Kolur!" I shouted. "What's going on? The storm!"

He looked at me, and he looked almost normal. Maybe a little older than usual.

"I'm trying to keep the boat steady, girl. What do you think I'm doing?" He sounded like himself. "Put a charm on her for us."

I nodded, taking deep, shuddery breaths. Maybe the strangeness earlier had just been my imagination. A little bit of fear creeping out to blind me. That could happen.

I rushed down below to gather up the lichen powder and the mortar and pestle. The *Penelope* tilted wildly, and everything slid back and forth. Dark seawater dripped down through the ceiling from the deck and stained the cot. I caught a few drops of the water in the mortar and braced myself against the wall as I sprinkled in the lichen powder. As I mixed them together, I muttered an incantation in the language of my ancestors, guttural and sweet at the same time. Magic thrummed through me. All that power of the islands, all that power of the winds, all that power of the north.

The boat tilted again, lifting up on the starboard side. I cried out and covered the mortar with one hand. For one long and terrifying moment, I thought we were going to flip, and then we'd freeze to death in the black and unforgiving sea.

But then the *Penelope* righted herself, and I cried out in relief and rushed up on deck to finish the rest of the charm.

The winds were worse now and laced through with tiny pellets of ice that struck my bare face. Kolur was still at the wheel, as calm as if the water was flat and the skies were clear. I smeared lichen paste on the masts and the railings, shouting the incantation against a storm. I was so cold, I could hardly think. When I finished, I slumped down next to the small, scattered pile of skrei, trying to steady myself as the boat rocked and the magic flowed out of my veins and into the wood of the *Penelope*. I could feel it working, distantly, like an overheard conversation. We kept rocking and swaying, but thanks to the charm, the ocean no longer washed over the railings, and the water already on deck was no longer frigid. The storm crashed around us but it didn't touch us.

I was exhausted.

Kolur looked over at me and gave a short nod of approval. "You did good," he said. "Kept calm under pressure. Very good."

He turned back to his sailing.

Yes, calm under pressure. He'd been *too* calm. But I was too tired to say anything about it. My limbs ached, and my eyelids were heavy. I pushed myself to my feet, leaned up against the mast.

"I need to rest," I said.

Kolur nodded again, this time without looking me at me. "Figured so. You go on down below, rest off the magic. I'll see us through the storm."

Something tickled in the back of my mind, a phantom thought that maybe I shouldn't trust him. But that was absurd. I'd trusted him for three years, and besides, he was Mama's best friend.

So I went down below and fell asleep immediately.

CHAPTER TWO

I woke up with a headache. Not a bad one, but painful enough to remind me I'd done magic the night before. I'd heard the more spells you cast, the fewer headaches you got, but I didn't see any of that improvement this morning.

I spent a few moments lying in the cot with my hands folded over my stomach, staring up at the ceiling, trying to sort out my thoughts. Because I was so bleary, it wasn't until I stood up that I noticed the *Penelope* wasn't moving.

Odd.

I shambled into the storage room and pulled out a canteen of water and drank it down. That cleared my head some. We still weren't moving. Had Kolur turned around and gone back home to the village after the storm? It didn't seem like him. We hadn't even brought in a full load of fish yet, and he didn't like pulling into the docks without one.

I pulled out another canteen, along with a jar of salted fish and a hunk of dark bread. It was the usual food we kept aboard and not really that appealing, but recovering from magic always makes everything taste better. I savored each bite, licking the salt from my fingers. I was feeling much brighter about the whole idea of being awake, and so I ran my fingers through my hair a few times and climbed up on deck.

The *Penelope* was moored at the docks, nestled in between a pair of unfamiliar red-tinted fishing boats. Kolur wasn't anywhere to be found: not at the helm and not up in the masts, either. Our small catch from last night was intact, encased in the soft blue glow of the preservation charm.

Well. Looked like I'd be getting to celebrate spring after all, although I knew Kolur would have it out for me if I left without helping him haul the fish down to the market. He must have walked over to the *Eel's Eye Inn* for breakfast. I dropped the gangplank and made my way down to the docks.

And froze.

These were not the village docks.

They looked near enough to them from up on the boat, but now that I was on land, I found that they were much busier, crowded and bustling like the docks in the capital. But these weren't capital folk – they didn't even look like Kjoran folk. Not that they had antlers growing out of their foreheads, but the men wore beards and long embroidered coats, and the women had their hair up in elaborate braids woven through with pale ribbons. As often as Bryn dressed up for her suitors, and as fond as she was of capital styles, I'd *never* seen her wear braids like these.

Panic gripped me again, cold and icy like the storm. I realized how foreign the voices chattering around me sounded. We all speak the same northern tongue, but from island to island, the accents change, and here the vowels were long and distorted, as if they were being shouted down a tunnel.

We weren't in Kjora.

When she was angry with him, Mama called Papa an *ice-islander*, a phrase from the language of the Empire, of which I could speak a little. Papa always retorted that he was a Kjoran, and I'd gathered over the course of my childhood that in the south, they saw the north as one place, the *ice-islands*, and not a collection of places, as we did. I had grown up in Kjora and so was familiar with Kjoran customs and practices. As far out to sea as I went with Kolur sometimes, I'd never stepped foot on another island.

Until now.

My head spun. I wasn't sure I could breathe anymore. Why had Kolur brought me here, to this foreign place? Had we been blown that far off course? I thought of the carved map Papa kept aboard the *Maia*. Akel was the closest to Kjora, a half day's sail. We must be there.

My initial panic receded then, and excitement rippled through me instead. My first time off Kjora. My first time having a proper adventure, just like Ananna of the *Nadir*.

I took a deep breath and wove myself into the crowd. I received a few strange looks, and I wasn't sure if it was because I was Kjoran or because I bore the imprint of Empire features. As I walked, I thought about how strange Kolur had been in the moments before the storm, like a man possessed. I'd say it was by magic if I didn't know better. Kolur couldn't call down the winds like that – my magic was the reason he brought me on board the *Penelope* in the first place.

And yet here we were, arrived safely on land by no action of my own.

I made my way along the narrow wooden walkways until I came to a trapper selling furs out of a cart. Vendors dotted up and down the docks, but he was the closest to the *Penelope*. I strode up to him and remembered the stories I'd heard about the bravery of Ananna of the *Nadir*. I reminded myself that Ananna was my true name.

"Excuse me," I said. "How long have you been set up here?"

He gazed at me over the stacks of pelts. "Why you asking?"

"I work aboard that fishing boat there." I pointed at the *Penelope*. "My apprentice master's awfully forgetful, and he didn't tell me where he was going when he left. I was hoping you might have seen him."

"He Empire like you?"

I shook my head, even though my cheeks burned. I wasn't used to people pointing out my ancestry. Everyone in the village had gotten over that urge a long time ago.

"Hard to say, then. A lot of folks came this way."

"He'd be dressed like a Kjoran. Brown hair. Only a little taller than me."

The trapper frowned. "A Kjøran, huh? I seem to recall spotting a fellow like that. Early this morning. Going into the city. But then, they all are." He grinned. He was missing a couple of teeth. "A bit far from home, aren't you, for your master to be leaving you on the boat?"

I scowled at him. "I'm not Empire! I'm from Kjora, too."

"I know. That's what I mean."

My stomach felt suddenly heavy. "What?"

The trapper jerked his head back toward the bustle of the town. "Kjora's a couple days' sail from here, ain't it? Never been off the island myself."

"A couple days? No." I shook my head, refusing to believe him. I told myself he was a typical landsman, that since he had no reason to sail the seas, he'd no reason to know the distances between islands. I only knew because of Papa's carved map. "Just half a day. We got blown off course."

"Half a day. That certainly ain't true." The trapper leaned back on his stool and gave me a long, appraising look. "Where exactly do you think you are?"

"Akel," I said, although my voice trembled.

The trapper stared at me for a moment longer. Then he laughed, his great shoulders shaking beneath his shaggy coat. I took a step back, glancing around, not liking this one bit.

"Stop laughing at me," I said.

"You ain't in Akel," the trapper said. "You're in Skalir."

Skalir. The whole world tilted the way the *Penelope* had last night. I grabbed onto the edge of the trapper's cart to steady myself.

"That's not possible," I said.

"No idea what's possible or not," he said. "But you're in Skalir."

My ears buzzed. Papa's map appeared in my head – the islands raised up in relief, the stain sunk deep into the wood. Skalir, past the Bathest Chain, past Akel, heading up toward the north, toward the very top of the world. The trapper was right; it was three days' sail, not even from Kjora but from the spot in water where the storm had hit us.

"Not possible," I said again.

The trapper squinted at me with suspicion, and I pushed away from him before he could say anything more. At first, I headed in the direction of the *Penelope,* but then I started worrying that it was still doused in whatever magic had brought us here in the first place. *That* magic – that must be why I slept so late. Working a simple protection charm had never worn me out so thoroughly before.

I turned away from the boat and walked toward town, my heart pounding. Something must have happened to Kolur; he wouldn't have left me alone otherwise. I could work a tracking spell on him but I didn't have the materials and I wasn't sure I'd be able to find them here. Or even afford them. Or if my magic would even work. Everyone said that magic changes as you cross the seas, and so the spells of Skalir might be spells I could never understand. I couldn't risk it.

I shivered and left the docks.

As crowded as the docks were, the town itself seemed small, little more than a settlement growing out of the cold, rocky ground. The wind blew in from the sea, smelling of salt and fish and the peculiar scent of late winter. There weren't as many people here, as if everyone wanted to cluster close to the ocean. I trudged down the main street, trying to be as inconspicuous as possible. It didn't much seem to work. Anyone out on the street stared at me as I walked past, and whispers trailed behind me like clouds.

Mama and Papa had both taught me pride. So I kept my head high and refused to look away if anyone caught my eye. But it was hard, not so much because I was ashamed but because I was scared. Scared that Kolur was gone for good, that some foul spell had stolen him away as I slept. Every child raised in the north hears stories about the Mists, those creatures from beyond even the uppermost part of the world. I didn't remember seeing any of their mist last night, that cold, gray blanket that can swallow you whole. But it had been dark and difficult to see.

Sea and sky, I wished I wasn't so far from the soil of my home. There's magic to keep the Mists at bay, but I still didn't trust that it would work here, even with the south wind.

So when I came across a wizard's shop, I ducked through the heavy, carved wooden doors, relieved at the sudden weight of magic around my shoulders. It was a small shop, dark, smelling of incense and blood. A girl stood behind the counter, chopping up dried marsh violets. She lifted her head when I walked in and frowned like she didn't know what to make of me.

"I'd like a protection charm." I pulled out the small pouch of gold discs Mama had me carry whenever I went sailing with Kolur. For moments like this one, I supposed. Papa always thought it was silly, that I should just carry Kjoran money, but Mama always insisted that he was shortsighted.

"We don't have many." The girl pulled out a tray, only half of the pockets filled with charms. They were basic things, built of lichen and stone. I ran my hands over each one, feeling out the magic. Even these simple premade charms work differently from person to person, and you have to make sure you're able to channel the charm's power properly before you buy.

The girl nodded approvingly.

When my hand passed over a bracelet made of twisted-up asphodel and threaded with tiny seashells, my whole body blazed.

"This one." I plucked it off the tray. The girl nodded and named her price. It was reasonable, and I was glad, because I didn't know the customs for haggling here in Skalir.

"Do you feel you're in danger?" she asked after I paid.

I slipped the bracelet onto my left hand. "I'm not certain."

She tilted her head at me. "If you're in trouble, the wizard could help you." *For a price.* She didn't say it aloud, but it was implied.

"Not necessary." I lifted my arm and shook the bracelet. With each movement, its power pulsed through me. Comforting. "But I am looking for someone. Another Kjoran. An older man. Brown hair."

"No one else has been in here for some time," she said. "I'm sorry."

I frowned and thanked her. I'd hoped that Kolur might have come here to gather up more premade charms for the boat.

Unless the *Penelope* had been damaged. Then the simple charms wouldn't be enough–

"Is there a repair yard here?" I asked. "Or a supply shop?"

"Are you *sure* you're not in danger?"

"Quite. I've just lost my apprentice master." I flashed a smile at her. "He tends to drink."

My answer mollified her curiosity. "The repair yard's not far from here. Walk left from the shop, and then turn toward the sea when you reach the prayer stones."

I thanked her again. When I walked back out on the street, I really did feel safer with my bracelet. The air was brighter, and I had a good feeling about the repair yard.

It didn't take me long to walk there. The prayer stones lay at the outskirts of town, a great pile of rocks worn smooth by the ocean, arranged in unfamiliar patterns in the frozen mud. We had prayer stones in Kjora, too, but the patterns were different, based on runes from the ancient tongue.

The repair yard was as small as the town, just a rickety wooden fence hemming in some broken-up lumber and a shack built of gray bricks. A single boat floated out in the water, one of its sails dangling at an unnatural angle. It hurt me to look at it, like I was seeing a broken arm.

This time, no one came out to greet me. I went up to the shack and banged on the door until a shriveled old man answered, his white hair tucked up in a startlingly red cap.

"Empire girl!" he cried when he saw me. "Do you like my hat?"

"What?"

"My hat. It was crafted from the finest Empire fabric over twenty years ago, by a sailor who lost his way. I helped repair his ship when no one else would, and he gave it to me as a gift of thanks."

"Oh." I pretended to study the hat like I had knowledge of Empire fabric. To me, it looked tatty and worn, but then, it was twenty years old. "It's quite lovely, yes. Wonderful workmanship." I had no idea if this was true. It was a hat.

The old man beamed. "What can I do for you, so far from home?" he asked. "Do you have a ship that needs repair?"

"Not exactly." The wind blowing off the water was as cold as the ice from last night's storm. I fiddled with my bracelet. "My apprentice master's gone missing. I thought he might have come here. We were in a storm, and he'd probably be seeking repairs."

The old man studied me, rubbing at his chin, his stupid red hat jumping in and out of my line of vision. "An apprentice master? So you aren't from the Empire."

"I was born in Kjora."

"Kjora! Still a long way from here." He nodded. "And your apprentice master, he's Kjoran, too?"

I nodded, not daring to get my hopes up.

"Aye, he did come by here, looking for parts."

I sighed with relief. "Not too short, not too tall? Brown hair?"

"And dressed like a Kjoran, yes. A bit grumpy."

That was definitely Kolur. "Oh, thank you, sir," I said, grinning wildly. "Do you know where he went? Did he mention anything?"

"He wasn't terribly chatty, but he did rush me about. Said something about having to meet someone."

My good mood evaporated. Meet someone? Who could he possibly be meeting? We had been blown here by accident.

I pushed the doubts aside. Maybe he had a friend here. Granted, I didn't know how, since no one befriends those from the other island, and besides, he hardly had friends in the village, save Mama. Perhaps he was asking around for a way to get us home.

"Did he say where?"

The old man shook his head. "But there aren't many places to meet here in Beshel-by-the-Sea. There's the lodging out on the edge of the woods, and Mrs Arnui's inn, in town."

I considered the two options. Kolur never liked to venture too far from the sea, so I figured it was safer to put him at the inn.

"Thank you," I told the old man. "That was very helpful."

His smile brightened. "If you need repairs, you know where to come."

I left the repair yard and made my way back to the village. The wind had picked up, blowing in from the north, cold tricky gusts that stirred up my hair and sent all the shopkeepers rushing to latch their shutters. I wrapped my arms around my chest and kept my head tilted down, checking the sign of each shop as I passed, looking for an inn. The wind blew. It didn't feel like Kjoran wind; it was sharper, and with a sweet scent to it, like ice berries or frozen flowers. A pleasant change from the brine of fish.

I found the inn easily. It was tucked down close to the docks, marked by a pair of thin, spindly trees that were out of place in the rocky landscape. *Inn*, the handpainted sign read.

I went in. The wind ripped the door from my hand and slammed it up against the wall, and every face in the room looked up at me. All the murmuring stopped. I froze, feeling vulnerable and afraid. I was in a strange place, and these people were all strangers.

"Shut the door!" A woman bustled up to me, her sleeves pushed up to her elbows. "You're letting in the Abelas." She grabbed the door and slammed it shut. "When they get like this, blowing down from the mountains, they'll stir up anything bad enough if you let them."

"Oh, I'm sorry." I straightened up my spine. "I'm looking for a friend. He's Kjoran."

"In the back." The woman sounded bored and harried at the same time. I wondered if she was Mrs Arnui. "If you want something to eat, let Addie know. We've got elk stew today."

· And then she scurried off to a nearby table, the benches lined with bearded fishermen.

I went toward the back of the room, looking for Kolur's brown hair. When I found him, he was facing away from the door, hunched over a bowl of that elk stew, talking to a woman. She glanced at me as I approached, the candlelight flickering in her eyes.

"Got a few weeks' time–" Kolur stopped and looked over his shoulder. "Hanna! You found it."

"Found it?" I stomped over to the table and slid into the bench beside him. "I've been looking for you all morning. I went to the repair yard and a magic shop and I had *no idea* – and why are we in Skalir? How is that even possible?"

My ranting was met with silence. The woman kept staring at me with a dark, hollow expression.

Then Kolur laughed. "Oh, you stupid girl, you didn't see my note."

I glared at him.

"I pinned it next to your bed. Told you exactly where to find me." He laughed again. "Guess you were in a hurry to get home? Thought we were in Kjora?"

The woman sighed and lifted one hand. A girl appeared. She was a smaller, shorter version of the woman who had yelled at me to shut the door, and she immediately refilled the woman's glass with frothy amber-colored ale.

"No," I said. "I thought we were in Akel. How the hell are we in Skalir?"

Kolur turned back to his stew. The woman took a long drink of her ale. Then she spoke. "You ought to just tell her, Kolur."

Her voice vibrated inside my head. It was rich and sonorous, like the bottle of Empire wine Mama opened up on her birthday one year.

"What's there to tell? Are you hungry, Hanna? I imagine you are, after that charm you cast last night. Addie!"

The girl appeared again.

"Bring Hanna here a bowl of this elk stew. And a glass of milk." Kolur peered at me. "Milk does wonders, helping you get over the magic exhaustion."

I wondered how the hell someone like Kolur would know that.

"I'm over it," I said. "I just want to know what's going on." The woman watched Kolur and me both. She was probably Kolur's age, but she didn't look as worn-down by life as he did.

"To answer your question," Kolur said, stirring at his elk stew, "we're in Skalir because that ice storm wasn't just a storm. There was magic in it."

"I figured out that much. What sort of magic?"

"The wild sort. It's of no concern to you. Just know that it brought us here. Probably would've blown us farther, if I hadn't cast a quick redirection charm. I knew Frida here could help us."

"Redirection charm?"

The woman flashed a quick, hard smile. "It's lovely to meet you, Hanna. I apologize for Kolur's rudeness." She held out one hand, long and tanned and graceful. "He should have introduced us right away."

I took her hand, hesitantly, and shook it. When our skin touched, my blood sparked; she was some sort of witch, to have such strong magic running through her body.

She smiled again, dropped her hand, and took a drink.

"Frida's an old friend," Kolur said.

"You don't have friends," I said. "And how did you cast a redirection charm? You can't do magic."

Kolur looked down at the table and didn't answer. Addie reappeared and set down a bowl of stew and a cup of milk. As much I didn't want to admit it, the smell of the stew made my mouth water and my stomach rumble. I really did need to eat.

I picked up the bowl and took a long sip. Kolur nodded approvingly. "Told you."

"When are we going home?"

There was a pause. Voices hummed around us, all speaking that strange, foreign dialect.

"You that excited to be back in the village?"

"No. I'm just curious." I gulped down my stew. It was delicious, the meat tender and falling apart, the broth flavored by herbs like the ones Mama grew in her garden.

"A couple days' time, most like." He stared down at his own stew as he spoke. "We'll get started repairing the boat tomorrow. There was a bit of damage, mostly magical. Frida should be able to take care of it."

"Not you? Since you can cast redirection charms now?"

"That was a fluke." Kolur took a drink of ale.

I kept eating my stew. A couple days' time on an island I only knew from the carvings on Papa's map. It was a sort of adventure, like the ones Mama used to have. Hanging around the Skalirin docks wasn't exactly the same as sailing a pirate ship through Empire waters, the way I used to pretend when I was a little girl, but it was as close as I was likely to come.

Still, doubt niggled at me. As excited as I was to see beyond the shores of Kjora, I couldn't shake the discomfort that something was wrong. Kolur couldn't do magic beyond the same few charms everyone can do, and it was strange that Kolur, who aside from his friendship with Mama was one of the most conventional Kjorans in the village, would have a friend on another island.

That his friend was a witch, well, that was even stranger. Exciting, too. But mostly strange. And I didn't know why.

Kolur set down his ale and leaned back on the bench. Something in his expression was off – not wrong, exactly, but *different*, the way the wind had felt as it blew through the town. It gave me the same sort of chill. He looked across the table at Frida and I followed his gaze, peering at her over my soup bowl. She stared back at me with eyes like oceans. They were just as unpredictable.

CHAPTER THREE

As it turned out, the repairs were even more minor than Kolur had suggested, and by the next afternoon the *Penelope* was fit to sail again. I hardly had to do anything at all, mostly just hand Frida foul-smelling powders and unguents as she made her way around the ship, casting unfamiliar spells. It was the closest I'd ever come to apprenticing as a wizard, and it was a disappointment to learn that it didn't feel all that different from apprenticing as a fisherman.

I could sense Frida's power crackling against my own, but there was a restraint to it. She wasn't showing me everything she could do. Every time I handed her something – some ground-up shells, a bit of dried seaweed – that magic would arc between us and then fizzle away, and I wondered what she was keeping from me. All her spells were sea-magic, something I was familiar with but hadn't really seen, and it was frustrating to sense her power but not be able to fully experience it.

I wondered if proper witch's apprenticeships were this frustrating.

Kolur watched the repairs from his usual place up at the helm, eating dried wildflower seeds. When I asked about them, he said they were a Skalirin specialty.

"How do you know about Skalirin specialties?" I said. "Are you telling me you've been off Kjora before?"

"I'm a fisherman," he said.

"That doesn't answer my question. My Papa's a fisherman and he's never sailed out of Kjoran waters."

Kolur just ignored me, though. "Here, try one." He handed me a wildflower seed. It was a small, dark dot in my palm. I glared down at it, angry with Kolur for keeping secrets.

"You wanted adventure," he said.

I wanted answers, too. Still, I tossed the seed into my mouth, figuring I could ask him again once we made sail. The seed burned my tongue and I spat it out on deck. Kolur laughed at me.

"Ass," I said, wiping at my mouth. "Is this really all I'm going to get to see of Skalir? Some burning seeds and a shabby dock town?"

"It's probably for the best," Kolur said. "Skalir's a backwards little island. Isn't that right, Frida?"

She glanced up at him from her place at the bow, where she was finishing the last of the repair spells.

"Not so backwards when you leave the shore and go into the mountains." She blew a swirl of glittering powder out into the water, and the ocean churned around us. "For good luck," she added, looking at me.

I'd never seen that kind of good luck charm before,

but before I could ask more about it Frida was walking back toward Kolur.

"Too many fishermen around," she said. "That's why Skalir seems so backwards."

She grinned, so I took it for a joke and laughed, even though I was technically a fisherman. But Kolur didn't find it so funny.

"Fishermen are honest folk," he snapped. "Unlike your lot."

"My lot?" Frida said. "You would know–"

"Hanna." Kolur stood up and shoved his package of wildflower seeds into his pocket. "Check with the shop to see if our supplies are ready."

I looked back and forth between Kolur and Frida, wondering what Frida was going to say that got Kolur all worked up. Kolur jerked his head at me. "Go on," he said. "Frida's done here, and I want to get to the water as soon as we can."

Frida crossed her arms over her chest. "You best do what he says," she told me. "Kolur never liked being disobeyed."

I scowled at both of them but I knew she was right, even if I didn't understand how. It still didn't make sense that Kolur knew so powerful a witch, that we just happened to land on the island where she lived, three days' sail from where we ought to be...

I didn't like it.

The supply shop was a little store right at the point where the docks gave way to Beshel-by-the-Sea proper. The owner recognized me when I walked in, even though I'd never met him before. Kolur must have told him to be on the lookout for a Kjoran-Empire girl. Not a lot of us around.

"You Hanna?" he asked, straightening up from where he'd been wrapping packages in rough tunic fabric.

"I'm picking up Kolur Icebreak's order." I stood in the doorway, fidgeting, looking around. It wasn't much of a store, just a room stacked with packages. I wondered what was in each of them. Goods from all over Skalir, probably.

"Certainly." The shopkeeper turned to one of his stacks. It was a dull sight, his hunched-over back, and I knew it was likely the last non-Kjoran sight I'd see for a good long while. "Here you are."

He dropped the packages on the counter. There were about ten of them, rather large, all wrapped in the same rough fabric. He read off the list – food mostly, dried fish and some sea vegetables, skins of fresh water. An awful lot for a three-day trip.

"Need any help carrying it to your boat?"

"No, thanks." I scooped the packages up by their tie strings and staggered out of the shop, where I called on the south wind to help lighten my load. Those ten packages felt like two as I walked back down the docks, the wind bearing the bulk of their weight. So far, adventuring was pretty dull. About the same as being in Kjora, all things told.

I carted the supplies back to the *Penelope* and set them up in the storeroom. The sun was sinking pale gold into the horizon, and I figured Kolur was anxious to be out on the open sea. So it was a surprise, when I climbed up from down below, to find Frida still on board.

And a bigger surprise still that she was standing over the wooden map with a sextant.

"What's going on?" I hissed at Kolur. "I thought she was finished repairing our boat."

"She is." Kolur stared straight ahead, out at the water. "I didn't ask her just to repair the boat, though. She's coming with us."

"What?"

Frida straightened up from the map and brought a roll of parchment over to the helm and handed it to Kolur. I fell quiet and watched her the way I would the poisonous spiders that crept through our house. But Kolur just glanced over the parchment once, nodded, and then rolled it up and stuck it in his coat pocket.

"Route calculations," Frida said to me.

"I know what they are." My confusion spiraled out like some unwieldy plant. Why was Kolur bringing a powerful witch back with us? Why would she agree to leave her home so easily?

What did they expect to *happen*?

"How are you going to get back to Skalir?" I said.

"Excuse me?"

"We're going home to Kjora. Don't imagine we'll ever come back – it was just a fluke that brought us here. So how are you going to get home?"

Frida glanced over at Kolur.

"Make sail!" he hollered out. "That means you, Hanna."

"Are we coming back here?"

"That ain't anything you need to worry about. Make the damn sail, girl."

"I'm on this boat, so it is something I need to worry about."

"I'm the captain, and I'm telling you it's not. So make the sail."

I glared at him, but I knew it was pointless; he was going to ignore me. So I did as he asked, dropping the sails down and tying them into place, my anger bubbling up under the surface. It was hard to concentrate. I kept glancing over at the helm, where Kolur and Frida stood side by side like old friends.

"Which direction for the wind?" I shouted at Kolur, my voice snappy with irritation.

"Oh, don't worry, I can do it." Frida strode to the center of the boat. My anger flared again. She lifted one hand. The direction of the wind shifted, filling up our sails and pushing us out away from the docks.

I gaped at her.

"You conduct through the air," I said, my anger with Kolur vanishing. "But earlier—"

"I do." Frida smiled. "I find simple water charms work best when repairing a ship. I can do both."

Both? That was a rarity. And maybe it explained why she was willing to leave Skalir so easily. That sort of power didn't make her typical of the north.

The wind gusted us out to sea. Frida walked back over to the map and looked over it again, nodding to herself. So she wasn't just a witch, she was a wind-witch. Same as me.

Maybe that was why Kolur brought her on board: because I wasn't good enough at magic, because I wasn't a proper witch. Ass.

I walked to the stern and leaned against the railing as Beshel-by-the-Sea drew farther and farther away. Their lanterns were already switching on, pale blue like the lanterns back at home. *Home.* Maybe when we got back, I'd convince Mama to send me to the academy to apprentice as a witch the way I wanted. I'd tell her Kolur was a liar. She didn't abide liars.

Frida materialized beside me, the wind blowing the loose strands of hair away from her face. A northern wind. She seemed to have an affinity with it, the way I had an affinity with the south. This fact irritated me for some reason.

"Have you left before?" I hoped I could get some information out of her if I came at it sideways.

"What?" She looked at me. "Oh, you mean Skalir. Yes, of course."

I looked down at the dark ocean water and shivered. She was so nonchalant about crossing the waters. I'd always wanted to try it, of course, but I was my mother's daughter, and that made me different from most island folk.

"I'm not from there, actually." She glanced at me out of the corner of her eye and smiled mischievously. I wondered if I looked surprised. "I was born farther north."

Farther north. I looked at her more closely. Her accent wasn't the same as mine, of course, but now that I thought about it, it wasn't the same as the Skalirins', either. More lilting, like a lute. And her black hair, that was unusual around Beshel-by-the-Sea, too.

"My mama sailed far north once," I said. "All the way to Jandanvar. She said it was full of wonders."

"Wonders." She nodded and looked back out at the land slowly diminishing into the sea. "Yes, I suppose you could call them that. But it's dangerous there, too. The Mists are closer, the cold is crueler. The people are further from human than in the rest of the world." She let out a long sigh. "I much prefer it here."

It rubbed me raw that Kolur had brought another wind-witch aboard, especially one who kept her power close by. But at the same time, I wanted to ask her about the north, about Jandanvar, about all those wonders Papa never expanded upon.

Kolur called her over to the helm, claiming he needed her advice. He didn't call me. So I stayed put, long past the moment Beshel-by-the-Sea vanished into the darkness, until all that surrounded us was water.

The next day, the ocean was as calm and smooth as glass, which meant there wasn't anything to do. Kolur handled the wheel and Frida tended to the wind and the sails, and that pretty much took care of all the morning chores aboard the *Penelope*. Under normal circumstances, I would have appreciated the chance to laze about on deck, maybe practice my magic. But every time I tried, I'd start dwelling on all of Kolur's and Frida's secrets. The fact that I'd been so neatly removed from any duties aboard the ship didn't help.

Midmorning, I gathered up the nets, preparing to cast them out into the sea.

"Girl!" Kolur barked. "What the hell do you think you're doing?"

"We're a fishing boat, aren't we?" I held up the nets. "Gonna do some fishing."

Kolur glared at me. "We already got a catch."

"Yeah, hardly anything. And it'll be all dried out from the preservation charm by the time we get home." I hooked the nets into place. "Might as well see what else we can find."

Frida watched us from the bow. Kolur stared at me for a few minutes, then pushed one hand through his hair.

"Liable to be disappointed in these waters," he muttered.

I pushed the nets into the sea. They fanned out and sank below the surface. Now I was back to where I started. Waiting.

Waiting.

Waiting.

Lunchtime came around and the nets still weren't full. We ate up on deck despite the cold, huddled around a little heat charm that Frida had cast. I'd never seen anything like it before, a perfect glowing ball the same color as the summer sun. It radiated warmth for a few paces, but it never got too hot, the way a fire would. The really remarkable thing was that it didn't seem to drain anything out of her. She'd fixed up the ship and she'd drawn down the wind and now she was heating the deck, too, and she didn't seem pale or worn out or anything.

I didn't know what to make of Frida. She was probably the most interesting person I'd ever met, and if she'd wandered into the village one afternoon, I bet I would have tried to be her best friend. But out here on the cold water, with all those looks between her and Kolur, and all those *secret*s, she left me nervous. Unsettled.

"That's some pretty interesting magic," I told her between bites of dried fish, trying to find out answers.

"Thank you." She smiled. "It's a northern charm. The winters are much longer up there."

"Northern?" I frowned. "Is it Jandanvari?"

She laughed. Kolur shifted a little in his place and stared off at the horizon.

"There are places in the north besides Jandanvar," she said.

I blushed. "I know. I just–" I tore angrily at a hunk of bread. "I was just curious."

"No, this particular charm isn't from Jandanvar." She drew her knees up to her chest. "I can show you some Jandanvari spells, though, if you'd like–"

"No." Kolur stood up and tossed his half-eaten fish back in the jar. "There'll be none of that on this ship."

"You're no fun." She winked at me, which I found startling. It made me feel like she and I were conspirators against Kolur.

"You're too reckless." Kolur stomped over to the wheel and whipped off the premade steering charm he'd bought from a wizard in the Kjoran capital. "Keep to the winds. What I brought you aboard for."

I frowned. My control of the winds was enough to get us home. It wasn't as if I'd never been aboard the *Penelope* before.

Frida laughed. "Is he always like that?"

Her question jerked me out of my thoughts. "Don't you know?" I said. "I thought you were friends."

"Oh, but that was a long time ago. He had a sense of humor then."

"How long ago?"

"Too long to count." She laughed. "We did have our adventures, though."

I looked over at Kolur. It was like I'd never seen him before. I'd always assumed he'd lived in Kjora his whole life, like everyone else in the village. He was a fisherman. Fishermen didn't have adventures. That was the whole problem with them.

Frida stood up and stretched. The wind swirled around her, its magic glinting in the sun. Back at home in the village, I would dream about looking like that, a proud wind-witch who had seen the world. It was one of my favorite daydreams this past winter, when the night crept in early on and the snow froze around our little cottage. Henrik would be playing by the fire, making nonsense noises to himself, and Mama would be singing pirate songs, and Papa would be repairing his fishing nets, and I'd look at all of them and know I wanted something more to my life. And so I thought about my future.

But looking at Frida didn't feel like looking at my future. It just made that future seem even farther away. Her life wasn't going to be mine; my life was going to be more like Kolur's, a bit of adventure in the past and nothing more. That's what comes from growing up in the north. Your life is bound by the rocks and the cold and the sea.

It was depressing.

I gathered up the leftovers from lunch and put them back in the food stores down below. Then I checked on the nets. They weren't full yet, but I was so bored, I pulled them up anyway. The catch wasn't *too* bad – mostly seaweed, although a few ling flopped among the ropes. I sorted them out and cast a new preservation charm over them. Kolur watched me, but he didn't say anything.

Night fell. We ate another meal by the light of the heat charm. I went down below and fell asleep.

The next day was the exact same. Still no chores for me to do, so I cast out the nets again. This time, I left them floating for longer. The wind gusted and swelled, ruffling my hair so badly, I finally combed it into two thick braids.

The wind was a true wind, not anything that Frida had manufactured, and it smelled sweet, the way the Abelas had back in Beshel-by-the-Sea. I stood up at the bow and let the wind blow over me, my eyes closed, feeling for the enchantment veining through the air. This was an old wizard's trick, meant to bring you more in tune with the world's magic. I tried to practice it as often as I could.

But today, I couldn't feel the magic, not exactly – or rather, I did feel it, but it seemed different, more of a presence than magic usually is. Like a predatory animal watching you from the shadows of a tree.

I didn't like it.

I opened my eyes and pulled myself back into my own head. The wind swept around me, although it no longer smelled of flowers. Maybe we were too far north. Maybe it was the Mists–

I shivered. No. The presence hadn't felt frightening; it hadn't felt dangerous. It was just *there*.

"Kolur," I called out, turning around to face him. "How long till we get back to Kjora?"

"You know better than to ask me that." True enough – never asking him if he were home yet was one of the conditions he'd set forth when he brought me on as his apprentice.

"Yeah, but there's nothing to do. You're not interested in fishing, and Frida calls down the wind and fixes the sails before I can–"

"Three days ago, you were griping about having to work. Now you're griping about not having to work."

I scowled at him. "I'm still trapped on your boat."

"That's because you're my apprentice," he said. "Now go on. Stop bothering me."

"You didn't answer my question."

"Cause you ain't supposed to ask it. Go check your nets."

I knew I'd lost, but I stalked over to the helm to see if I could glare an answer out of him. Kolur didn't even acknowledge I was there. As far as I could tell, he thought the only thing that existed in the whole world was the *Penelope* and the vast shining expanse of the sea.

Eventually, boredom got the best of me in my standoff. I went back to my nets.

Still not full, even though I'd left them out for a couple of hours longer. I sighed and hauled them in. Less seaweed this time, but there was a hunk of glacier ice. I frowned. There weren't any glaciers this far south, and the water was too warm this time of year for the ice to have floated down–

And then I saw something else, something that froze all the air out of my body.

A capelin, long and thin and gasping for air on the deck. I knelt down in the tangle of nets, not noticing the cold seawater soaking through my trousers. I scooped the capelin up in my hands. It slapped against my gloves, leaving a scatter of scales in its wake.

You couldn't catch capelin in our waters. They were northern fish, and they never came this far south. Skalir was farther north than Kjora, certainly, but we should be firmly in Kjoran waters by now, and this fish, this narrow, gasping fish, should not be here.

With a shout, I flung it back into the nets. Tears prickled at my eyes.

We weren't going south to Kjora.

We were going north.

"Kolur!" I screamed. "What are you doing? Where are you taking me?"

My voice bounced off the cold. The air vibrated. Over at the navigation table, Frida set down her sextant. Kolur kept staring at the horizon.

"Kolur!" I scooped up the capelin and raced over to the helm. He looked at me, looked at the fish.

"What is this?" I hissed, shaking it at him.

"It appears to be a capelin."

I hurled the fish back out into the water. "It doesn't swim this far south. Which means we aren't south at all, doesn't it?"

Kolur fell silent and my anger coursed through me. Not just anger, though – fear, too, a little prickle of it. I'd trusted him. Mama had trusted him. And now he had spirited me away. Even if I had always wanted to go on an adventure, I wanted to do it on my terms. Not Kolur's.

"Frida!" he called out. "Do you think you could take the wheel? Don't like using the steering charm unless I absolutely have to."

A pause. The *Penelope* rocked against the waves. That cold, sweet-scented wind ruffled my hair.

"Of course," she finally said, and she set down her sextant and walked over to the helm. I recoiled from her when she passed, no longer admiring her magic but fearing it, fearing what she might be capable of.

She didn't do anything except take the wheel from Kolur, who turned to me, not looking the least bit guilty.

"I suppose we should talk," he said.

"Talk?" I shrieked. "*Talk?* What are you doing to me?"

"Nothing." He walked over to the port railing and leaned against it, the wind pushing his hair away from his eyes. I joined him, my whole body shaking, and not from the cold.

"I'm not doing anything to you." He glanced over at me. He looked older than usual, like the last few days had drained the life out of him. "You are right, though; we're not sailing back to Kjora."

It was a strange relief to hear him admit it. I slumped against the railing and wrapped my arms around my chest. "So, where are we going?"

"North." Kolur squinted into the sun.

"Well, that's obvious. *Why* are we going north?"

"Just an errand I have to take care of."

"An errand? An *errand*?" I threw my hands up in the air in frustration. "You couldn't have told me about it?" Then I peered at him, considering. "Why'd you bring me, anyway? You clearly don't need me."

Kolur hesitated.

"Well?" I snapped. "I know it's not just because you thought I'd have a good time. You're the most unadventurous person I've ever met." Even though I wasn't so certain of that now.

Kolur let out a deep breath. "I didn't know about it until after we had made sail. I had to make a quick decision, and I chose to bring you."

I stared at him. "The bones," I said, remembering the way they had scattered across the deck, foretelling times of strife and strangers coming to town. "I knew what I saw."

Kolur looked away from me.

"And you lied to me. You said they spelled out the same thing both times."

"I know what I said." He ran a hand over his wind-tangled hair. "I didn't handle it as well as I should have."

"You think?"

He gave me a dark look. "Well, you're always saying you wanted an adventure."

"You still lied to me." I pointed back at Frida. "Besides, you don't even need me. That's why she's here, isn't it? 'Cause you need someone trained to do magic? Real magic?"

Kolur gave me a long look and didn't answer.

"Sea and sky, why didn't you just say from the beginning–"

"It's difficult to explain." He gave me a weak half smile. "If I'd turned around to take you home, I'd never have made it. But I swear I'll have you back home in only a few weeks' time."

"A few weeks?" My chest tightened. "Mama will be worried sick. Papa, too – they'll come looking for me."

"I sent word that we were delayed."

"You *what?*" The whole world spun around. Kolur kept staring at me, as unperturbed as if we were arguing about the fishing schedule or repairs to the boat. "You told *them* but you didn't tell me?"

"I had my reasons," he said quietly.

I tore away from him, shaking with fury. Frida looked at us from her place at the wheel, the wind tossing her braid around. Everything was falling into place. The extra supplies. Frida joining us on the trip. Kolur's strangeness during the storm–

"You caused this." I whirled around to face him. "You made all this happen. I don't know how, but you – you're planning something."

He didn't deny it.

My eyes were heavy, and my face was hot. I raced over to the stairs and climbed down below. As soon as

I was off the deck, the tears spilled out. I thought about Mama receiving word that I'd be home in a few weeks. It was from Kolur; she wouldn't think anything of it.

He'd betrayed me. He'd betrayed *her*.

I slammed the door to my cabin and shoved the trunk of old sails up against it. I hoped that would be enough to hold him – I hoped he wouldn't get Frida to use magic. Then I dug through my stack of clothes until I found that charm I'd bought in Beshel-by-the-Sea. I'd taken it off when I'd boarded the boat, thinking I was safe.

I slipped on the charm, and its thin protective spell rippled through me. I collapsed down on the bed and took deep breaths as tears dripped down the side of my face.

I didn't know if the bracelet would keep me safe from Frida's magic. It certainly wouldn't take me home, where Papa could soothe me the way he had once when I was a little girl, telling me that all liars are punished by the ancestors. But it was better than nothing. Even so, I lay there weeping, with no idea what to do next.

I woke with a jolt in the middle of the night. My face was sticky with dried tears, and the charmed bracelet had twisted tight around my wrist. I couldn't see anything. I was in a void.

No – I just hadn't activated the lantern before I fell asleep.

I crawled out of the cot and felt around until I found the lantern's familiar round curves. "Light," I whispered, and it blinked on. The cabin looked as I had left it. My clothes were flung across the floorboard; the trunk was still shoved up again the door.

The *Penelope* rocked and creaked, sailing us to whatever fate awaited in the north. My stomach rumbled. Of course. I'd missed dinner.

I shoved the trunk aside and eased the door open. Kolur usually slept up on deck, next to the helm, but Frida had been sleeping down in the storeroom. I wanted something to eat, but I didn't want to see her. I supposed that was the trouble with hiding on a fishing boat – there aren't many places to hide.

Still, I crept into the storeroom, taking care not to step on the noisier boards. The storeroom was flooded with dark blue light from the lantern, and I could just make out the shape of Frida curled up in a hammock in the corner. Moving quickly, I grabbed a jar of dried caribou and some sea crackers and jam, along with a skin of water, and then hurried back to my room to eat.

It was a satisfying enough meal, since we hadn't been at sea long enough for me to be sick of it, but when I finished, I had no desire to fall back asleep. My thoughts kept swirling around, churning and anxious. I imagined Frida sneaking into my cabin and casting some dangerous curse on me, and I rubbed at my bracelet, trying to make the image go away. It didn't.

Plus, my chamber pot needed emptying.

I held out as long as I could, not wanting to risk facing Kolur up on deck. I resented him for keeping secrets from me, for keeping his magic from me. In the gentle rocking of the boat, I had the unnerving thought that maybe

Mama'd known about his past, too, and maybe that was why she'd arranged for me to apprentice with him.

Or maybe not. I took a deep breath, grabbed the chamber pot and left my cabin.

The *Penelope* rocked back and forth, and I pressed one hand against the wall to steady myself. The wind was howling outside, a low, keening moan that sent a prickle down my spine. I'd have thought it was Frida's doing if I hadn't just seen her sleeping.

With practiced movements, I climbed up on deck without spilling the chamber pot. The wind gusted around the boat, slamming into the sails and kicking up the ocean in frothy peaks that appeared now and then over the railings, illuminated by the magic-cast lanterns. At the horizon, Jandanvar's lights cascaded across the night sky, swirls of pink and green. You could see them even in Kjora, and it was a comfort to see them here, in unexpected waters.

The first thing I did was check for Kolur. He was over by the helm and sleeping, a blanket tucked around his shoulders.

I made my way to the starboard railing and chucked out the mess in the chamber pot. It all disappeared into the churn of the sea. I set the pot down at my feet and leaned against the railing. The air had that scent again, sweet like berries and flowers. Except nothing about it made me think of spring.

It was cold.

Death-cold, Papa would say, but I stayed out in it anyway. There was a crispness to it I found refreshing after being cooped up in my cabin. I wasn't used to being inside, and I'd always preferred to be out-of-doors. I did understand why Kolur would rather be at sea than back in the village, trapped in his shack on the beach. But that still didn't explain what we were doing out here, why we were sailing into the north. I'd be home in a few weeks' time, he'd said, so we couldn't be going far. Maybe it had something to do with his old life in Skalir. A fisherman's debt? Payment to a former apprentice master? Perhaps he'd gone too far into unfamiliar waters before I met him, and he had old ties to sever.

A lot of possibilities, to be sure. None of them made me any less angry with him.

The lanterns cast long shadows across the water that rippled with the waves, moving like the ghosts in Papa's warning stories. It was mesmerizing, the inky black of the night sea, the blue glow of the lanterns, the stars glittering overhead. My thoughts unwound from me, still conjuring up reasons for Kolur to sail us north with a trained wind-witch. Maybe he was cursed and finally found a cure. Maybe *she* was cursed, and he was the cure. It would be just like the story Mama had told me about Ananna – I used to pretend I was Ananna before she was a ship's captain, travelling across the desert to cure the curse placed on Naji of the Jadorr'a. Maybe I was on the same sort of journey now.

Something splashed in the water.

I jumped back from the railing, startled. Or maybe this was about the Mists. I hadn't considered that possibility. I hadn't wanted to.

Another splash. This time I realized it came with a shadow, one that moved differently from the others. I leaned over the railing, peering close, my heart racing. In truth, this didn't seem like the Mists. They always came with omens, with mist and gray light. Maybe this was just a whale. Even though we were too far north, and too early in the season, to see one.

Another splash. I grabbed one of the lanterns and dangled it over the water, trying to get a better look.

There was something below the surface. Too small to be a whale and too thin to be a seal.

I took a step back. Under other circumstances, I would have called for Kolur. But not tonight; I was still angry with him. I touched my bracelet instead.

A head emerged from the water. A young man's head, pale hair plastered to his skull, seawater running over his skin in rivulets.

I shouted and dropped the lantern overboard, then immediately turned to Kolur, afraid I'd woken him – but he slept on.

The lantern's glow sank all the way down into the ocean's depths. I cursed. I'd have to explain that eventually.

"Oh," said the young man. "You dropped something."

His voice was strange, melodious and reedy, like a flute. I was too scared to move. He swam alongside us, his face turned toward me. It was almost a human face, one with all the marks of beauty – sharp cheekbones and a long, thin nose and large, pale eyes. But that beauty was what made it unnerving. I'd seen handsome men before, and I'd seen exquisite women, and it wasn't until this moment, in the shivering dark, that I realized every single one of them possessed some minor imperfection that let you know they were human. The more I looked at this young man, swimming like a dolphin alongside the boat, the more inhuman I found him.

"What are–" I started in a fierce whisper.

The young man dove beneath the waves.

The wind surged. I clutched the railing so tightly that my knuckles turned white. My bracelet was freezing against my wrist. I waited for gray mist to curl off the water, for a gap to appear in the sky filled with unearthly light. I waited for danger.

But nothing happened.

Kolur slept on.

The *Penelope* continued on her path to the north.

The ocean was empty.

CHAPTER FOUR

Three days passed and I didn't see the boy again. I wasn't frightened of him, exactly, but when I crept up on deck at night, I wasn't certain I wanted to see him. I thought he might be part of the reason Kolur was sailing us north.

After those three days, I decided not to keep myself locked in the cabin during the day. It was too much, being alone with my thoughts like that, with all my anger and frustration and confusion swirling around inside my head. I didn't want to hide – I wanted answers. Besides, fuming in my cabin was even more boring than doing chores.

When I finally wandered up on deck, nothing had changed: Frida still mapped out our path through the water. Kolur still steered at the wheel.

"Decided to join us, huh?" Kolur grinned. It was colder now than it had been a few days ago, despite the sun shining up in the clouds. No heat charms burned on the deck. I thought about Mama's garden back in Kjora, all the seeds tucked into the mud and waiting for the air to turn so they could punch their way up to the surface. Henrik and I had helped her plant them, the way we did every year. She never told us what seeds we were given, and it was a surprise every spring when they revealed themselves.

It was almost spring there. But it didn't feel like spring here.

"Are you going to tell me where we're going?"

"North." Kolur pointed up to the sky, as if the world were a map.

I glared at him. "Well, if you're not going to answer my questions, do you at least have anything for me to do?"

Kolur shrugged.

"Maybe you should have thought of that before you dragged me out on your errand."

Over at the navigation table, Frida lifted her head, the wind tossing strands of her silvery-brown hair into her eyes. "I do," she called out.

I frowned. Glanced at Kolur. He was staring out at the water, lost in the motions of the *Penelope*.

"You can come over," she said. "I won't bite."

I walked across the deck, rubbing at my bracelet. It held the warmth of my skin, so I knew I didn't face any immediate harm.

"Our path is going to get dangerous," Frida said.

"I thought this was just a simple errand."

Frida smiled. "The danger isn't the errand; it's the path." She pulled the cover over the carved map before I could see where that path led us. "The ice hasn't completely broken up yet, so we run the risk of icebergs. Kolur tells me you can do a bit of magic? I may need help with spells, and I thought we could practice."

"You want me to help you but you won't even tell me where we're going?" Heat flushed in my cheeks.

Frida looked at me, her head tilted like a bird. "Kolur asked me not to."

I twisted around and looked at him through the blustering wind and the flapping sails. He was ignoring us both, as was his way.

"Why?" I turned back to her. "What harm could it do? It's not like I have any choice here."

Frida smiled knowingly. "That's what I told him. But he's worried about you doing something that could get yourself hurt."

I hugged myself, trying to conjure up some warmth.

"Shall I show you the magic we'll be doing?"

"On what? There isn't any ice around here."

"Ah." Frida nodded. "Yes. I see what Kolur was worried about now."

"What?" I hated this, the way they both kept talking around me, dropping hints. Like they were playing some stupid game.

"There is ice here. Come." She walked over to the railing. I waited a moment to be contrary. Then I followed out of nothing better to do. The water was choppy and dark green, almost black: a color that made me think of emptiness. "It's hidden, drifting beneath the surface. I have a spell working to melt it away before it hits the boat." She glanced at me out of the corner of her eye. "That's why I'm not burning the heat charms."

I had wondered, but she didn't need to know that.

"Kolur worried that you would run off when we next

made port, that you'd try to steal a boat to sail your way back home." She laughed. "I told him you seem capable enough. You're his apprentice, after all."

I squeezed the railing and wondered where we were going to make port. It was hard to remember the carved map from Papa's boat, but I was pretty sure there were chains of smaller islands this far north. Not that I'd ever heard anything about them. Papa was always saying that there was enough wonder in the waters of Kjora to last a lifetime.

"Where are we going to make port?" I said.

"Ah, already plotting your escape, I see."

"I'm not going to steal a boat," I snapped. "Kolur's going to take me home, isn't he?"

"Of course." Frida smiled. "But your mother is a pirate."

I rolled my eyes. "You can't sail these boats alone, even with magic. I'm not an idiot."

Frida laughed. "It's been done before, I imagine. But yes, you'd be safer with a crew. Honestly, his real concern is that you wouldn't know this part of the world. It's dangerous, more dangerous than the southerly islands. Not just because of the Mists–" she gestured at my bracelet and I covered it protectively with my other hand "–but because of the land and the sea themselves. You're not used to it. Now watch." She braced herself against the railing with one hand and lifted the other in a slow, graceful gesture. Her wrist swirled and swayed, and her fingers rippled.

The wind shifted.

It had been blowing in from the southeast, the sails catching it so as to propel us northward, but now it was blowing entirely from the north, and there was a melancholy to it from the magic.

Over at the helm, Kolur cursed. "You'll break the masts!" he shouted.

"Ignore him," Frida said. "Look at the water."

I did. Spots of brightness appeared on the surface, like spangles of sunlight. Except they didn't line up with the sun.

Frida exhaled slowly.

The spots of brightness glimmered. For half a second, I saw what Frida saw – ice. The bright spots were chunks of ice, invisible in the swirl of the waves without the aid of enchantment.

And they were melting.

Their light bled into the ocean water, bright on dark, a beautiful swirl of color, like Jandanvar's lights, like the moon dancing with the night sky.

And then it was gone.

Frida let out her breath again, this time in a long unpracticed rush. She grabbed the railing with both hands and leaned back, stretching.

"So that's how you melt the ice." She straightened up and grinned at me. "You can do it with sea-magic as well, but I thought you'd prefer the wind."

I felt a twinge of annoyance because she was right, but it passed quickly enough, swallowed up by a lifetime of dreaming I could become a witch.

"I was curious which direction, though." Frida's

eyes sparkled. "Do you know yet? It took me a bit of exploration before I figured it out."

I didn't want to answer at first, but at the same time, it was a chance to talk about my magic with someone who understood, and I didn't get that opportunity often. I sighed and braced myself. "I'm pretty sure it's the south wind." Everyone always laughed when I told them that, and said how obvious it was. But I'd actually inherited it from Papa. Mama's magic was all based in the soil.

But Frida only nodded. "You should find this charm easy, then. When we sail across more ice, I'll show you how to do it."

I stared out at the dark water. It was good to have a job aboard the ship again.

Even if I had been dragged out here against my will.

I went up on deck that night, late, long after everyone had gone to sleep. It had become a habit these last few days, a way of having the *Penelope* to myself, even if just for a little while.

The wind was calm, nudging us gently along our way. I walked over to port side and leaned over the railing, staring down at the water. The lanterns' light reflected back at me, but I didn't see anything swimming alongside the boat.

I still thought that I might have imagined him. But I walked around the perimeter anyway, checking the water. Kolur snored, a soft rhythm that lined up with the motion of the *Penelope*. At the stern I stopped and let out a deep breath. No boy. Maybe I really was going mad out here. Maybe it was the far north making its way into my thoughts. Changing them.

Water splashed against the side of the boat.

I leaned over the railing immediately, gripping tight. A shadow flickered through the water.

"Hey," I hissed, forgetting the possibility of madness. "Hey, are you down there?"

A pause. The wind shifted directions; the sails swiveled into place, their magic crackling around me with the same melancholy I'd sensed before.

Then that pale face appeared, glowing in the water like the moon.

"You were casting magic earlier," he said.

I shivered. My heart pounded.

"Not me," I said in a low voice. "The witch on board."

"You mean you're not a witch?"

I shrugged, nervous but a little pleased, too, that he'd mistaken me for a proper witch.

He dropped below the water. I was certain I wasn't imagining him now, and all the many explanations for his existence passed through my head: he was a ghost; he was a water spirit made manifest; he was a merman, a new kind that lived in icy waters.

Or he was from the Mists.

He reappeared without warning. I gasped and stepped back. The boy frowned.

"Don't be scared of me."

It took me a moment to find my voice. "Why not?" I leaned closer. Sprays of freezing water splashed across my face. But the boy didn't seem cold at all.

"Because I'm here to help you." He bobbed with the waves. "My name is Isolfr."

"What *are* you?"

"Does it matter?"

"Yes!" My answer came out louder than I'd intended, and I glanced over at Kolur. He was still asleep. "Yes," I said, more quietly. "I don't make a habit of trusting boys who can swim in ice water."

Isolfr gave me one perfect, dazzling smile. "I'm not a normal boy."

"I can see that."

A wave crested and he rode with it, rising up alongside the boat. The water sparkled around him like it was full of stars.

"You still didn't answer my question," I said. "What are you?"

"What are you?"

"I'm human! You have to know that. Are you from the Mists?"

I spat out the question without meaning to – it's dangerous to be so forthright with someone from the Mists. I regretted it immediately, too, and my whole body went cold, and I took a step backward, shaking in the wind. But my bracelet remained lifeless, inactivated, on my wrist.

Isolfr looked scandalized.

"The Mists?" he said. "No, never. It's true I'm not human, but you don't need to be human to live in this world, do you?"

Quiet settled around us, and I eventually shook my head.

Isolfr smiled again, although not as brightly as he had earlier. His smile was lovely, like the paintings in the capital, and I didn't like that I thought that.

"You never told me your name," he said.

I hesitated. I got no sense of danger from him, it was true. He waited for me to answer, moving with the rhythm of the waves. In a way, he reminded me of the illuminated ice Frida had shown me that afternoon. He was that lovely, that unearthly.

"Hanna," I finally said.

Nothing happened except that Isolfr smiled again. "It was wonderful to meet you, Hanna. I look forward to working with you."

He dove down into the depths.

"Working with me?" I said.

I stayed up on deck as long as I could stand it, shivering in the cold as I waited for him to return, to explain himself, but he never did.

When I cleared breakfast the next morning, I pulled out the bones from the fish we'd eaten and scraped them as clean as I could. They were small, flimsy things, but combined with the bones from lunch and dinner, I should have enough to cast a fortune-telling charm of my own. I didn't expect them to tell me what Isolfr was or what he wanted – a creature like that had surely protected himself with magic – but I did plan on asking where Kolur was sailing us to. Just because he wouldn't answer my questions didn't mean I couldn't get answers.

I wrapped the bones up in a handkerchief and slipped

them under the blanket on my cot. Then I went back on deck, where Kolur and Frida had started up their duties for the day. A week in and we'd established a routine, one that hardly involved me. If Kolur was too lazy to return me and so had to force me to accompany him on his errand – I certainly wasn't going to call this an adventure, because it was far too dull – he could at least have found something for me to do.

The sails curved outward under the force of the brisk, strong wind, looking like fluffy white clouds against the cold steely sky. The air smelled sweet. I pulled myself up from the ladder and closed my eyes and concentrated, trying to feel for that presence I'd felt earlier–

But there was nothing there.

"What the hell are you doing?" Kolur's voice interrupted my concentration. I opened my eyes.

"Nothing," I called back. "Just like you want."

He shook his head and kicked at the boards. "Looked like you were in a damn trance. Don't get like that out here, girl. It could mean something dangerous."

"It wasn't anything dangerous. I knew what I was doing." I walked over to him. Frida was hunched over the map, as always, tracing a path with her finger. Yesterday, I'd tried to slide up beside her and peek at our navigation plans, but she'd slammed the lid shut with a gust of wind before I could see anything.

"Fine. But I don't know that." Kolur glanced down at me. "You know it's not just icebergs we have to worry about out here."

He was talking about the Mists. I suppressed a shiver.

"Funny," I said. "Frida told me the exact opposite."

Kolur rolled his eyes, but Frida smiled at us from across the boat.

"Frida's a troublemaker." Kolur paused. "You want to take the wheel for a little while? Should be fine, what with her melting charm going."

"Sure." It was something to do, and when I took the wheel from him, I felt the strength of the ship beneath my hands as it cut through the water. Kolur slouched beside me, his arms crossed over his chest – waiting for me to mess up, no doubt.

"Is it just killing you?" I said. "Letting me do some work for once?"

"Focus on the seas, girl."

We sailed on. The ocean glittered around us; the wind flapped at the sails and brought that scent of cold, frozen flowers. I thought about Isolfr emerging from under the sea, claiming we were going to work together.

"Kolur?" I said, still looking out at the horizon.

"Tired already?"

"No." I chewed on my bottom lip, trying to figure out what to say. As angry as I was with him, he needed to know about Isolfr. He was right – we were far north, and the waters were dangerous. Keeping Isolfr a secret meant putting the *Penelope* in danger.

"Well? Spit it out, girl."

"Last night, I saw a boy swimming in the water beside the boat. I spoke to him, and he said his–" I stopped. Kolur had wandered over to Frida, and they stood side by side, staring down at the navigation table.

Ice welled up in my stomach.

"Kolur!" I shouted. "I was talking to you."

He lifted his head. "What's that? You tired already?"

My hands trembled, my head spun and anger flushed hot in my cheeks. The *Penelope* veered off to the port side, and Kolur gave a shout and came running up to me. He yanked the wheel out of my hands and righted our path. The sails snapped. Dots of sunlight scattered across the deck.

"Are you sure you're okay?"

"I'm fine. You're the one who keeps ignoring–"

He turned away from me and stared out at the water. The wind ruffled his hair. "Maybe we can have you send a note down to your mother next time we dock. Think she'd like to hear from you."

For a moment, I was struck by this new piece of information – the next time we dock? Where was it? Someplace with messengers, if we'd be able to send a note.

But then the implication of his promise struck me heard. He'd talked about docking, but not about Isolfr. He didn't hear me. I brought up Isolfr and he didn't hear me.

I stumbled away from him without answering. The wind roared in my ears.

Magic could do that. Magic, and not much else.

That night, I crept up on deck, the way I'd done every night since we left Skalir. But tonight was different. Tonight, the air itself felt sinister, like the wind was laced with poison instead of enchantment. I had my bones with me, still wrapped up in their handkerchief. And I intended to get some answers.

Kolur was sleeping at the helm, the steering charm glowing in the darkness. I crept up to the bow, where the wind was strongest, and closed my eyes to get a feel for its magic. It was strong tonight, a glimmer behind my closed eyelids, a tremor in my muscles. I pulled the wind's strength into me so that it was racing through my blood, sparking and shining. I opened my eyes and dumped the fish bones into my palm. They jumped with enchantment. My whole body thrummed, the magic rising and falling with the swell of wind.

I murmured the incantation and scattered the bones across the deck. Kolur snored in the distance. The bones arranged into their patterns. At first I thought it was a scatter of islands, some archipelago in the north that I didn't recognize, and my heart leapt – was this where we were going? Jandanvar wasn't an island chain, I knew that much. But then I looked closer and saw that the bones had fallen into bland nonsense: Friendship. A long journey. Magic.

"Worthless," I muttered. I gathered them up and tossed them again, this time trying to concentrate on a specific question: *Where are we going?*

The bones clacked across the deck. They had fallen into the exact same formation as before.

I batted them away in frustration, sending them scattering toward the mast. Kolur slept through it all. I stood up and shivered in the cold. Water splashed around the *Penelope's* prow, spraying me with a frozen mist. Moonlight bounced off the water.

"Hanna."

I jumped. The voice was melodious and soft. Inhuman.

"You!" I grabbed the railing and leaned over the side. Isolfr floated in the water, his eyes wide and shining, gazing up at me. "Did you put a spell on Kolur and Frida?"

He slid into the water so that his shoulders and neck and most of his chin were submerged.

"You *did*." I clung to the railing like it could save me. "Kolur!" I shouted. "Kolur, wake up."

"He won't." Isolfr's voice was quiet, a rush of whispers to blend in with the roar of the sea. "He won't wake up."

I stared down at him. Cold horror crawled up the inside of my stomach. "What did you do to him?"

"Made sure he slept through the night." Isolfr rose out of the waves, looking indignant. "Maybe I was helping him. Frida Kuhn, too." He wore a dark tunic and his pale skin gleamed in the moonlight. "I just want them to sleep."

"No, you don't." I wished now I hadn't kicked my bones across the deck, since I would have liked something to throw at him. "What are you doing? What do you want?" I paused. "What *are* you?"

His eyes went wide again. If I hadn't known better, I'd have thought him scared.

"Well?" I said.

He dove under the water.

I cursed and screeched in vexation. Across the boat, Kolur snorted but didn't wake up.

"Answer me!" I shouted into the water. Isolfr was down there, a dark shadow moving beneath the waves. "Tell me what the hell is going on. What do you want?"

The shadow moved back and forth. I was certain it would disappear. But then Isolfr's head crept up, water streaming through his hair. He looked like silver.

"Am I going to get an answer out of you?" I demanded.

"Only if you ask the right question." His lifted his chin, almost like he was trying to be brave. My heart slowed. Maybe he really was scared. Now, there was a thought. That this strange shimmering magical creature was afraid of *me*.

"What are you?"

He shook his head.

"What do you want?"

He paused. Opened his mouth. Closed it. The water sloshed around him. Finally he said, "To help."

"Help with what?"

"I can't tell you yet." He paused. "There are – factors."

I sighed. "Fine. Why did you enchant Kolur and Frida? They ignore me if I try to tell them about you."

"They can't know about me." His eyes flicked back and forth. "It would be – dangerous right now. I can't reveal my identity to them. But I can reveal it to you."

"I don't know your identity."

"I told you my name."

I sighed and leaned my elbows against the railing. Even with my coat, I was getting cold out here. I rubbed my arms. It didn't do much.

"Are you cold?" Isolfr rose farther out of the water. "I can show you how to create a heat charm."

I looked at him, considering. The wind blew straight through me. But I shook my head. "It'd be easier if you just gave me some answers."

"I've given you what I can."

I sighed. "Why is it dangerous for you to tell Frida and Kolur who you are?"

He hesitated. "It's quite complicated," he finally said. "But Frida Kuhn has – a history. She's known to be unstable."

I glanced over my shoulder, at the open hatch leading down below, where Frida slept. Kolur had said Frida was a troublemaker–

"Don't lie to me," I said.

"I'm not." Isolfr shook his head, throwing off dewy droplets of ocean water. "I'm just saying she's a powerful woman."

I laughed. "Sea and sky, are you scared of her?"

Isolfr floated in the water and didn't answer me.

"What did she do?" I hesitated. "Am I in danger?"

"Not from her." Isolfr bobbed with the swell of a wave. "She wouldn't hurt you. But she did some magic, back when she was training in Jandanvar, that harmed my brother."

"She trained in Jandanvar?" I was startled and the question came out too loudly, my voice echoing out across the night. Isolfr dived below the water.

"Oh, for–" I rubbed my forehead. This was starting to get tiresome. "Come back up!" I shouted. "I'm sorry I startled you."

His eyes appeared. His nose. His mouth. He really did have a lovely face.

"So she trained in Jandanvar and hurt your brother." I sighed. "And you don't want her to know you're here."

He nodded. "She's frightening."

"Fair enough." I didn't add that he seemed a bit skittish in general. "All right, one more question. Do you know where we're going?"

He nodded. The sea foam shone around him. "You're going to a place in the north. But I can't say more than that yet."

"Jandanvar?" I leaned over the railing, far enough that my coat was dampened with sea spray. "It's Jandanvar, isn't it?" Anger swelled inside my chest. "That place is halfway to the Mists! They let people from the Mists wander their streets. What's wrong with Kolur?"

Isolfr didn't say anything.

I sighed and stepped away from the railing. The wind played with my hair. *A place in the north*. Well, that was more than Frida and Kolur had told me, at least straight on.

"So, why will you talk to me?" I said. "Am I not as frightening as Frida?"

"No, of course not." Isolfr gave a disarmingly handsome smile. "I am to help you, like I said, to work with you. What you said about Jandanvar isn't entirely true, by the way."

"What?"

"That it's halfway to the Mists. It's in this world."

"I know that," I said. "But they still let the Mists through there. And it's a place of dangerous magic; that's what everyone says." It had never occurred to me that witches trained in those cold, frozen lands, casting spells up to the swirl of Jandanvar's lights.

"People live there," Isolfr said.

"Not human people."

"Frida is human, and she lived there."

I scowled at him.

"You are right to fear the Mists, though. Those who mean us no harm never leave Jandanvar." He lifted his chest out of the water and looked me straight in the eye. I trembled from the cold. Still, I didn't dare leave him to slink down below where I could crawl into my bed sheets until I found warmth. He was giving me answers.

"You should watch for mist on the water," he said. "A certain type. Very thick."

"Oh, I know," I said. "What do you think I'm wearing this bracelet for?" I lifted my wrist up and shook the bracelet for him to see. It glowed in the moonlight.

Isolfr frowned. "That's weak magic."

"It's better than nothing." I folded my arms over the railing, and my breath puffed out as I spoke. "Besides, any child of the north has been trained to look out for the Mists since we were babies." I counted off with my fingers. "Unnatural gray mist. Folk with flat gray eyes. Unusual star patterns. We learn the constellations just so we can tell if the Mists have been changing the night sky."

Isolfr almost looked disappointed. I figured he had his whole speech worked up, trying to warn me about the Mists. "But many humans have gray eyes."

I shrugged. "Mama told me you'll know the difference when it's the Mists and when it's just a human."

His shoulders sagged and he shook his head, flinging dots of water across the ocean's surface. "It's not enough.

You need to learn to recognize those creatures that are particular to the Mists. The ones that the people of the Mists control." He looked at me. "Here on the open sea, they'll fly or they'll swim."

"So does everything else."

He gave me an annoyed look. "Yes, but these will be creatures unlike any you've seen before. They communicate on the veins of magic running through our world, so you'll *feel* them coming, a tremor on the air."

I looked away from him, out to the wind-beaten ocean, and shivered.

"They often blend in with the light and shadow, reflecting their surroundings like mirrors. You have to look for disturbances just out of the corner of your eye." He paused, treading water and gazing up at me. "Has that ever happened to you? Have you ever seen something move just on the edge of your vision, but when you look over, nothing's there?"

I toyed with my bracelet, spinning it around my wrist. "Sure. Happens to everyone, doesn't it?"

"*That's* the Mists," he said, "moving along the roads between worlds. Be careful if you see it."

I nodded. The cold was working its way through my coat. I couldn't stay out here much longer.

"Be careful," Isolfr said, and then he dove back into the water.

This time, he didn't emerge again.

CHAPTER FIVE

We continued on our journey to the north, and I continued my nighttime visits with Isolfr. Talking with him was like trying to figure out a puzzle: I'd ask him questions, he'd give me vague answers, but only if he was of a mind to. Frustrating, to be sure, but exciting too. Something to distract me from the boredom of life at sea.

"So, if you won't tell me what you are," I said, leaning up against the railing, a blanket pulled around my shoulders, on top of my coat, "can you at least tell me where you're from?"

Isolfr bobbed in the water. He looked like a patch of moonlight.

"I'm from up there," he said, and pointed straight to the stars.

"The sky?" I said. "You're from the sky?"

He nodded. "I miss it, too. My family has a palace in the air, and it's quite a thing to see."

"I'd imagine so." I'd no idea if he was joking, if this was in any way an honest answer. I'd never heard of creatures living up among the clouds, but then, neither

Mama nor Papa knew about much in the way of spirits.

Whatever Isolfr was doing down here, I suspected it was more involved than protecting the *Penelope* from the Mists. I also suspected he didn't want to do it. Now, he never came right out and *said* that, because Isolfr never came out and said anything, at least not anything useful, but I got the sense of it anyway from how wistful he'd look when he talked about his home up in the clouds.

And then one night, when we'd been talking for a week or so, he startled me with a sudden burst of straightforwardness.

"Do you trust me?" he said.

I blinked at him in surprise. I was out at the bow, our usual spot. The nights kept getting colder and colder, and the stars were sharper now, like flecks of diamonds up in the sky.

"What?" I said.

"Do you trust me?" He sounded out of breath, like he was nervous. He lifted himself up out of the water, his eyes fixed on me.

"Truthfully?" I hesitated. Isolfr looked so hopeful I didn't want to tell him no. "I'm not sure."

He furrowed his brow and dropped low into the water. Even in the darkness, I could tell my answer saddened him.

"Wait," I said. "It's not – please don't take it personally."

He lifted his eyes, and that wounded expression made his features even more unearthly.

"You have to admit you're a little hard to trust," I said. "Since you can swim in freezing water and claim you live in the clouds." I paused. "And you keep warning me about the Mists."

"That's to help you." He pushed himself up. "I want you to trust me," he said. "I have to show you something and I don't want you to be afraid."

A chill went through me, and I wrapped my arms around chest to keep warm. "This is new," I said.

"I've been delaying it." Isolfr looked down at the water. "Kolur is a fool, you know, and he's on a fool's errand."

"I'll have to take your word for it, because I certainly have no idea what he's doing. I keep pressing both of them, but they never give anything away. I'm not even sure when we'll be making port next." I clung to the railing and pressed myself over the side of the boat. The sea spray stung my face and made my eyes water. Clouds drifted over the moon, turning everything dark. "What do you want to show me? Is it related to where we're going?" I felt a little thrill of curiosity – maybe I'd finally found a way to get Isolfr to tell me what was going on.

"No." He hesitated. "It's related to – it's from – the Mists, actually."

"The what?" I jumped away from the railing. The open ocean was too open, and I felt exposed. "No. Absolutely not. You won't even tell me what you are, and now you–"

"I'm not from the Mists!" He drew himself up and his skin gleamed and his eyes flashed with a ferocity I would never have expected from him. "I'm trying to *protect* you from the Mists. And that's why I need to show this to you. *Please.*" A wave swelled and almost swallowed him up. He looked deflated after his outburst, a piece of silk caught on the current.

"I was tasked with warning the *Penelope* of the danger she's sailing into." Isolfr's voice was quiet. I had to strain to hear it over my racing heart. "I was asked to show you the threat you've been facing. I've put it off, because–" The waves surged again. "Because I was afraid. But I can't delay any longer. So even if you don't trust me – you'll have to trust me."

He smiled then, that charming bright smile, but I could see through it. And what I saw was fear.

I thought about my family's stone cottage on the road to the sea. I thought about Mama's garden, the way it looked in the summer, when all the herbs were blossoming and the vegetables were growing. I thought about Henrik playing in front of the fire, about Papa coming home from his fishing trips smelling of the ocean, about Mama singing pirate songs as she swept dirt out the back door.

I wondered if I'd experience any of it again.

I looked down at Isolfr floating there in the dark ocean. His eyes reflected the starlight. In the last week, I'd begun to set aside the reality that he wasn't human. I hadn't even realized I'd been doing it until now.

"Please," he said.

"What are we sailing into that's so dangerous?" My voice wavered. "Just tell me. I've thrown the fortunes, and I didn't see anything–"

"Because this part of your future is blocked. But you're traveling north, to the far north, the top of the world." Isolfr swam up to the *Penelope* and touched his hands to her side, the first time I'd ever seen him do so. Nothing happened. The boat kept moving through the water. The protection charms didn't even ripple.

That, more than anything, convinced me.

"Jandanvar?" I said.

He didn't answer.

I threw my hands up in frustration. "I still don't understand why you won't just tell Kolur, if this is so dangerous. I don't have any control over what he does."

Isolfr's face darkened. "I can't tell him. I'm sorry."

I shook my head and the freezing wind blew my hair into my face. "This is pointless, Isolfr. Fine. Whatever you need to show me, show me."

There was a long pause. The wind picked up, blowing in from the north. I wrapped my arms around myself, trying to keep warm. One hand brushed against my bracelet, and the magic in it hummed, tell me everything was all right.

Isolfr climbed over the railing.

Out of the water, he moved like a dancer, graceful and serpentine. When both feet were on deck, he looked at me shyly. His hair clung to his cheek. Water pooled at his feet and shone on his skin. That dark tunic was plastered against him.

"Hello," he said, like we hadn't just been speaking.

"Hello yourself. Are you sure you're not cold?" I nodded at his soaking tunic.

He shook his head. The *Penelope* rocked in the frigid wind.

"Well?" I said. "What is it you want to show me?" My heart started beating fast when I asked the question. And the boat's rocking made my head spin.

Instead of answering, Isolfr began to sing.

I was startled to hear which song: it was one in the old language that I knew well, about an ancient queen who was the first to sail between the islands. A wizard's song. The words were carefully chosen, the sort of words with magic in them that would weave in with the invisible veins of magic flowing all around us.

As Isolfr sang, he knelt down on the deck, his eyes closed. He lifted his left hand in an arc, palm flat, and his right hand thumped out a beat on the deck. The wind roared, bringing snow and chips of ice and a faint sparkle that looked like stardust. I was too astonished to be afraid.

My eyes itched and watered, and I rubbed at them. Splotches of light appeared on my closed eyelids.

When I opened my eyes again, I was no longer standing on board the *Penelope*.

I screamed and whirled around. We weren't even at sea anymore. The sky overhead was the thick golden color of autumn sunlight. The ground beneath us was flat and reflective, like a mirror. When I looked down, I saw myself staring back at me.

My chest hurt, and I took deep breaths, trying to capture air. "Isolfr!" I shouted. "What the hell did you do to me?"

Someone grabbed my hand, a touch gentle and cold. Isolfr. I shrieked and pulled away from him, terror vibrating inside me. He let me go, saying, "Wait. Hanna."

"Where are we?" My voice bounced around in a tinny, haunting way. "What did you do? Sea and sky, I should never have trusted you! You're a monster, aren't you? You–"

He grabbed my hand again and squeezed. "You're safe," he said. "I swear it."

I shook my head, but my panic was ebbing in spite of myself. The golden light cast a sense of calm over everything. It was obviously enchanted, but it didn't strike any warnings with the magic residing inside me, or the magic residing inside my bracelet.

"We're in a liminal space," Isolfr said. "The place between worlds. No one can hurt us here. Feel." He squeezed my hand tighter. "Concentrate. You're a witch; you can feel it. We're safe."

His hand was as cold as the night air aboard the *Penelope*, but it was pleasant, like the day after the year's first snowfall. I concentrated, steadying my breath. He was right. That sense of calm came from a protection spell, a sort not so different from the one Frida had cast over the *Penelope*. Only, it was deeper, and older, and stronger.

I'd never felt magic like it.

"We'll only be here a few minutes. I want you to meet someone, but we have to do it someplace safe." Isolfr let go of my hand and raised his own hands up over his head as mirrors of each other. "Gillean of the Foxfollow, I call you!"

His voice rang out, sonorous and rich. It didn't echo emptily the way mine had. I stared where Isolfr stared. I had no idea what I was going to see.

Shadows appeared, moving together into vague shapes. They lightened; they distorted. It was a man. A skinny man, with a mop of tousled gray hair and a shuffling, awkward walk. When he saw Isolfr, he let out a sigh.

"Mr Witherjoy!" he exclaimed, clutching at his chest. "Oh, you had me for a fright."

"I'm sorry, Gillean, I couldn't warn you."

"Your name's Isolfr Witherjoy?" I said.

Isolfr tilted his head. "It's both. Hanna, I'd like you to meet Gillean of the Foxfollow."

Of course it was both. I'd just said that. I was about to protest when Gillean turned toward me, and my body froze.

His eyes were gray.

Matte gray, like stones.

He was from the Mists.

He gave me a bow, practiced and easy. I stared at him in horror.

"You lied," I said to Isolfr, my voice deep in my throat. "You are from the Mists."

Gillean laughed.

I turned sharply to him, wishing I had a weapon beyond my bracelet. I didn't keep a knife on me, not when we weren't bringing up the nets. There was no reason.

"Forgive me," he said, and he smoothed down his dusty old jacket. "The notion that Mr Witherjoy would be from the Mists–" He chuckled again and shook his head. "I assure you, he's quite of your world." Gillean's expression softened slightly, and he said, "And I don't mean to harm you. I can't harm you, in fact, even if I wanted to."

The golden light brightened, and my thoughts were suffused with peace. A world built of a protection charm. This would be a place to live.

"Why do you bring me here?" I asked.

"I was wondering the same thing myself," Gillean said. He looked at Isolfr. "You said you wouldn't need to speak with me again, after the last time."

"I know. I'm sorry. My orders changed."

Orders? Who was he working for?

"I need you to tell her about Lord Foxfollow," Isolfr said.

"Who?" I said.

Gillean's face went pale. He trembled and rubbed at his shoulder distractedly. For all the stories I'd heard about the Mists, my first encounter with a man from those lands wasn't particularly frightening. And yet not even that golden light could melt away the tiny chill of fear still crawling under my skin.

"It's all right," Isolfr said gently. "It'll be just like before. I need her to hear, though, from you. If I could have found another way to do this, I would have."

Gillean hesitated. "And you're sure I'm protected?"

Isolfr paused, just for a fraction of a second, before answering yes. It left an uneasy feeling in my belly, that pause.

"I was valet to Lord Foxfollow," Gillean told me. "He is a dangerous man, my dear. He has tired of all the power in our world, and so he wants to go after yours."

"Is that where Kolur's going?" I said. "To meet with this lord?"

Gillean didn't answer. He had a glazed look, like the past had entangled him completely.

"I served as valet to his father, too," Gillean said. "That had been pleasant enough. But when he died, and this Lord Foxfollow assumed his title—" He closed his eyes. Isolfr moved forward by a step, one hand held out as if to catch Gillean before he fell.

Gillean took a deep, shuddery breath and regained his composure. Isolfr stepped back. "Oh, it was awful, my dear. He's an awful man. You wouldn't know it speaking to him, not at first, because he's quite charming. He always knows what you want to hear. It was through pure manipulation that he gained all the lands in Mists. But I don't imagine your world will go so easily. You humans have always put up a fight."

I was at once horrified and bewildered. Of course the Mists had tried to gain access to our world before – Ananna had stopped one such man, and her lover Naji had done the same long before he met her. But Ananna was a pirate queen and Naji was one of the Jadorr'a, and it made no sense to me that Kolur would be swept up in that sort of destiny. He was a fisherman. And not even a very good one.

"But the worst is when Lord Foxfollow's charm fails him." Gillean let out a ragged breath, and Isolfr moved close to him and put his hand on his arm. Gillean nodded. "When he can't manipulate you into doing what he wants, he sends out his horrors. They were formed out of the magic of our world, a dark spell banned many decades ago. Lord Foxfollow pays no attention to such rules. His horrors take no solid form. They're constantly shifting, constantly *changing*. I can't imagine the havoc they would do here if they were released. I remember when he sent them after his cousin Rothe, when he learned that Rothe had been meeting with one of Foxfollow's rivals. It wa–"

Another ragged breath. Tears shimmered on his cheeks. Isolfr wrapped his arm around his shoulder with a gentleness I didn't expect.

"It's all right," he said. "You don't need to go on if you don't wish to."

Gillean sighed, a shuddery, start and-stop noise. "Thank you." He looked up at me. "Forgive me, Miss Hanna. I wanted to be more helpful to you."

He seemed so small and frightened, standing there in the golden light. He wasn't what I imagined the Mists to be at all.

"It's all right," I said. "I think you have – helped me." That wasn't true; I still didn't understand why Isolfr had brought me here, or what Lord Foxfollow had to do with Kolur. But Gillean looked so shaky and awful that I couldn't express my confusion out loud. I didn't want him to feel his pain had been for no reason.

"Give me a moment," Isolfr said. "I want to see him back to his home safely." He and Gillean walked several paces away from me. I fiddled with my coat and watched as Isolfr conducted a simple protection ritual. Wizard's magic; human magic.

Cold swirled through the liminal space, the first wind since we had arrived. I could tell that it came from somewhere else.

Isolfr kissed Gillean on the forehead, and then Gillean evaporated on the wind.

Everything stilled.

Isolfr turned back to me. I straightened up, ready to demand answers. Before I could, though, Isolfr said, "Blink."

"What?" I willed my eyes to stay open.

"Blink."

"No. Tell me what's going on." I opened my eyes a fraction wider. "You warn me about all this danger, and then when I ask where you're going, you just say *north?*" My eyes were dry and itchy. "You tell me to watch for the Mists, and then you bring me here and show me this poor terrified man who tells me that a man is after us, a man who's a terror in a land of terrors."

"It's not a land of terrors," he said quietly.

"Shut up!" My eyes burned. "He's going to send horrors after us? *Why?* What did Kolur do? Just tell me wha–"

We were standing aboard the *Penelope*. The wind rattled the sails. Kolur snored over by the helm. Everything was dark.

Gods damn him. I'd blinked.

"Thank you." Isolfr materialized at my side, his skin glowing silver like magic. It made him lovely to look at, but I shoved him away, furious.

"Tell me what's going on!" I shouted.

"I am!" Isolfr twisted his pretty features into a scowl. "Lord Foxfollow knows that Kolur is coming. I can't warn Kolur myself, because it will only make matters worse. Kolur doesn't like me. So I'm warning you."

"What? Kolur doesn't like you?"

Isolfr pointed out at the sea. "Those terrors that Gillean spoke of are tangible. Real. Lord Foxfollow will find a way to send them through the gaps between the two worlds. I can't tell you what they'll look like, because they'll adjust to whatever veins of magic they came riding in on. They may be beautiful; they may be ugly. I hope they won't look like any creature you've ever seen before, but I'm not sure I can guarantee that, either."

He took a deep breath. I gaped at him and shivered in the cold.

"I'm trying to keep you safe," Isolfr said. "It's my duty. I don't have any say in the matter. I can't explain further, not right now. But I won't let Lord Foxfollow hurt you. Any of you."

He stopped, his chest heaving. I'd never seen him so sure of himself, and it disoriented me, to see him standing on the deck instead of swimming in the sea, his expression burning and intense.

"I'm sorry," I said. "I just don't understand."

Isolfr's shoulders slumped. He looked sad. "You will, eventually. I promise." He put one hand on the ship's railing. "But you can understand this: feel the magic." He looked me right in the eye, and for a moment I was mesmerized. "Feel the wind. Don't worry about the direction. You're a strong enough witch that when the horrors come, you'll feel a shift, like the whole world's gone dark."

My heart fluttered at the thought that I was a strong enough witch, and so I nodded even though it wasn't much to go on. But before I could ask him to clarify, he vaulted over the side of the boat with a splash.

When I rushed up to the railing, the water was empty.

CHAPTER SIX

I didn't see Isolfr for four days.

It wasn't for lack of trying. I went up on deck at night, standing in the sweet-scented wind while Kolur snored on unawares. But the water stayed dark and empty, and I felt a dull ache inside my chest. Maybe I'd been wrong to trust him – he'd toyed with me, then left me alone without any real answers.

One night, I felt a presence on the wind, a sense of intelligence swirling around me. I tensed and grabbed for my bracelet, thinking back on the warning Isolfr'd given me about sensing the Mists' horrors. But this presence wasn't a horror. It was simply there, surrounding me and the boat and the ocean itself, like it belonged in this place.

During the days, I spent most of my time hanging around Frida, studying her hand movements as she called down the winds. Papa could do a bit of wind-magic, and he'd taught me what he knew, but it wasn't much. Frida was a real witch. Sometimes when she was tracking our path on the carved map, I stood a few paces away, behind the mast where she couldn't see me, shadowing her movements with my own hands. I wasn't trying to cast her spells. I just wanted to understand how the movements felt. She moved more like a dancer than a witch. Maybe that was the trick.

The day after Isolfr took me to the in-between place, I spent the morning watching her throw new protection spells over the boat.

"They wore out more quickly than I expected," she told me, rubbing the bannisters with sparkling ground conch shell. "The north is tricky."

My stomach tightened up. "Maybe it's not the north," I said.

She looked at me, her eyes clear. "Did something happen?"

I hesitated. Kolur still wouldn't listen if I tried to mention Isolfr, but Frida was a *witch*. She had trained in Jandanvar.

"This boy, Isolfr," I said. "He's been swimming alongside the boat. I let him aboard last night and he didn't hurt me at all, and I'm sorry if–"

But Frida had moved down the railing. The wind whipped her braid around, and she lifted her head and squinted at me. "You have to do much more spell repair once you pass Skalir. Everything's thinner here."

I sighed and dropped my head back. The sky was empty, a flat grayish-blue that reminded me of the Empire mirror Bryn's mother kept in her bedroom. So Frida wouldn't listen when I said Isolfr's name, either.

In those four days, we never saw any land, only hunks of icebergs that Frida or I melted or moved with wind magic. They made me feel lonely, those icebergs, drifting out here in this emptiness on their own.

One day at lunch, we all sat huddled around a heat charm, eating the dried salted fish from our stores. We still had enough for a couple of days of normal eating, plus more if we skimped. Neither Frida nor Kolur had said anything about it, though.

"How long till your errand's done?" I said, breaking the silence.

Kolur glared at me.

"I didn't ask when we'd be back home." The sails creaked overhead. "Just about your errand."

Frida sipped from her waterskin, silent.

"I told you, girl, it'll only be a couple of weeks, and then I'll have you safely back on Kjora."

"It's been a couple of weeks." I pointed at the remains of our meal. "Are you planning to stop anywhere soon to restock? We're going to have to start taking rations, you know."

Kolur gave me a cool look and then turned to Frida. "How close are we to Juldan? I imagine we could stock up on supplies there."

"Oh, not far. A day's sail. Half a day if I can get the winds to behave. It's a bit out of our way, but nothing too terrible."

Juldan. I thought about Papa's carved map. Isolfr had told me the truth, then; we were far north, although not as far as Jandanvar.

But Juldan wasn't our destination. We were just resupplying.

I frowned across the meal at Kolur, wondering how much longer until I'd get to go home. I'd be much more excited about this adventure if we were actually doing something.

Kolur seemed to make sure he looked everywhere but at me.

I lay in bed that night, unable to sleep. Frida had done up the navigation calculations and announced that we'd be sailing into the Juldan port late tomorrow morning. My mind spun with plots to keep Frida and Kolur on land, to convince them to forget their madness and sail back to Kjora. Passage on a ship back to Kjora would be too expensive for a fisherman, and passenger ships were rare besides, so I figured I wouldn't be getting home otherwise. But maybe I could try to convince a crew into letting me join them. Ananna had done that. She'd spun a good yarn about betrayal and set sail that very evening. Maybe I could manage the same when we were in Juldan. I could call down the winds, after all, and it wasn't like Kolur needed me, what with Frida on board. Besides, if I joined with a crew, maybe I'd have a chance for a proper adventure, like the kind in stories.

But then my thoughts wandered away from the north. What if sailing home to Kjora meant that this Lord Foxfollow would follow us there? What if going home meant bringing horrors back to my parents and Henrik and Bryn?

I wondered if that meant I believed Isolfr. If I trusted him.

Things didn't make sense.

I stayed awake through the night, staring up at the lantern's light sliding back and forth across the ceiling. The air crackled like a storm was coming. My body buzzed. I rolled over onto my side and slid my hand under the knot of fabric I used for a pillow.

Sparks shot up my arm, radiating out from my bracelet.

I shrieked and yanked off the bracelet and stumbled away from the cot, dragging blankets and my makeshift pillow with me. The bracelet glowed.

I knelt down beside the cot, my breath caught in my throat. The air around the bracelet throbbed, humming with enchantment. Slowly, I reached out with one finger and poked it, this time prepared for the spark. It trilled up my arm, igniting all the residual magic inside me. I closed my eyes and grabbed the bracelet in my fist and concentrated–

Gray mist. Sharp, curving claws. Black ocean water. Light. Light. Light dripping like blood. Mist.

A scream.

I dropped the bracelet and jumped back. The air was still crackling around me. I leaned up against the wall and took deep breaths and tried to decide what to do. Kolur, I had to warn Kolur. Or Frida. No, she would have sensed the magic before I did, she should already know–

I heard a noise.

It came from up on deck: a slurred thump, a muffled shout. I cried out and then slapped one hand over my mouth. I was so scared that I started to cry.

Footsteps bounded past the cabin door, coming from the direction of the storeroom. They disappeared and reappeared overhead.

I was too frightened to move. I closed my eyes and strained to listen. The wind whistled around the *Penelope*, and it sounded as if it were weeping, too.

I thought I heard voices, droning with a low murmuring panic.

Sweat prickled over my skin.

Someone shouted.

I couldn't stay here. Isolfr had warned me about this. He had chosen me for whatever stupid reason, and now that the time had come, I just stood in my room and cried.

Kolur and Frida were hurt or dead, and I was left alone on the *Penelope* to die, too.

I snatched up the bracelet. It was cold, but it didn't make me see anything, thank the ancestors. I took a deep breath and eased open the cabin door. I leaned against the frame. I listened.

Voices.

As quick as I could, I darted into the storeroom and grabbed the big straight knife we used to clean fish. It still glittered with scales from the last time I'd used it. I held the knife close to my chest. My bracelet burned me, it was so cold.

I slid forward, cautious, terrified.

The boat rocked with the weeping wind.

I finally reached the ladder, but my fear had me paralyzed. Voices drifted down from the deck, fevered and distorted from the wind. One of them sounded like a woman's. Frida. Maybe she was hurt. Maybe I could save her. I'd never saved anybody. But Mama had. And Papa, too. Maybe there was a first time for everything.

I clutched the ladder and heaved myself up, the knife sticking out at an awkward angle from my right hand. The cold wind blew over me. It smelled of the sea, and it smelled of blood.

I peeked my head up out of the hatch. All the lanterns had burned out and everything was cast in silver from the moonlight. Two figures were hunched over at the bow of the ship. A woman, a man: Frida and Kolur.

Frida's long, dark braid swung back and forth in the wind.

"Kolur?" I gripped the knife more tightly.

Kolur turned toward me. Something lay at his feet. "Hanna, get down below."

"No! What's going on?" I scrambled the rest of the way up on deck. Frida looked at me as well, her expression unreadable. "What is that?" I pointed with the knife at the lump at their feet. It didn't move.

The deck was smeared with brightness.

"Well?" I moved forward, faking a bravery I did not feel. "What is it? What's going on—"

I froze. The sails snapped in the wind.

The thing at their feet was a body.

A body on the deck. A body that bled light.

Isolfr. In the moonlight, his body shone like alabaster. I shook and trembled and a bile rose up in my stomach. The boat seemed to tilt on the waves.

But then Kolur moved toward me and no longer blocked the body's face, and I saw its features twisted up in an expression of fear.

It was Gillean.

Gillean of the Foxfollow.

The knife clattered to the deck. I stumbled backward. My foot caught on the edge of the hatch. Kolur grabbed me and pulled me forward. The sudden movement made my head spin.

"I don't know what's going on," Kolur said in a low voice. "I woke up, and I found–" He nodded his head in Gillean's direction. "You probably shouldn't see it."

I yanked away from him. The world seemed to have less air in it, like we were all underwater. Gillean stared blankly at me in the moonlight. Light smeared on his face, and there were ragged tears in his jacket, all soaked with that same bright blood. Bite marks. Slash marks.

From sharp, curving claws.

Frida put her hand on my shoulder. "Kolur's right," she said. "You should go down below. It's safer. We don't know how this man got here, but he's from–" She hesitated. "He's from the Mists. You can tell from the way he bled."

"I do." The confession erupted out of me. "I know how he got here." A tear streaked down my face. Another. Another.

"You what?" Kolur stomped up at me and looked me hard in the face. "What? How could you possibly know–"

"I have told you!" I shouted. "Isolfr, the boy in the water! He introduced me to– to–" I couldn't say Gillean's name. My voice trembled. "It's Lord Foxfollow. He has horrors."

I could tell they didn't remember anything about Isolfr. And why would they? They were enchanted.

I tore away from them, my tears hot and frustrated, and ran to the railing. The water was dark and still. No Isolfr.

"Where are you?" I whispered. I could feel Kolur and Frida staring at me. The horrors traveled on veins of magic, that was what Isolfr had said, and I had felt it earlier, the magic harnessed by my cheap protection charm from Beshel-by-the-Sea.

I grabbed the railing tight and closed my eyes and tried to feel the magic on the air. It hummed around me. Normal.

"What are you doing?" Frida's voice was too close. My eyes flew open. She stood beside me, the wind tossing her braid out over the water.

"I'm feeling for disruptions in the magic." I managed to keep my voice calm. "Lord Foxfollow killed Gillean – that man – and brought him here. Because he was–" I couldn't keep my voice calm for long. "Because he was trying to help me." The tears came again, this time so many that I could no longer see anything but smears of light. Frida drew me in close to her, and I buried my face in her shoulder. She smelled of life on the sea.

That kindness surprised me.

"The magic's fine," she said. "I felt the disruptions, too. That's why I ran on deck. But I assure you that whoever was here is gone now."

I pulled away from her and wiped my eyes.

"I didn't see anything," Kolur said. "Didn't hear anything, either." We all looked at each other. Not at Gillean. "I woke up when Frida came on deck." Kolur was pale in the moonlight. "Whoever it was didn't seem interested in hurting me, at least."

"We're under a spell," Frida said. "That's the only explanation. But I can't feel it."

"It's Isolfr!" I said. "Kolur never wakes up when I talk to him."

But they both ignored me. I couldn't feel Isolfr's magic either, only the wind, cold and sharp and steady. I looked out at the water. There was still a chance that Isolfr was responsible for all of this, that Lord Foxfollow was a fiction he'd created. He'd put Kolur and Frida under a spell, after all. Maybe I only trusted him because he was so disarming, so shy, so beautiful.

And yet my bracelet never burned when he was near.

"We ought to give him a funeral," Kolur said, interrupting my worry. "Some kind of ritual. Get him off the boat, at least."

Frida didn't say anything.

"Bad luck to toss a man unceremoniously into the ocean," Kolur said. "Creates ghosts, and you don't want them hanging around a boat."

"He's from the Mists." Frida's voice rang out. "Even you aren't that softhearted, Kolur."

Kolur frowned at her. "Ain't about being softhearted. You know that. You've seen it."

There it was, some hint at their history. But I wanted a funeral for Gillean, too, and it wasn't because of ghosts. "No," I said, and sniffled. "No, he needs a funeral. He wasn't a bad person. He tried to help us."

"What are you talking about? You've never seen him before."

I sighed with frustration. Isolfr claimed he wanted me

to trust him, but he also made me keep his warnings from Kolur. His logic was incomprehensible.

Frida smoothed down her shirt with her hands, a nervous gesture. "In all likelihood, this is a Mists trap."

"It's not." Kolur turned away from her. "If it was a Mists trap, we'd be trapped."

I shivered.

"Hanna, come help me." Kolur dragged the chest containing our spare sails out from its place beside the masts. I glanced at Frida one last time, but she was gazing out at the ocean. She didn't look happy. I left her there and went over next to Kolur. He pulled out a stretch of fabric.

"Oh, drop the damn knife, girl. Frida'll watch out for us."

"She doesn't seem happy about us doing this."

"She hasn't had the run-in with ghosts that I have. I don't want to risk it." He nodded at me. "Help me with this sail. We'll wrap the poor boy up nice and neat."

I jammed the knife into the belt of my coat so I wouldn't have to set it down. Then I grabbed the rest of the sail and hauled it out of the chest. "Do you know any rituals?" I said. "Funeral rituals? For the Mists?"

Kolur stopped and squinted up at the moon. "What makes you think I know rituals for the Mists?"

"You've been keeping a lot of secrets lately."

Kolur looked at me. "My history ain't *that* interesting," he said. "And anyway it'd be dangerous to get involved with Mists magic. Northern rituals are fine. Just trying to keep the ghosts away."

"Are you sure?"

"Know more about it than you do."

I rolled my eyes. He glanced over at Frida, who was watching us with her arms crossed over her chest. "You ever think that maybe this doesn't have anything to do with us?"

She glared at him darkly and didn't respond.

It's a threat, I thought, but I didn't bother saying it aloud. Isolfr's spell would guarantee they forgot it as soon as the words left my mouth.

"We need your help," Kolur said to Frida. "You can keep watch over here."

Frida sighed and walked over to us.

"This is dangerous," she said, looking at the sail I cradled in my arms.

"You think I don't know that?" Kolur gestured at me to hand him the sail, but I hesitated.

"How dangerous?" I said.

Frida swept her loose hair away from her face and looked at me. "We don't always know what the effect of using our rituals on someone from the Mists will be," she said. "Our rituals might attract Mist attention."

"But I know damn well what's going to happen if we just toss him in the water," Kolur snapped. "The spirits'll be on us before morning. You know it, too." He jerked his chin at Frida. She looked away, scowling.

"We're not in a good position," Kolur told me. "But I'm willing to risk it."

I nodded. I didn't want to toss Gillean into the ocean without a funeral, either. He had tried to help me. He had been kind. Maybe our magic wouldn't mix badly with his. Maybe the Mists had left our world and wouldn't see what we had done. Maybe some things are just worth the risk.

"Now let's see that sail," Kolur said.

This time, I offered it to him. He grabbed one end and walked across the deck, spreading it out flat.

We worked in silence until Frida said, "I assume you keep a jar of anointing oil on board?"

"Bad luck not to." There was no gloating about Frida giving in. Everything was quiet and somber.

Frida nodded and went down below. Kolur and I stood side by side next to Gillean. The sail we'd draped over the deck lifted up on the wind.

I shivered.

"You cold?" Kolur glanced at me. "I'll tell Frida to charm one of her heat globes."

"No," I said. "I'm not cold."

The night seemed endless, swarming around us, trapping us. When I looked over the railing, I couldn't tell where the ocean ended and the sky began.

"Probably some victim from one of their squabbles," Kolur said. He shifted awkwardly, and I knew he was trying as best he could to be a comfort. "They'll send 'em through sometimes. Way of getting rid of the bodies."

There was no point in correcting him, so I just said, "All right."

Frida climbed back on deck. She had the little stone jar of anointing oil – it was whale fat, really, that had been infused with herbs and blessed in a ceremony out on the wilds of the tundra. All sailors kept a jar on board, in case of death. Without the ritual, a soul would be trapped in our world as a ghost, one of the legion of the dead who haunt the living. And you didn't want a ghost aboard a boat.

I thought about that time when I was a little girl and Papa made us all go inside and bar the doors. "They didn't do the ritual," he'd said, and all night we heard the shrieking and howling of that lost soul weaving its way through the village. So while I wasn't sure if the anointing oil would work on Gillean either, I didn't want to risk hearing those awful cries again. A cold wisp of dread twisted inside me and whispered that Gillean's death was my fault, that it was *Isolfr's* fault. He'd made Gillean speak. But Isolfr wasn't here to do his duty and bless the deceased. It fell to me.

"I'll do it," I said. "I'll bless him."

Kolur looked up. He'd already opened the jar. "You sure?"

At his side, Frida frowned.

"Yes. It's supposed to be a woman, anyway."

"It's supposed to be an acolyte of Kjorana," he said. "Which you are not."

I scowled. "I can stand in her place. Let me do it."

Kolur glanced at Frida, who remained stone-faced. But he handed me the jar without more fuss. It was heavier than I expected and warm from where he'd been holding it. I knelt down beside Gillean. His blood glowed all around me. Up close, his face seemed – surprised more than scared. I'd never seen someone die before. Maybe it was a surprise for your life to be snuffed out of you.

I dipped my thumb into the oil and took a deep breath. There were tears in my eyes. He'd been kind to me. He'd tried to help me, best he could. He wasn't the way the people of the Mists were supposed to be at all.

He'd been kind, and now he was dead.

I turned my face away from Frida and Kolur so they wouldn't see me crying. I pressed my anointed thumb against his forehead. His skin was warm like he was still alive. Startled, I snatched my hand away, expecting him to move. But he didn't.

In a blur, the incantation came to me – I'd learned it as a child, like all children of Kjora. "Release his soul to the great sea," I whispered. "Let him find his way home." I touched my thumb to both of his cheeks, then to his mouth.

A sighing filled the air, like a hundred birds taking flight at once. But there were no birds here. As quickly as it came, the rustling was gone, and I was certain I had imagined it. For a moment, I thought I saw a shimmer floating above Gillean's brow, like a slick of oil across the surface of water, but then that was gone, too.

I straightened up and wiped my eyes as discreetly as I could.

"We'll need to wrap his body," Kolur said softly.

I nodded and set the jar aside. Frida moved to help us, all three of us kneeling alongside Gillean and then pushing him at the count, *one two three,* onto the sail. Now that he was facedown, I could see the huge, jagged tears in his back, all glimmering silver.

"Something bad happened to him," Kolur said, looking sideways at Frida. "Something very bad."

"I can see that," she said.

I didn't want to think about Gillean's wounds.

Together, the three of us wound Gillean up in the sail. His blood glowed dully through the fabric, like burnished moonlight. Kolur nodded at me, and he and I picked him up, end to end. It felt like casting a fishing net into the water. But this was all we had.

I reminded myself that Gillean's body was just a shell, that with the anointment Gillean himself had fled to the great sea, where he'd swim among the souls of ancient fishes. It was only his body going into the northern waters.

Only his body, torn to shreds.

Gillean's body landed with a splash and bobbed up and down with the waves. Kolur muttered a prayer to the ancestors and then turned away, but I stayed in my place, expecting Isolfr to appear.

He didn't.

The swath of fabric drifted off into the moonlight.

When I turned around, Kolur and Frida were huddled close to each other, not speaking. I watched them across the deck. Frida was the first to break the silence.

"I'll cast another protection charm," she said. "You likely just sent out a beacon for the Mists."

Kolur grunted. "You'd rather we keep the body on board, let him be a beacon for ghosts?"

She didn't answer, only looked at me one last time. I stared back at her, and I got the sense she was studying me, trying to make sense of what had happened. I tensed and waited for her to say something. But she didn't.

Frida faced the north and lifted one hand against the

wind. The sails groaned as the wind shifted. I walked over beside Kolur, my arms wrapped around my stomach. I wanted to draw into myself and disappear.

"Don't worry, girl," he said. "I'm sure it was just bad luck."

I wondered how many times he was going to repeat that. I hated hearing it. I hated that I couldn't correct him.

"Still, I gotta admit, I'm not looking forward to sleeping up here alone." He looked over at Frida. The wind blew her hair straight back away from her face, and her magic settled over us, prickling and almost warm. "It's gonna be a long night till morning."

"I'll stay up here with you," I told him. "To keep you company." I smiled a little. It was the right thing to do, just like anointing Gillean and sending him out to sea despite the danger, even if Frida didn't see it that way. "I don't imagine I'll be getting much sleep tonight."

He laughed, although the laugh was thin and nervous. Frida's protection charm pulsed through the wood of the *Penelope*. She dropped her hand and the sails swung back to accommodate the northern wind.

She walked over and stood beside us. "I'll stay on deck tonight, too," she said. "It's not a night to be alone."

I wasn't going to argue that point, and I wasn't going to deny the protection of Frida's magic, either. Better to have it there than nothing at all.

Dawn broke after an uneasy night. I only realized I'd fallen asleep when I awoke to a beam of pink sunlight settling across my face. I was curled up beneath a pile of seal furs, sleeping on a hammock I'd tied between the foremast and the mainmast. Frida slept on beside me. Kolur was up at his usual place at the wheel, sleeping too.

Everything was calm.

I crawled out of the hammock and stretched. My head was fuzzy. In the soft light of morning, it was hard to believe that last night a man, a man who'd been trying to help me, had died. Except I didn't have to believe it. I knew it had happened, and the pale stains soaking into the wood of the deck were just more proof.

I wanted to distract myself, so I set about checking the rope and the enchantment on the sails. I made sure that all the other magic running the boat was in order. Frida's charm was still in place, strong and steady. All of Frida's navigation notes were locked away, but I checked the carved map, placing my finger on the spot of ocean where I thought we were. Juldan was only a few fingerwidths away.

The *Penelope* glided slowly through calm waters. I wandered over to the bow and cast the charm to look for ice, just to have something to do. But I didn't find any; the water stayed dark and murky as always. In truth, I was as much watching for Isolfr as I was for ice. But I wasn't sure what I'd say, what I'd do, if I found him.

He'd put Kolur and Frida under a spell. Maybe he'd done the same to me.

I leaned against the railing, breathing in the cold scent of the sea. I wondered if Gillean's soul had found its way. Even in the calm, lovely morning, remembering his face made my stomach flop around.

I was still staring out at the water when I noticed something flicker beneath the surface.

"Isolfr?" I whispered. "Is that you?"

No answer.

"If it is, you better get up here. Something terrible has happened, and–"

The flicker beneath the surface skipped away. Probably just a fish. I leaned back.

The flicker returned.

It was stronger this time. Brighter. It didn't move like a fish. *Flicker* wasn't really the right word – *swirl*, maybe. Like cream dropped into the hot black coffee Mama fixed sometimes.

Only this felt – sinister.

And my bracelet was growing cold.

I didn't move from my spot, only kept my gaze on the place where the brightness swirled around in the water. Maybe it was magic left over from the ice-finding spell. But if that was the case, I knew, then my bracelet wouldn't be burning into my arm.

The swirl thickened, became solid. It rose out of the water, a thick gray mist.

"Kolur!" I screamed. "Frida!"

The mist rose and rose until it formed the shape of a person. Two bright eyes appeared. They blinked once.

The magic inside of me rioted.

The mist-man disappeared.

"Hanna!" Kolur pulled me away from the railing. "Don't let them see you."

I was dizzy. Frida was already at the railing, drawing up the wind. I closed my eyes and concentrated, trying to feel for abnormalities. But my heart was racing too fast. I couldn't get a hold of anything.

"They're close by." Frida turned toward us. "That was a scout. We need to get down below, into the cabin. Hanna and I–" She hesitated, just for a second, her eyes flicking over to Kolur. He stared blankly back at her. "Hanna and I will have to use what magic we can down there. It'll be easier to protect a smaller area."

Kolur nodded. "Hanna, do as she says. Gather up your strength, girl."

I wasn't sure that was possible right now. "This is because of us," I said. "Because of the body. They followed it–" I felt sick. The funeral rituals. All I'd wanted was to honor Gillean, and now look what had happened.

"Don't think about that," Frida said. "Come." She put her hand on my back and turned me toward the hatch leading down below.

And then we both stopped.

I was certain we saw it at the same time.

A warship, towering toward the sky, big enough to cast a shadow over the *Penelope*. It looked carved out of gray stone, and towers rose up from its deck instead of masts, all of them billowing mist.

It was sailing right toward us.

I froze in place, trapped by the warship's shadow. Beside me, Frida cursed, then shouted Kolur's name.

"I see it!" he called out, his voice strained and small.

The ocean churned around the warship's prow, frothy and gray-white. I couldn't see anyone moving on its deck. It was a hollow, empty ghost.

"It's the Mists, isn't it?" I asked.

Frida hesitated for a moment. Then she said, "Yes. I think so."

After we had cast Gillean into the sea, he had drifted toward the west, sinking as he went. Trailing light. And now this ship, huge and monstrous and run by magic, was sailing toward us. From the west.

I thought it was the right thing to do, casting the rites. He died because of me. But now we were going to die, too.

Kolur shouted behind me. I couldn't make out what he said, his words distorted by my panic. But Frida called out, "Right away!" and bounded off.

I still couldn't move.

"Hanna!" My name rose out of Kolur's shouting. "Hanna, get the hell away from the railing!"

An enormous dark wave, rising from the warship's path through the water, swelled underneath us. The *Penelope* rocked back and I went skittering across the deck, landing hard on my back next to the masts. For a moment I stared, dazed, at the pale blue sky.

"Hanna!"

The boat lurched.

That broke me out of my spell. I scrambled to my feet, clinging to the mast for support. Kolur glared at me over at the helm, where he was fighting the wheel for control of the *Penelope*.

"Turn the sails!" he roared. "That ship's not turning away."

I nodded.

"Don't use magic. It's too dangerous right now." The wheel whipped out of his grip and went spinning, and the boat spun with it. Everything tilted to starboard. I toppled sideways, grabbing onto a loose rope before I tumbled over the railing. As soon as we righted again, I went to work, loosening the knots and dropping the sails. Kolur's words echoed in my head – *don't use magic.* I listened to him. Now was not the time to be contrary.

We rocked back up. I stopped thinking about Kolur's orders and just acted on them. I'd shifted the sails plenty of times without magic, but always on calm seas, and never when the situation was so dire.

The boat tilted again. Freezing seawater splashed over me, so cold I gasped and nearly dropped the rope. Shivering, I drew the rope tight and tied it off in its new position, although my hands trembled so badly, I was afraid I wouldn't be able to make the knot.

I tied off the second rope just as the boat lifted up on a great wave. For a moment, we stayed there, at its peak, higher than a fishing boat should be. The air sighed around us. The warship was close and so tall that it blocked out the sun, and I clung to the mast and stared up at it. Figures stood up on deck now. Men with no faces, lined up in rows, watching us.

It was the longest second I'd ever known.

And then we plunged back down. Seawater poured over the deck, burning with cold.

In the shock of that freezing water, magic stirred. Wild magic, tumultuous and deep and unfathomable. I held on and stared at the dark gray side of the warship, and I knew I was going to die.

Water rose up around us, glittering in the sun.

The magic tasted like salt on my tongue.

And then the ocean crashed down on the *Penelope*, and for a moment, all I saw was light splitting through the murk, and all I felt was a cold so deep, it sank straight to the marrow of my bones.

Then darkness.

CHAPTER SEVEN

In my dreams, I heard the sharp cry of a seabird.

My dreams were unclear, nothing but murky shapes in the dark, momentary dots of brightness, a sense of floating in thick air. That bird cry was the only moment of lucidity.

It happened again, louder.

Again.

The murk brightened and cleared away. I felt the ground beneath me, rough and cold, and I smelled pine. In the distance, someone sighed, over and over.

I pushed myself up to sitting and blinked, trying to clear out the shadows. Slowly, shapes formed: a march of trees in the distance, smooth gray pebbles underneath me, the ocean. That was the sighing, I realized. The ocean, rolling in along a shore.

I was on a shore. I was dry, by some gift of my ancestors, and I was alive.

I stood up, my legs shaking. The tide was out and dark seaweed dotted the beach in clumps.

There was no warship anywhere.

Relief flooded through me and turned to hysterical laughter that echoed up and down the beach, blending with the rush of the waves. I turned in place, taking in my surroundings. I didn't see the warship, didn't see any hint of the Mists at all – but I didn't see Kolur either. Or Frida. Or the *Penelope*.

"Shit," I whispered. A wind blew in from the north, tousling my hair. I turned left and right, trying to decide which direction to go first. We must have washed ashore Juldan, protected and unharmed – there had been that surge of magic before the world went dark. It wasn't borne by the wind, so it wasn't Frida's. It had been borne by the sea. Kolur? I couldn't imagine it. Of all the explanations of his behavior, the idea that he was a powerful wizard was the most absurd. I just couldn't accept it.

Following some instinct burning inside of me, I went left. The wind pushed me along. I still wasn't entirely in my right mind; everything was trapped in a pale haze, and I stumbled over the unfamiliar beach, afraid of what I would find. Or of what I wouldn't.

I didn't know how long I walked. Everything on the beach looked the same – the trees, the seaweed, the stones. Despair crept up on me, worse than the cold.

Maybe I wasn't alive at all. Maybe that's why I was dry. This wasn't a blessing from my ancestors at all. I stopped walking and stared down at the ground, and tears welled up in my eyes. I'd never felt so empty, so alone.

And then I saw it. A piece of broken board. Smooth, polished birchwood.

The same as the *Penelope*.

I bent down and picked it up. It was damp with seawater, but other than that, it was just a broken splinter of wood. Seeing it gave me a shuddery feeling like I was too cold.

I tucked it under my arm and kept walking.

As I walked, I found more hunks of wood, all that same polished birchwood as the *Penelope*. That shuddering turned heavy and settled in my stomach, and I walked as quickly as I could. It didn't take long before I saw a dark lump farther down the beach. It didn't look like a ship, even a wrecked one. I stopped and stared at it, still holding that first piece of wood close to my heart. The lump looked like a much larger version of the clumps of seaweed that had washed ashore.

The north wind blew. I moved forward.

The lump was a towering mass of seaweed, dark and stringy and swaying back and forth from the wind. It was taller than me. As tall as a fishing boat.

The sick feeling intensified.

"Hello?" My voice sounded small. "Kolur? Frida?"

I edged closer to the mound of seaweed. The air crackled with leftover sparks of magic. This was the *Penelope*, I was certain of it, but she'd been transformed. Magic can do that, when you use too much at once. It changes the ordinary into the extraordinary.

I reached out my hand, the hand wearing my bracelet, and ran my fingers over the seaweed. It made a chiming noise, and the blood in my hand jolted. Beneath the sweep of seaweed, I could make out the dark wood skeleton of the *Penelope*.

A boat was one thing. But if Frida and Kolur had still been aboard when this happened–

"Kolur!" I shouted, louder this time. My voice carried on the wind. "Where the hell are you?" I whirled in place, feeling wild and out of control and alone. The whole world was empty. "Kolur!" I screamed. "*Kolur!*"

"Quiet, girl. You make enough noise to wake the dead."

I thought I imagined his voice at first. It seemed to come from everywhere. But I realized that was just the wind, and when I whirled around, kicking up sand, I saw him shambling toward me. He was pale and his face was ragged, but he didn't seem hurt.

"Oh, sea and sky, you're alive." I slumped with relief. "I thought I was alone here. I thought I was *dead*–"

"Not so lucky, I'm afraid."

I scowled at him for making such an awful joke. But he only squinted up at the *Penelope*. "Shit," he said matter-of-factly.

"Will Frida be able to fix her?" *Was Frida even alive?* "Or are there wizards in Juldan–"

Kolur glanced at me, frowning. "I don't know. Probably have to get a new one."

"A new–" The air escaped me. A new *boat*? "We can't afford that, can we?" Did Kolur have money? Why hadn't he sent me home in Skalir?

Kolur shrugged. "Depends on where we are. Not every transaction requires money."

"Depends on where we are?" I blinked and looked around, at the sea and the trees. "Aren't we in Juldan?"

Kolur looked over at me. "There was magic involved

in setting us free," he said after a moment. "Surely you felt that. We could be anywhere."

Frida. Or maybe Isolfr. He could swim in the frozen ocean; perhaps he could channel enchantment through it as well.

"We need to find Frida," Kolur said. "I take it you haven't seen her."

"You mean you haven't?" My sick feeling returned, stronger than before. Isolfr might have sent us here, but Frida would be the one to get us home. That was the whole reason Kolur had brought her aboard.

"She'll be around her somewhere." He walked out past the remains of the *Penelope* and gazed down the shoreline. "This way." He pointed to the left.

"How do you know?"

"Just a feeling. Come on."

I joined him, and we walked down the beach in silence. The old magic radiating off the boat muffled the air around us, muting everything. I hadn't noticed how drained the colors were until I saw the *Penelope*. Now I couldn't not notice.

We hadn't been walking long when I spotted a streak of brown against the gray expanse of the rocks. "Look, there." I pointed. The streak wasn't moving. "You think that's her?"

"Might be. Too far off to tell." But Kolur broke into a jog and I followed along behind him, cold air burning in my lungs. When I was close enough to see it was Frida, I began to run.

She didn't move.

I knelt down beside her and pressed my fingers under her nose. Still breathing. Kolur's footsteps crunched over the stones. He wasn't in much of a hurry.

"Frida!" I shook her arm. She had all the magic; she would be able to get us to safety. "Frida, wake up."

Her eyelashes fluttered. I shook her harder. By now Kolur had joined us, and he said, "Frida, open your damn eyes."

She did.

"Well, that was exciting," she said. "You know I hate the water, Kolur."

Kolur laughed. "We do what we have to do."

"What?" I said.

They both ignored me. Frida sat up and shook out her hair. Then she patted it with one hand. "Dry," she said. "Thank you."

I swiveled to look at Kolur. There was no way he'd done this. Kolur bought his charms from shops in the capital. He made me do all the magic on board the *Penelope*. He was a fisherman, not a wizard.

But Kolur didn't respond to Frida's thanks, just stuck out one hand to help her to her feet. She accepted it and, once standing, put her hands on her hips and glanced around.

"Where are we?"

"Don't know," Kolur said.

"The *Penelope*?"

"Damaged," I said. "Magic-sickness."

"Figures." She took a deep breath, clearly less upset by this situation than I was. Both of them were, but

Frida's nonchalance was more frustrating. Kolur never told me anything. But Frida was a witch, a real witch. She had been to Jandanvar; she had seen the magic at the top of the world. And all the little charms she'd taught me aboard the *Penelope* didn't make up for the fact that she kept Kolur's secrets for him.

I was worked up enough to demand an explanation when Kolur said, "I figure we should keep walking west. Bound to run into someone sooner or later."

"How do you know that?" I said. "How did any of this happen? How are we all still alive?" Questions tumbled out of me, one after another. "And that warship! What happened to it? Is it going to come after us?"

"Oh, it's still out there," Kolur said. "But we got some time before it comes after us again."

"How do you *know* that?" I shrieked, but I knew I wasn't getting answers from either of them. They were already walking down along the waterline, heading to the west.

I hated them both. I was glad they were alive, but I hated them more than I ever hated anyone. Even Isolfr. He had at least *warned* me about the Mists. Not that I'd been able to do anything about it.

I ran after Kolur and Frida, stumbling over the stones. They both trudged along in silence. We followed the gentle curve of the beach, not passing any houses or boats or people or animals. No signs of civilization. Uneasiness peeked through my anger, and I thought about the chains of uninhabited islands, places where no creatures could survive.

"How do you know we're going in the right direction?" I asked when I couldn't stand the silence anymore. "There's nothing here but trees."

Kolur glared at me. "I know, girl." He jerked his head off to the west. "We landed a bit farther off than I expected." He turned away and took to walking again. Frida did her best to ignore both of us.

"Than you expected?" I caught up with him. "So you can do that kind of magic, then?"

Kolur grunted. "Plenty of people can do that kind of magic."

"Sea and sky, I am so sick of you not answering my questions."

"Stop, both of you." Frida stood a few paces ahead of us, pointing at the sky. "There's smoke."

She was right; a thin gray twist curled against the sky.

"Ah, finally." Kolur took off again. I glowered after him. I'd every intention of returning to that conversation, even if I had to make him listen to me.

Seeing the smoke did give me hope, though. There were others here. We weren't stranded on one of the empty islands.

It didn't take long before we had circled around the bend and come across a round fabric tent. Smoke drifted out of a hole at the top of the roof. There was no garden, only hard frozen soil, but the rocks had been arranged like a path leading to the tent's opening, and that gave it a feeling of permanence.

"Huh," Kolur said. "Don't look Juldani, does it?" He glanced at Frida, but she only shrugged.

I had no idea what a Juldani tent looked like. My anger with Kolur flared again, that he'd lived the sort of life where he would know that, and he chose to keep it a secret.

Kolur walked up to the door and tugged a rope attached to a metal bell. A few moments later, an old woman answered. Her hair was knotted up in a brightly embroidered scarf that made her face look perfectly round.

"Excuse me, ma'am," Kolur said, speaking with a sharp, prickly dialect I didn't recognize, "but would you mind telling us what island we're currently on?"

The woman scowled at him. "Lost your way, did you?" Her dialect wasn't the same as the one Kolur spoke, but it wasn't much closer to the Kjoran way of speaking I was used to.

"I imagine this must happen to you frequently," Kolur said. "Weary, confused sailors finding their way to your door."

This didn't sound like him in the slightest. He was being polite, for one. I didn't like it. I snuck a glance at Frida, but she had her arms crossed over her chest, looking bored.

"No," the old woman said, "it doesn't. Because most sailors aren't so stupid as to get blown off course." She poked her head farther out the door and looked at each of us in turn. "Not much of a crew."

"They're better than they seem," Kolur said.

That *really* didn't sound like him.

The woman made a scoffing noise. "You're in Tulja," she said.

Tulja. The name was foreign and unfamiliar, and I was struck with a flurry of panic that it wasn't Juldan, or even Jolal, which was only a day or so farther north. Tulja? I couldn't even remember it on Papa's carved map.

"Rilil is up the road there, if you're looking for sailing work." The woman scowled at us again. "Now, if you'll excuse me, I have business to attend to."

She yanked the curtain shut. Kolur turned to face us, and before I could start in on him, Frida did it for me.

"Tulja!" she said. "You brought us to Tulja?"

There it was again, the idea that Kolur had done magic.

"Didn't mean to. It's farther north than we were, though." Kolur grinned. "Let's see what we can find in Rilil, shall we? I hope someone's selling a boat." He breezed past us and made his way to the frozen dirt road the woman had pointed to. I hung back with Frida.

"How did he bring us here?" I asked her.

She sighed and ran her fingers through her hair. "I'm not the one to answer that, I'm afraid."

"Gods! No one will tell me anything."

"Because you're young and ignorance will better serve you. Come, before Kolur leaves us behind."

I couldn't believe she'd said that to me. I stood in front of the old woman's tent, watching Frida hurry to catch up with Kolur. Ignorance would better serve me?

I thought of Isolfr then, and Gillean. Isolfr had tried to tell me about Lord Foxfollow, and Gillean had died for it. And look at all the good it had done. The warship still attacked us. We were still trapped here on Tulja – wherever Tulja was.

I realized Kolur and Frida seemed in a mind to leave me. "Wait up!" I shouted, and ran up the road to catch up with them. Panting, I said, "So where is Tulja, exactly?"

"North," Kolur said. "A bit longer of a sail than I expected."

"How long?"

He didn't answer.

"How long, Kolur?"

"Nothing you need to worry about. We'll be in the town soon."

I fumed. My anger was like magic, propelling me along the slippery, miserable road. I gave up trying to ask questions, because I knew it would just leave me angrier than I had started. My mood did not make for a pleasant walk.

After a while, we began to pass more signs of life. There were round white tents, and a handful of little stone huts, and fences that held in great shaggy horned creatures that stared at us with the doleful eyes of deer and caribou. Every now and then, we'd pass someone standing outside one of those houses, and they studied us like we were a danger. That sense of hope I'd got from the smoke seemed ridiculous now. So there were people. What if they refused to help us? Or mistrusted us enough to attack us?

Civilization suddenly seemed more dangerous than the wild.

The ground was patched with snow, and ice daggers still hung from some of the fences. We were much farther north than we should be.

Eventually, the tents and grassland gave way to something like a proper town, although the buildings were really just mounds dug out of the earth, some of them augmented with stone or grass roofs or scraps of that same thick fabric that had made up the old woman's tent. Everything was crammed in close together. The roads remained unpaved, and the signs hanging next to the doors were painted with unfamiliar letters. Pictures, really. I squinted at them as we went past, but I couldn't read them.

Kolur could, however, because he stopped in front of a sign jammed into the ground next to one of the larger mound-buildings and said, "We need to eat. Get up our strength."

I wasn't hungry. But Kolur and Frida both ducked inside, and I wasn't about to let them leave me alone.

It was a mead hall – the sort of thing, in Kjora, you'd find standing alone in the wilderness. It was odd to see one in a town, even as small and semi-permanent a town as this one. Faces turned toward us as we walked in. Mostly men, their hair long and plaited. They turned away from us just as quickly. It was a relief to know we weren't of interest.

Kolur led us to a table in the back, one that was shoved up against a stone-lined wall, underneath a sprawling set of antlers. "Sit here," he said. "I'll tell the mead master we'll be wanting some food."

I hadn't realized how exhausted I was until I sank onto the hard, roughhewn wood of the bench. My legs seemed to dissolve away from me, and every joint in my body was filled with a dull, distant ache.

"He's right, you know." Frida peered at me in the smoky candlelight. "We need to rest. Gather our strength. That magic took a lot out of us."

"The magic," I said. "It wasn't yours."

"I won't give you your answers." She tilted her head. "Ask Kolur."

"Kolur won't tell me anything." I glared down at the table. Voices rose up in waves, laughing, shouting lewd remarks at one another. It was the sort of place Mama would love but wouldn't let me go; the sort of place Papa would hate, and not on my behalf, either.

I missed them.

"They've got eel pie on the menu today." Kolur's voice boomed out behind me, and he slid into place on the bench, depositing a trio of mugs filled with frothy dark ale. "Drink up. You too, Hanna." He nudged the mug toward me. I just stared down at it balefully.

"How did we get here?" I asked.

"We walked."

I lifted my face to him, my cheeks hot with anger. My hands shook. "You know that's not what I meant."

"For the grace of the ancestors," Frida said, "just tell her." She sipped at her ale. "This whole thing hasn't exactly been the quick errand you promised me, either."

"What is going on?" I shouted, loud enough that it caused a momentary pause in the surrounding chatter. Kolur ducked his head and looked down at his ale. I was too angry to care. "An errand?" I hissed at him. "And the Mists are after us – I know who was behind that warship. Lord Foxfollow."

I was hoping Isolfr's spell wouldn't work when we were on land, hoping that it was tied in some way to the *Penelope*. And for a moment, it looked like my hopes might pay off – Kolur's eyes flickered with confusion. "How did you–" He stopped himself. "Drink your ale, Hanna. Food will be here soon."

He was still blocked. I slumped down and took a long drink in frustration. The ale was bitter and thick, like soil. Drinking it made my stomach woozy.

How did you, Kolur had said. How did I what? How did I know? Was he familiar with Lord Foxfollow?

"The Mists," I said. "Lord Foxfollow. Why are they after us?"

Kolur and Frida stared at each other across the table, Frida glowering at him like she wanted to scold him.

"We'll be gone months," she said.

"Months?" I squeaked.

Kolur looked at me then. He swirled his ale around in his cup. "She's right," he said. "I should tell you."

I didn't believe he would. This whole conversation was piecemeal anyway, what with how he couldn't hear half the things I had to say.

"The Mists are after us," he said.

"I know!" I slammed my cup down. "I've been saying–"

"Specifically, they're after me. I thought I'd be able to avoid them while I took care of things, but–" Kolur scratched at his head. "I haven't been entirely honest with you."

Frida gave a snort of laughter, but I just glared at him. "I noticed."

"I don't mean just in the last few weeks. I mean – well, pretty much since I met you. Since I met your mother." Kolur drained the last of his ale and wiped his upper lip dry. "I ain't a fisherman. At least, not by training. I'm a wizard. A water-wizard. I learned my trade on the seas of Undim, in the far north–"

"Almost to the top of the world." I was suddenly too dazed to be angry. The magic during the battle had belonged to him. And if he trained on the Undimian sea, that put him in a very special class of wizards indeed. Most people do magic. But only some people can *do* magic, can do it well enough to make it their calling. Those people learned at the Undim Citadels. That was where I'd always wanted to learn.

"Then why–"

"It's a stupid story." Kolur laughed a little. "There was a woman. A, well, a queen. The Queen of Jandanvar."

"The *what*?" I squawked, loud enough to draw stares.

"I met her shortly after I finished my training. She came out to see all the new wizards, in this big glass boat, the sunlight sparkling everywhere–"

"Get on with it," Frida said.

Kolur shot her a dark look. "Fine. We met. Fell in love. You know how it is."

I didn't really, but I didn't say anything.

"But the problem with falling in love with a queen is there's a certain expectation that you'll be king." He grunted and turned toward the center of the hall, where a big clump of sailors was singing old drinking songs. "I didn't want that. I didn't even want to live in Jandanvar, much less rule it. I tried to convince her to run away with me, down to the south, the far south, to the Empire. But she wasn't going to do that. We were at a bit of a stalemate."

"A stalemate," Frida said. "You're both stubborn asses; that's the problem."

"What does this have to do with anything?" I said. "You're this great wizard and you've been living as a fisherman for the last ten years? All because you didn't want to be king? Who doesn't want to be king?"

"Anyone with half a thought in his head." Kolur leaned back. "I went to the Citadels because they recruited me. I had the touch, they said." He wriggled his fingers. "But I'd always wanted a simple life."

I rolled my eyes.

"I was a fool," he said, "to leave her the way I did. I got scared. But that's why we're out here, to set things right." He glanced at Frida, glanced back at me. "We're going to Jandanvar."

I stared at him. His admission rang in my ears. I knew it.

"When I called on the favor of the sea, I asked her to take us as far north as she could. That brought us here, to Tulja." He coughed. "We're about three months' sail from Juldan."

All the sound went out of the room. My ears buzzed, my heart raced. Three months away. "Were we – have we been *out* for three months–"

"Oh no," Frida said quickly. "Only about a day or so. We traveled on the magic."

I looked at her, and then I looked at Kolur, and then I took a drink. It burned the back of my throat.

"It was quite safe," Kolur said. "No need to worry."

I glared at him. "I didn't even know you could do that sort of magic until just now. Don't tell me it was *quite sa–*"

"Three eel pies." It was the server, a girl in a long brown dress. She dropped the pies on the table along with a trio of dinner knives. The pies smelled salty and rich, and my stomach flipped over a couple of times.

"Ah, that's better." When Kolur cut into his pie, steam billowed up into the air, and the smell of cooked eel was even stronger.

"You really ought to eat," Frida said. "It can make you sick if you don't."

I glared at her, but I knew she was right. If we'd been traveling along veins of enchantment, my body would need to fight off that desire for transformation that occurs whenever too much magic gathers at once. I cut off a tiny slice of pie. It was better than I expected, the wild taste of eel tempered by some pungent, savory herb I couldn't identify. With that one bite, I realized just how hungry I was, and I ate the rest of the pie quickly, hardly stopping to taste. Having a full belly renewed my strength. And renewing my strength gave me even more incentive to get answers out of Kolur.

"So why are we sailing to Jandanvar?" I demanded. Kolur was only half finished with his pie, and he glanced up at me, amused. "What does all of this nonsense you've told me have to do with the Mists?"

"Done already? And you're the one who said you didn't need to eat."

"Kolur," Frida said, making his name into an admonishment.

I pushed my plate aside and leaned over the table, still glaring at him. He sighed and set his knife down.

"It's not nonsense," he said.

I waited for him to explain.

"It's my life." He laughed, bitterly. "My whole life, that I threw away. The Mists are after us because the queen is set to marry one of them."

"What?" I said. "Why would she do that?"

"The boundaries are thinner at the top of the world. The Jandanvari have more connections with the Mists." He shook his head. "She's the first to marry one of them, though. I don't know what's she's thinking, agreeing to that damn Lord Foxfollow."

When he said the name, he seemed to speak into a vacuum. There was a dullness to his words.

"Yeah," I said. "I know who Lord Foxfollow is."

But Kolur ignored me, as I expected. "I don't know much about him. He's powerful, from what I understand. I don't know why she agreed–" He stopped, and I couldn't tell what emotion was trying to work its way out. "We're sailing to Jandanvar to stop the wedding."

I stared at him. He wouldn't look at me, only picked up his knife and cut off another hunk of pie.

"We're what?" I said.

"Going to stop the wedding."

My ears were buzzing again. My whole body felt hot.

"We were almost killed by the Mists," I said, quietly and evenly. "A man, an innocent man, was killed for trying to warn us. We risked our lives on the magic."

Kolur was making every effort not to look at me.

"All so you could win back some queen!" The words erupted. "A woman *you* abandoned. You had your chance, Kolur. And now you're bringing the Mists down on me and on Frida and on *everyone* – just because she's marrying someone who *isn't you?*"

Kolur stared down at his pie. Frida sat off to the side, staying still, staying quiet.

"Well?" I asked.

Kolur lifted his head. "Yeah," he said, "that's about the whole of it."

I screeched in anger and shoved away from the table. The plates and cups rattled. "That's stupid!" I said. "And dangerous! Why didn't you just sail off on your own? Why'd you have to bring me with you?"

"I told you." Kolur's voice was firm. "I had no idea until we were out on the water. When I threw the bones, trying to find the skrei, that's when I saw that I was going to lose her if I didn't–"

"I don't care." I curled my hands into fists. "I don't care about your stupid queen, Kolur. Do you have any idea what you've gotten us into?"

"More than you," he snapped.

I screeched again and stood up. I knew plenty. I knew more about Lord Foxfollow than he did. More about how dangerous he was, more about the sort of weapons he used. And if I said anything about it to Kolur, my words would slip out unnoticed, all because Isolfr had cast some idiot's spell on him.

It was starting to make sense to me, in the senseless way that magic often goes. Isolfr was probably a subject of Jandanvar. They weren't quite human; everyone knew that. It seemed odd that the rest of Jandanvar wasn't protesting this marriage, but perhaps they weren't aware of the extent of Lord Foxfollow's cruelty. Or perhaps he had most of Jandanvar under some sort of Mists spell. And if Isolfr knew Kolur was coming, through magic or divination, he saw some possible hero. And so he intercepted us, gave me the warnings... I still didn't understand why he was keeping it all secret from Kolur, or why he was forcing me to keep it secret. What had he said – he wanted Frida's help but he was *frightened* of her? Sea and sky and the ancestors.

No one would tell me the truth. And I was sick of it, sick of being a puppet they pushed around whenever they needed.

I slammed out of the mead hall and into the freezing sweep of the town, ignoring Kolur as he called out my name. The sky was starting to darken, later than it had in Kjora. Now that I was out of the smoky, rowdy mead hall, my thoughts settled a little. I was three months away from home, and adventuring wasn't remotely like it had been in the stories about Ananna. I might as well be home in Kjora for all the excitement I was having here in Tulja, and I realized, stalking through the freezing wind, that Kjora was exactly where I wanted to be. Kjora, where spring brought warmth and our houses weren't mounds in the dirt. But I had no money, no boat. I refused to stay with Kolur, and I refused to

help Isolfr at whatever he was trying to do. That did not
leave me with many options – the only thing I had to
trade was my half-formed magic and my skills aboard
a boat.

A boat.

The old woman had said the docks were here, and we
were close to the sea besides, having followed the shore
to get here. I walked up to a woman sweeping out her
shop with a straw broom, the handle wound up in blue
ribbon.

"Excuse me," I said. "Excuse me, how do I get to the
docks?"

She squinted at me. "Come again?" Then she frowned.
"Empire?"

Her accent was thick. I shook my head. "Not Empire.
Kjoran."

"Oh. Yes." That seemed enough for her. Kjora was a
long way away, and maybe she thought of it as part of
the south. "Where would you go?"

"The docks."

"Oh! The docks. Yes." The pointed to the west. "That
way. Follow the signs."

"I can't read the signs."

She frowned again, like she was puzzling through
what I'd said. "Oh, I see. Kjoran. First street on the right
will take you there." She gave a satisfied nod rather than
a smile.

I thanked her, hoping that was enough to find my
way. I pulled my coat tighter around my chest and
walked until I came to the first crossroads. A sign hung

from a pole jutting sideways out of the ground, painted with those same unfamiliar letters I'd seen everywhere. I studied them for a moment, but it wasn't any use. I was too far from home.

For a moment, I was almost knocked out by a dizzying wave of fear. I couldn't even read the signs. I'd never been on my own before, not even in Kjora.

This was a specific kind of loneliness, I realized. One that was born out of fear.

Then the wind shifted, and I got a whiff of the sea, briny and comforting in the way that it smelled just like the sea at home. I decided to take it as a sign from the ancestors that I had made the right decision. I walked the rest of the way down the road. All the flapping tent-buildings of the village disappeared, replaced with rocky soil and smatterings of pine trees. My fear returned, sharp and sudden as a blade. I wondered if the woman had steered me wrong, if she'd sent me into some sort of trap just because she took me for Empire.

I wished I had a knife, at the very least.

But then I heard shouts, men's voices calling out fishermen's cues. I recognized most of them – some things are standard across the islands, I supposed.

I went around a bend in the road, my heart pounding, and came to the docks.

There wasn't much to them. Not like the docks at Skalir or even back home in the village. Just long slabs of barnacle-encrusted wood jutting out into the choppy water and a handful of rickety boats bobbing in the waves.

My spirits sank at the sight of it.

I'd been hoping for sailing ships big enough to make the journey south, but I knew immediately there was nothing but fishing boats here, most of them smaller even than the *Penelope*. If I wanted to sail home, or even to the closest island, I wouldn't be doing it today. Or any time soon, most like.

I didn't see anyone who looked like they might be a dockmaster – figured, in a place this small. So I straightened my shoulders and walked over to a trio of fishermen standing next to a worn-out old cog, the same sort as the *Penelope* and thus practical for longer trips. They fell silent as I approached, staring at me like I was a ghost.

"Excuse me," I called out, conjuring up my bravery. "I'm looking for work."

The fishermen blinked at me. For a blinding moment, I was afraid they didn't understand me. But then one, the youngest of the three, spoke up.

"Most men around here won't hire an Empire sailor."

"I'm not Empire; I'm Kjoran."

The fishermen conferred amongst themselves, muttering and grunting, the way men do. I shifted my weight, embarrassed at the thought of them talking about me.

The younger sailor turned to me. "You sound Kjoran."

"That's what I just told you. I've never been farther south than the Sunbreak Sea."

He laughed. He wasn't handsome, exactly, not like the suitors Bryn was always entertaining – too weatherworn, his skin patchy and red from all that time spent out at sea. But his face was friendly, despite him thinking I was some Empire spy.

"There's not a lot of work around here." His accent wasn't as thick as the shopwoman's, which I was grateful for. "Not a lot of fishermen on this island. Just Geir, who works alone, and Baltasar's boat, which is the biggest around." He jutted his chin inland. "Most of Tulja raises yaks. You got any experience with yaks?"

I shook my head. "I can do magic."

The fisherman turned back to the others and took to muttering again. I strained to listen to what they were saying, but their accents were too thick and their voices too low.

He turned back to me again. "What sort? Sea magic?"

"Wind." I held up my hand. "You want to see? I know plenty of protection charms, and I can set the sails so you won't have to mess with them when we're out on the water."

The young fisherman turned to one of the elder ones, a fellow with a bushy yellow beard and rheumy eyes. He nodded, once, and I took a deep breath and concentrated, pushing aside all the turmoil from earlier. The wind was gentle, but it was blowing in from the southeast. Made my job easy.

I closed my eyes and hummed to myself, and the strength of my ancestors rose up inside me, drawing forth the magic inherent on the air. The wind shifted so that it was blowing straight from the south, and it brought with it the scents of home – Mama's iceberry pie, the soap for bathing we kept in a little ornamented box, the herbs growing in the garden next to the front door. My hair whipped around my face and my coat whipped around my legs and I opened my eyes and the three fishermen were all staring at me in wonder. Behind them, the sails of the fishing boat rattled and flapped; I couldn't do anything with them if she wasn't moving. But I could sculpt a protection spell, and I did, weaving the wind into a blanket that settled over all of us, me and the fishermen. It was thick as smoke.

"Good enough for you?" I asked, out of breath from holding the magic.

The younger fisherman laughed. "C'mon, Baltasar, that's better than anything Reynir's ever conjured up."

The man with the yellow beard harrumphed. "Don't take much to beat out Reynir. You can stop, Empire girl; I've seen enough."

I let the magic drop. The protection shimmered away; the wind settled and shifted out of the southeast again.

"I'm not Empire," I said. "My mama was, technically, but she was a pirate, so she never pledged allegiance to the Emperor. And my papa's family has lived in the north all the way back to the time of Helgi."

The younger fisherman grinned at me. After a moment's hesitation, I smiled back.

"Please," I said, and I addressed Baltasar, speaking as formally as I could. "I was washed ashore when my boat was attacked. My captain–" I figured that was better than saying *apprentice master* "–led me astray about why we were going north. I'm just looking for a way to earn money to support myself."

Baltasar studied me. He tugged at his beard. I held my breath like I was about to drop underwater.

"Fine," he said. "I'll take you on. Be here tomorrow at dawn. We'll be catching lisilfish."

I didn't know what lisilfish were, but at least I had a way home. And that was the best news I'd known in a while.

CHAPTER EIGHT

My new fishing boat was called the *Annika* and it was
a good sight larger than the *Penelope*, despite being
moored here at these sad little docks, on an island
more known for raising yaks than catching fish. The
fisherman who got me hired, Finnur, told me that the
crew was pretty sizable, about ten men all told. Well,
eight men and two women, me included.

After Baltasar hired me, I wandered back into Rilil
to try and find a place to sleep for the night. We had
a three-day run out to the Blackened Sea tomorrow,
so at least I'd only have to spend one night in an inn.
However, I was wary of coming across Kolur and Frida.
I'd run straight from the mead hall to the docks without
giving much thought to either of them, and I was still
angry at the way they'd dragged me north and kept
secrets from me and put me in danger of the Mists.

I asked directions to the closest inn from a woman
selling hunks of charred meat from a cart, right at the
edge of the docks. She frowned at me, made me repeat
myself a couple of times, then pointed me off to the

west. The inn proved easier to find than I expected, since beneath the picture-letters was the word *inn* itself, spelled out for travelers, I guess.

It was one of the more permanent buildings, with actual stones stacked up around the mound, and a real wooden door. I went in. The room was dark and smoky from the fire burning in the hearth, but an old man was behind the counter, cleaning out ale mugs.

"Can I help you?" he asked without looking up.

"I need a room. Just for one night."

"Very well. Fifteen stones."

I stopped. "Stones?"

"Aye, what we pay with up here." He squinted up at me and set the mug aside. "You don't got none, do you?"

I pulled out my pouch of gold discs and counted out fifteen of them. Then I laid them on the counter. "I've got these."

The man stared down at them. They looked flat and dull in the lantern light.

"No good here," he said, and chuckled. "Haven't seen discs in a while, though." He pinched one between his thumb and forefinger and held it up. My stomach felt heavy.

"What do you mean, they aren't good here?" I asked. The man looked at me. "I mean, they're gold. That's good everywhere."

"Good in the southerly islands, not the northerly ones. If you want to stay at my inn, you got to round up fifteen stones." He tossed my disc back on the pile. It hit the others with a flat metallic ring. "Not going to steal it, girl. I told you, they're worthless."

I swept the discs back into my pouch, keeping my head low because I was afraid I might start crying and I didn't want him to see. Kolur had betrayed me, and here I was trapped in a land where I barely understood the language and my discs didn't have any value and so I couldn't even buy a room at the inn. I bet Kolur knew about Tuljan stones. I bet he had whole piles of them sewn into his boots.

All I had was the *Annika*.

I mumbled a thank-you to the innkeeper and walked back down to the docks. My limbs were heavy and the air seemed colder than it had before I left. I wrapped my arms around myself, trying to warm up. It didn't work.

The *Annika* sat where I'd left her, tall and majestic in the thin sunlight. Baltasar and Finnur and the others weren't standing on the dock anymore, but the gangplank was down and I figured since I was technically an *Annika* fisherwoman, I had permission to climb aboard. So I did.

The deck had that eerie empty quality ships get when they're moored on land and aren't ready to sail yet. Except it wasn't truly empty. Baltasar was up at the masts, tugging on the ropes and fooling with the sails, with the help of a spidery, gray-haired man I hadn't seen before.

"Excuse me," I called out.

Baltasar glanced up at me. "Don't need you till tomorrow, sweetheart."

I walked up to him anyway. "I'm in a bit of a predicament," I said.

Baltasar laughed, his attention back at the ropes. The other man, though, kept sneaking glares at me, his brow furrowed. I tried my best to put him out of my mind.

"It turns out I can't pay for a room at the inn with my gold discs," I said.

The wind picked up and one of the sails yanked out of the spidery man's hand. He cursed and went chasing after it, shouting something back at Baltasar. His accent was so thick that I didn't catch it except the words *witch* and *what she's done* and *don't trust*.

"You hush up, Reynir!" Baltasar snapped. He turned to me. "Don't mind him. He's angry we're replacing him on the masts. But he's a sea-wizard, and he's never been able to control the wind."

The loose sail flapped out over the edge of the boat, and Reynir jumped up to try and grab it. He wasn't having much luck.

"See what I mean?" Baltasar laughed again. "Now, what's your worry? Something about gold?"

"I can't pay for a room at the inn," I said.

Baltasar nodded.

"And I can't stay with my old captain, since we had a – a falling-out, and it'll be too cold for me to sleep out in the open, and–" I stared at him pleadingly. "This is an overnight boat, isn't it, sir? Please, you can take it out of my pay, but I've got nowhere else–"

Over on the starboard side, Reynir managed to wrestle the sail away from its freedom. Baltasar held up one hand.

"You can sleep aboard tonight if you want. Down in the crew quarters. Nothing fancy. I'll be here myself."

He shrugged. "Might do you well to get used to the boat and her sails." He nodded over at Reynir, who was pulling the loose sail back into place, scowling all the while. "No way you can do any worse than Reynir."

"I heard that!" Reynir shouted back, and he glared at me one last time. Baltasar just found it funny.

"Oh, thank you," I said. "I promise you, you won't be disappointed in me."

I didn't sleep well that night. The crew's quarters were cold, even with the heat globes Reynir produced for me and Baltasar – I suspected he'd made mine weaker than he ought to. Plus, I was fretting about my future, which never makes for a restful sleep. In the end, I wrapped a warm sealskin blanket around my shoulders and went up on deck. Better than hanging in that uncomfortable hammock, waiting for sleep to overtake me.

The docks were quiet and dark. I walked up to the railing and looked down in the water, but Isolfr wasn't there.

Good. I think I wanted to see him less than I did Kolur.

The wind blew over me and the magic sank into my skin. Everything felt as it should: no disruptions, no sense of darkness on the horizon. No Mists.

For a moment, a small and shivering moment, I let myself think that it was over, and that was enough for me to go back down to my hammock and finally fall asleep.

Not that my sleep was restful. I was jarred awake the next morning by Reynir, his thin, pointed face like a remnant of a nightmare. "About to make sail," he snapped. "Better go out there and prove what you can do with the winds."

The morning was a blur after that. The sun was just starting to rise as the crew stormed aboard, and their laughter and groans and roughhousing finally woke me up completely. Reynir, who turned out to be the boat's fortuneer, gave me the directions to the Blackened Sea with a scowl, and I called down the winds and the *Annika* sailed off to the west.

Since I wasn't a strong witch like Frida, I had to stay up on deck the whole time, in case the winds shifted directions or there were other unforeseen problems. It was dull work and cold, but fairly mindless, and I was able to watch the crew ready the nets and prepare the preservation charms. I wasn't a part of a crew at all. Sometimes it felt like watching a play.

At lunchtime, Finnur brought me a jar of dried and salted meat. He said it was yak's meat.

"Thought you might be hungry," he said.

I was, and I smiled at him in gratitude. "Thank you," I said.

"You got to soften it in your mouth first," Finnur said, pointing at the jar. "Like this." He pulled out a strip and tossed it into his mouth, and his jaw worked around a bit. "Don't try to chew till you can." He spoke around the hunk of yak's meat. "Not the best meal out there, but better than nothing."

I nodded, grateful for his kindness. I pulled out a strip of my own, studied it for a moment, and then slid it into my mouth. Finnur was right; it was tough as tree bark. I let it sit under my tongue, tasting the salt.

"So do you know what kind of fish we're after?" Finnur asked.

"Baltasar told me." I paused, trying to remember. "Lisilfish, wasn't it? I don't know them."

"Wouldn't imagine so. They ain't much in the way of southern fish." Finnur leaned up against the mast. "Trickier than skrei or ling. With normal fish, you can just drag 'em up on deck and let 'em suffocate. Not so with these buggers." He pulled away from the mast and walked over to the railing, gesturing for me to join him. I did. The fishing net trailed out behind us, glimmering in the pale northern sunlight. Light flashed beneath the water, and my heart jumped with it, but Finnur said, "That's the lisilfish there. You can see 'em flickering."

"Is that what makes them trickier?" I leaned farther over the railing. I couldn't get a good glimpse of them, but they seemed to be swimming among the nets like any other fish.

Finnur laughed. "No. You'll see when we drag 'em aboard." He stared thoughtfully out at the water. "Baltasar says it's cause they swam south from Jandanvari waters, and that makes them smarter than most fish."

Hearing the name *Jandanvar* made me dizzy. I thought of Kolur the last time I'd seen him, his face illuminated by the murky light of the mead hall. Then I thought about Gillean. I pulled away from the railing and pretended to test the wind, just in case Finnur was of a mind to keep talking about Jandanvar. But one of the crewmen called him over to help with a tangled net.

We dragged the nets in late in the afternoon. Baltasar rang the big brass bell that hung from the highest mast and shouted, "Net time! Net time!" He handed the wheel off to one of the younger boys and jumped down from the helm. "You," he said, "Empire girl. Stand off to the side. You'll just want to watch the first time."

"I've brought in fish before," I said.

"Not like this, you haven't. Stand off to the side."

I did as he asked. He wasn't Kolur; I couldn't sass him and expect to have a job the next time the boat went out to sea.

He wasn't like Kolur. Definitely a good thing in my mind.

I took a place over on the port side, close to the masts in case trouble stirred up with the wind but still in good view of the net. Half the crew crowded around. I frowned. Seemed a lot of men to bring in just one net.

"Grab the net!" Baltasar called out. Everyone did as he asked, winding their fingers up in the ropes and bracing themselves against the deck. "Hold!"

They held. The boat rocked back and forth; the wind rippled through the sails. The tip of my nose burned from the cold.

Everyone seemed to be holding his breath.

"Draw!" Baltasar shouted, and in one great gasp of effort, every single one of those fishermen heaved at the net. Water splashed up along the side of the boat and the net erupted into the air. It was full of tiny silver sparks that threw bits of light all around the deck.

It went up into the air.

And it *stayed* in the air.

I'd never seen anything like it, this net of fish floating over a boat like those brightly colored kites children play with during the windy months. It swayed back and forth, showering water over the fishermen, who grimaced and grunted and chanted something in a language I didn't recognize. I felt like I needed to dart forward and help, but whatever magic this was, I didn't know it.

"Drop!" Baltasar shouted.

The chanting swelled. The air rippled. And then, with a rush of coordinated movement, the net slammed against the deck.

It stayed there.

The crew burst into shouts of joy, laughing and slapping at one another's backs. Finnur made his way over to where I stood watching. He was soaked with seawater, his hair plastered in dark ribbons against the side of his face.

"See what I told you?" he said. "Tricky."

I looked over at the net. Someone had already cast the preservation charm, and one of the crew, the other woman, was loosening the net so she and another crewman could dump the fish out properly. I wondered why they cast the preservation charm first, but then I saw that the fish were still moving, swimming around the air like it was water, hemmed in by the shimmer of the preservation charm.

"They aren't dying," I said.

Finnur shrugged. "They don't die easily, no. Natan puts a poison in the preservation charm to slow their hearts. It takes a minute to work. Says it's not painful."

"And people want to *eat* these?"

Finnur laughed. "It's a Tuljan delicacy, actually. Lisila. I'll have Asbera make it for you sometime. The poison can't hurt humans."

I looked at him. He seemed serious, not like he was going to make fun of my supposed Empire ways.

"Really?" I said.

He nodded. "Asbera makes some of the best on the island. That's why I married her." And he pointed to the fisherwoman, who was standing with the other crew and laughing now that the lisilfish were all out of the nets.

The rest of the trip continued much like that first day. We caught seven more nets' worth of lisilfish, moving from place to place according to Reynir's calculations. I controlled the wind the whole time and never once let us blow off course, but Baltasar wouldn't let me help draw in the nets.

"Maybe next time," he grunted when I asked him about it. "You need to learn the spells first."

We arrived back at the Rilil docks midafternoon during the third day, exactly when Baltasar promised we would. That level of honesty was a refreshing change of pace. The stores of lisilfish weighed down the *Annika*, and it took the entire crew to bring them to the market, where Baltasar sold them to a tight-faced, thin-lipped young man who tutted over the size of the fish. Still, Baltasar haggled him to a price of nearly four hundred stones, and I could tell by the whoops of excitement from the crew that it must be a good deal. We each got an equal share. When Baltasar handed me my pouch, the stones clacking together, I felt a surge of pride. With Kolur, I'd only been an apprentice, and so my share was always small and went straight to Mama besides.

"A job well done," Baltasar said. "Next trip planned is two days from now. You'll be there."

I nodded, pleased. I shook the bag of stones and opened it up. They actually were rocks, sea stones that had been polished down into evenly sized discs about the same size as my gold ones. What a difference materials make.

A couple of crewmen muttered cold words to each other, and I had a creeping feeling that they were about me. But I told myself not to be bothered. The captain appreciated my work, and I was paid, and if I could put up with that islanders' paranoia that is the trademark of the north, I'd get home for certain.

"Good haul this trip." Finnur sidled up alongside me, Asbera at his side. "And two days without sail. A nice break."

I nodded, but his comment struck me in a cold place. I still didn't have anywhere to go. I tightened my grip on my wages. Finnur and Asbera both stared at me. Then Asbera frowned.

"You don't have a place to stay," she said in a soft, whispery voice I would not have expected to belong to a fisherwoman.

I considered lying, but Finnur had been so kind to me that I didn't want to. I shook my head. "I can find something," I said. "I know there's an inn–" But it would cost fifteen stones a night. With two nights, I'd have spent almost all of my wages. I wouldn't be able to save anything. And even though sailing aboard the *Annika* had been a fine experience the last three days, I still didn't want to spend the rest of my life in the little earth-mounds of Tulja. I wanted a way home.

"Oh, don't stay at the inn," said Finnur. "It's filthy. The old man who runs it never airs out the beds." He nodded down at my wages. "With all we got today, you'd have enough to put in for a room at the boarding boats down on the docks' edge. You won't save much from today's payment, but you'll have plenty once we get back from our next trip."

My heart sank. I looked back and forth between Finnur and Asbera, who stared at me with identical expressions, calm and sympathetic. I looked down at my wages.

"What about food?" I muttered.

"Oh, don't you worry about that," Finnur said. "We'll cook for you." He grinned. "I promised you I'd have Asbera make lisila."

"You didn't tell *me*," Asbera said, but she laughed. "Yes, we don't mind. We've plenty to share."

I hesitated. I wanted to trust them, but I'd trusted so many people since I'd left Kjora, and none of that trust had worked out. Kolur and his lies. Isolfr and his – I still didn't know what. Because of him, I'd seen a dead man, and I'd almost died myself.

"We really don't mind," Asbera said. She leaned in close to me and lowered her voice. "And we're not frightened of the Empire like the rest of these louts."

I scowled. "I'm not from the Empire. My mama was born there, that's all."

Asbera brightened. "Well, then, we really have nothing to fear. Come, let's take you to the boarding boats."

And against my better judgment, I relented. I was tired and sore from the last three days of work, and I knew I needed to think in the long term if I was to ever leave.

"The boarding boats," I said. "All right."

Finnur laughed and slapped me on the back. We left the merchant. The rest of the crew had dispersed, and the docks were more bustling than I'd seen them before, what with all those one-man sailing boats coming in from the sea. Asbera and Finnur led me past the crowd to a collection of ramshackle, sailless boats roped and moored together. A wooden sign flapped from a pole jutting sideways out of the ground, but like all the signs here, I couldn't read it.

"Here we are," Finnur said. "Let me take you to see Rudolf. We can get you set up while Asbera cooks."

Everything was happening so quickly. I nodded, and Asbera trotted off to a narrow dinghy that bumped up against the pier.

"So you just live here?" I asked. "On the water?"

"Yes. Most of the crew does." Finnur shrugged. "It's cheap. And we don't have to maintain anything while we're gone." He led me down a rickety wooden walkway to a junk painted with more unfamiliar letters. Finnur banged on the side of the boat and shouted, "Rudolf! Got someone who needs a place to live!"

There was a pause. The boats knocked against each other, a pleasant, hollow sound. Then footsteps echoed from the deck of the junk and a man's face appeared over the railing. He was even more weatherworn than Kolur. He scowled at me.

"Empire?" he barked.

Before I could explain, Finnur said, "No, she's from Kjora."

"Southerly." The man – Rudolf – made a coughing noise. "Well, as long as you can pay, you can stay here." He rapped his fingers against the railing. "Fifty stones a month."

I felt like I'd been stabbed through the stomach.

"Don't be an ass," Finnur said. "Me and Asbera pay thirty."

Rudolf scowled. "I don't know this girl."

"She works aboard the *Annika*. Baltasar's word ought to be good enough for you."

Rudolf paused. I reached into my coat pocket and rubbed my fingers against my wages. Thirty a month was a good sight cheaper than thirty for two days.

"Fine," Rudolf said. "Thirty stones, once a month. That don't cover food, girl. This ain't an inn."

"I know it's not, sir." I counted the stones out into my palm, dismayed to see almost all of my wages disappear. Rudolf dropped away from the boat's railing, and I stood waiting for him with the stones piled high in my hand. A few moments later, he reappeared at the top of the gangplank. I handed him his payment and he counted it out and nodded once, satisfied.

"You've got the *Cornflower*." He deposited the stones into a worn-velvet sack that he tucked away inside his coat. Then he pulled out an enormous metal ring, jangling with keys of all cuts and sizes.

"Can't do much with the deck," he said. "I keep an eye out, got a couple of charms up. May or may not keep someone off. But you can lock up the captain's quarters and the storage room well enough. Recommend you keep your valuables in there. Ain't responsible if they get stolen."

"Of course. I understand."

Rudolf pulled off a long, slender key from the ring and handed it to me. "Finnur can show you where it is. Ain't that right, Finnur?"

"Sure thing. It's right next door to us." He grinned at Rudolf. Rudolf scowled in return.

"I don't get payment on the first of the month," he said, "I'll send my dogs after you."

And with that, Rudolf hauled himself back up his ladder and disappeared over the railing.

"Don't worry about the dogs," Finnur said. "All you have to do is feed them sausages and they'll be rolling around on their backs, waiting for you to play with them." He laughed. "Come on, I'll show you the *Cornflower*."

We walked down to the edge of the pier. I still had this dazed, edgy feeling, like it was a huge mistake giving my money to that man. Of course, I hadn't had that feeling in all the time we were sailing north from Kjora, so maybe my intuition wasn't what it should be.

Finnur reached down in the water and picked up a thick salt-encrusted rope that was tied to the pole jutting off the pier. He tugged on it, and the dinghy drifted toward us, bobbing on the water.

"Unfortunately, we're not pierside," he said. "But it's not a big deal, taking the dinghy."

He let me step on first. It sank a little beneath my weight, but it was dry and solidly built. Finnur rowed us around the tangle of moored boats. The rope attached to the rowboat was long enough that it uncoiled out behind us, disappearing beneath the water's surface. When we came to another junk with *Crocus* painted across the side, he jabbed the oar straight down into the water, locking us into place.

"That's where Asbera and I live," he said, pointing at the *Crocus*. "The *Cornflower*'s right there, just down that gap. We should be able to climb over from the *Crocus*."

I nodded dumbly and watched as he crawled up the ladder onto the deck of his boat – of his home, I reminded myself. And I thought then of my own home, my real home, landlocked and built of gray stones. I couldn't see much of the *Cornflower* from here, only a strip of peeling gray wood rising out of the water and some sailless masts, part of the forest of masts that made up the boarding boats.

"You coming?" Finnur was aboard the *Crocus* now, standing beside the ladder, waiting.

"Yeah, sure." I made my way up the ladder, looking over at the *Cornflower*. I saw more of it the higher I climbed, but there wasn't much to see. Just a moored cog. It was hard to think of it as a home.

Like a gentleman, Finnur helped me over the railing. The deck of the *Crocus* didn't look like any boat I'd been on. No sails, and the wheel had been removed at the helm. There were pots filled with lichen and little blue flowers and shrubby, tough-looking herbs. Tall glass jars sat at random intervals, half full with gray water. Ropes of dried vines hung from the masts, twisted together into figures that looked human and animal at the same time. Protective charms, most like.

"You can see the *Cornflower* from the starboard side." Finnur pointed. "No one's lived there for a while, but Rudolf usually keeps the empty boats clean."

I nodded and walked over to the side of the boat. The *Cornflower's* deck was empty except for a pot of its own, lichen dangling over the sides like a waterfall.

"It's warmer down below," Finnur said. "We can see about looking for a plank to get you across the way. But it'll be nice to have a rest first, don't you think?"

"Sure." I looked away from my new home and followed Finnur down below deck. I expected it to look like the *Penelope*, may the gods take her: sparse and empty save for stores and fishing supplies. But it didn't. It was hung with brightly colored tapestries and stuffed with carved wooden furniture. There was a hearth, just like in a house, filled with hot, glowing logs. Asbera was there, her hair tied back, stirring a great cauldron of something that smelled like fish and spices and made my stomach grumble.

"Hello, Hanna." She glanced at me over her shoulder and smiled shyly. "Did Rudolf give you a fair price?"

"I guess," I said. "I don't know."

"Thirty stones," Finnur said. "What we're paying."

"Oh, good." She gestured at the table. "Please, have a scat. I'm afraid the lisila isn't quite ready yet. We still have tulra ale, don't we, Finnur?"

"We do." Finnur ducked out into the corridor, his footsteps echoing around the room. I sank into one of the chairs, exhausted. I hadn't realized just how much so until now, after three days on the *Annika* so soon after being washed ashore by magic. Really, I just wanted to sleep.

Finnur returned with a mug of some frothy amber liquid that I assumed was ordinary ale until I sipped it, and found that it was sweet and buttery and not at all fermented.

"Tuljan specialty," she said. "We make it out of the tulra flower, from the far north."

She smiled, but I stared down at the foam in my drink. The far north. It seemed that even when I left Kolur, the top of the world was still haunting me.

Asbera sat down across from me with her own mug, and Finnur sat beside her and rested his hand on her arm.

"Everyone wants to know what brought you to Tulja," Finnur said.

Asbera sighed and slapped at him. "That's rude."

"Well, it's true!"

"It's fine." I stared down at my mug again. I didn't want to tell the truth, at least not the whole truth. "My ship wrecked here, like I said. Had a falling-out with my captain." I shrugged. "We weren't supposed to go this far north."

Finnur gave a nod like he understood everything. Asbera stood up and checked the cauldron bubbling on the stove.

"I'm grateful for the work." I paused, still not sure how much I should tell them. "But I'd like to try and sail home to Kjora if I can. I miss my parents."

"Ah, yes, I miss mine, too," Asbera said from the stove. "They're yak tenders, you know, out near the base of the mountains." She grinned at Finnur. "This one came by looking to trade pelts for Baltasar. He'd only just been taken on as an apprentice. He wound up living in an old yurt for the better part of the winter." She laughed, and Finnur gazed up at her the way Papa would gaze at Mama sometimes.

"That's a nice story," I said, and then, because I felt a need to fill the silence in a way that wouldn't involve explaining why my captain had been sailing us north in the first place, I told them about Mama and Papa, and how Mama'd served aboard the *Nadir* and decided she loved the north more than she loved the south. That drew smiles out of Finnur and Asbera both.

"That's why the Empire's always trying to claim our islands," Asbera said. "Because they all know deep down it's better here."

I laughed at that, even if I didn't know myself one way

or the other. I'd only ever belonged to the north, even if Mama's ancestors, warm and smelling like honey and spices, spoke to me sometimes through the winds.

Asbera checked the cauldron again, and this time she clapped her hands together and said, "Oh, praise joy, it's ready. I'm *starving*. Aren't you, Hanna?"

I nodded. "Three days with nothing but salted fish–"

"Oh, don't even say the words." Finnur slapped his hands on the table. "Here, Asbera, let me help. Hanna, you stay. You're our guest." He got to his feet and pulled carved wooden bowls out of the cupboards next to the hearth. Asbera spooned the bowls full of lisila and then delivered the bowls to the table. The lisila was a sort of stew, with a creamy white broth that shimmered like moonlight. It smelled of herbs, fragrant and grassy like summer.

"Once you've had a taste of this, you'll wish everything else you ever eat is lisila," Asbera said.

I assumed she was joking, or boasting, as cooks do. But when I sipped from the rim of my bowl, I could hardly believe that what I tasted was real. The flavor was savory and so complex I couldn't quite define it, but as soon as I tasted the lisila, I wanted more. It didn't help that I was so hungry. I'd slurped down half my bowl when I glanced up and found Asbera and Finnur laughing at me.

"Told you," Asbera said. She sipped at her own bowl and closed her eyes. "As good as I remembered."

"It's the lisilfish," Finnur said. "They cook down and create – *this*." He gestured at the bowls.

"Shame they're so expensive."

"Oh," I said, cheeks warming. "I didn't know. I'll be happy to help pay–"

"Nonsense." Asbera shook her head. "You need to save your money, like you said." She smiled and took another sip from her bowl. "I'm sure you'll find some way to repay us in the future."

I nodded. I certainly hoped so.

But more than that, I hoped that Asbera and Finnur were as normal as they seemed, and that the rest of my time in Tulja would be as simple and satisfying as my evening aboard the *Crocus*.

CHAPTER NINE

After dinner, Finnur helped me get settled aboard the *Cornflower*. It was a much smaller boat than the *Crocus*, but belowdecks was well cared for: the holes in the ceiling patched, the floor dry. The hearth had been cleaned of old ashes, and there was an actual bed in the captain's cabin, with a small, hay-stuffed mattress. After weeks of sleeping on cots and hammocks, I found it an unimaginable luxury.

I slept easily that first night, deep and steady, although I dreamed, something I hadn't done aboard the *Annika*. My dreams were strange but not unsettling: I was at the base of a tall, rocky mountain, surrounded by yaks that snuffled and pawed at the frozen ground. Wind roared over the mountains, coming from the north. It smelled of tulra ale and seemed to have a voice of its own, whispering my name, telling me I was safe. I believed it. I was certain it came from Finnur and Asbera.

When I woke, sunlight was spilling in through the doorway. I'd left it open in the night. I got up and stretched, feeling refreshed for the first time in weeks. A cask of lisila sat on my bedside table, left over from left night – Asbera had given it to me when I left the *Crocus*. I ate it quickly, and it was just as delicious for breakfast as it had been for dinner. Finnur had told me there was a shared well in the center of the town, so I dug around in the storage room until I found some empty skins. Then I went up on deck.

The air was cold and bright and still. The deck of the *Cornflower* was bare in comparison to the deck of the *Crocus,* but I had no intention of draping it with plants and charms. That would suggest I planned on staying here for a long time, and I didn't. My bracelet could protect me for the time being.

The dinghy was still where we had left it the night before, lodged in the space between the *Cornflower* and the *Crocus*. I lowered myself down and rowed to the pier. The docks were mostly empty, just a pair of fish-boys running errands back and forth between the boats and the shops in the village.

Everything felt as much like a dream as the base of the mountain had.

I followed Finnur's directions to the well. To my relief, no one was there, and I filled up the skins and dropped them in my bag. I realized I didn't want to go back to the *Cornflower* yet. There wouldn't be much to do besides sit on my cot and count down the days until we made sail again.

So I walked through the streets of Rilil, weaving through the mounds of earth and piles of stone. Most of the doorways were graced with twists of vine, simpler, more decorative versions of the charms Asbera and Finnur kept on their upper deck. I hadn't taken those vines for charms when I'd been walking through the town with Kolur and Frida; in fact, I'd hardly noticed them at all.

Thinking on Kolur and Frida made me feel all twisted up. It had been easy to forget about them those three days at sea, but now that I was back in Tulja, I knew there was a chance I'd run into them. And I didn't want that.

I passed the last semi-permanent building, and the road opened up into a huge field dotted not with yaks like I expected but with the same round, leathery tents that the old woman had lived in. They were clustered like people drawing together for warmth, and smoke drifted out of the tops of most of them. Far off in the distance rose a mountain, purple-gray in the misty air. It looked like the mountain from my dream – but then, all mountains tend to look the same.

I turned and walked in the opposite direction. The waterskins were starting to get heavy, but I still wasn't in a mind to go back to my boat. Too dull and lonely, sitting down below by myself.

Eventually, I came to the other end of the village, to the road leading down to the ocean. I dusted some old snow off a nearby stone and sat down and took a drink of water. Birds circled overhead, crying out to one another. I smelled salt and fish. It was peaceful, in its way. Peaceful and lonely.

And then I heard singing.

It was distant, coming from the direction of the beach. I couldn't make out the words, but as I listened, music joined up with the singers' voices, a jangly, rhythmic instrument that I didn't recognize. Part of me thought that maybe I should leave, that I was hearing something I wasn't meant to as a daughter of the Empire and the southerly islands both, but I stayed put. The music grew louder. I realized they were singing in the language of the ancients.

Figures appeared on the bend in the road, moving in a procession through the cold, gray air. And they weren't human. They were monsters.

All sorts of monsters, some with great shaggy coats and others with sharp, needly beaks and still others like men built of straw. My fear paralyzed me in place. I thought of the warship slicing toward the *Penelope*, thought of Gillian's dead body. I thought of the Mists.

The monsters moved closer. One of them, a creature with a bulbous, oversized boar's head, shook a ring of metal that flashed in the thin sunlight. Another carried a torch that guttered and sparked an unnatural orange-gold.

They come on the veins of magic–

Isolfr's words appeared unbidden in my head, and without thinking, I reached out to the magic on the wind, testing, trying to find that sense of *wrongness–*

There was none. The magic was calm, peaceful. Nothing wrong, nothing dangerous.

The figures drew closer. I scrambled off my rock and crouched half behind it, clutching my bag tight, too afraid to take my eyes off these monsters. The singing poured over me.

Not a single one of the creatures' mouths moved.

I frowned. That didn't make sense.

As they passed, the straw-man turned his head, pale gold shedding off him. His eyes peered out of the mound of straw. They were dark and benevolent – human.

They were human.

The monsters sang, but their mouths didn't move.

Masks, I thought, and I straightened up, still trembling. None of the other costumed men looked at me; they just continued their procession into the village. The torch sent sparks and smoke up into the sky, and I felt the shudder of its enchantment, a warmth and protection I hadn't expected.

At the first shop, a family stepped through the curtain in the doorway, a man and his wife, their little girl. The girl tossed something at the procession – it looked like dried flowers. She didn't seem scared, only grateful.

I slumped down on the rock, sighing, and watched the procession make its way through Rilil. Magic trailed in its wake, settling over the village like a balm. Magic, it was just magic. Protection.

It just didn't look like any protection I had ever known.

The *Annika* left for another trip two days later. Couldn't come soon enough. I'd spent the rest of my money on food and wasn't able to save anything for the trip home. I hoped this payment would be as large as my first, since I wouldn't have to worry about doling out most of it for a place to stay.

Asbera and Finnur were already aboard when I climbed onto the deck in the pale early morning hours. Asbera smiled like she was glad to see me.

"Hanna!" she said. "I hope you're settling in all right." I hadn't seen either of them for those two days, since I didn't want to come across as a burden. I was glad to see her, though, since I had questions, mostly about those costumed men and their magic.

"I am." But I didn't have time to say more than that, since Baltasar blundered up on deck. Reynir stumbled behind him, reading fortunes from a little scrap of scroll. He glared at me when he saw I was back.

"Gather round!" Baltasar shouted. "We're going southeast today, looking for lampreys. Reynir here says we can make the catch of the season if we can get there before those damned Kjiljans."

The crew applauded and stomped their feet against the deck. A little thrill of excitement worked through me, too. Maybe the catch of the season would be enough to get me home.

"Well, what are you waiting for?" Baltasar cried. "Get on with it!"

The crew erupted into action. So much was happening, I didn't have time to think – and I was grateful for that after spending the last few days doing nothing but thinking. I called the wind into the sails while a couple of crewmen aligned the spars. The *Annika* pulled out into the water and swung around, moving parallel to the shore, heading west. The land was dotted with those little round tents, gray smoke twisting into the air.

We sailed.

It took most of the day to get to the southern point where Reynir claimed we'd find fish. Most of the crew spent the time lolling around the fires, throwing dice and playing Hangman's Gambit, another gambling game Papa had taught me to play last year. No one asked me to join them. Which was fine, seeing as how I didn't have any money to gamble.

Still, I felt isolated standing there among the masts, watching the men throw dice and count out stones. They got to wait out the trip, but I had to control the winds. I'd never thought of it as especially tiring magic, but the *Annika* was much bigger than the *Penelope* and it proved to be more work than I was used to.

The sun finally started to sink into the horizon. The winds shifted to the northeast, and so I didn't have to control them as much. I was grateful for the break. But then I took one look around the deck, at the fires glowing in the darkness, and suddenly felt very lonely.

"Are you hungry?"

It was Asbera. She'd been scrambling up on the masts all day, where the men were afraid to climb, and so I hadn't seen much of her.

"Yeah," I said, grateful to have someone to talk to. "It takes a lot out, controlling the winds."

She grinned. "I bet." Then she handed me a fish that had been grilled by the fires. "Finnur caught them earlier. Fishing off the side like a child. No one believed he'd actually get something." She laughed.

"Thank you." I stared down at the fish, its scales

blackened by the smoke. My stomach grumbled, and I peeled the flesh away from the bones and nibbled at it. Skrei. Nice to eat something familiar. It reminded me of Kjora.

I expected Asbera to leave me and go back with the others, but she stayed by my side.

"The wind's shifted," she said. "You don't have to keep controlling it, do you?"

I shrugged. "I don't mind." I took a bite of fish to keep from saying anything more.

"You shouldn't let the crew get to you," she said.

"I'm not."

She smiled and the skin crinkled around her eyes. "They'll exclude you until they don't anymore. It's our way here in Tulja. We can't help it."

Part of me wanted to believe her and part of me didn't care because I just wanted to go home.

I finished the fish and tossed the bones overboard. I checked the water, the way I did whenever I was at the railing, looking for a shadow beneath the waves, a glimmer like moonlight. But there was nothing there. Isolfr had dragged us into danger and then he'd abandoned us.

"How do you like Tulja so far?" Asbera asked. "Aside from–" she waved at the crew "–all that. I really do promise it'll get better. They just have to get accustomed to you."

I hesitated, trying to think of a diplomatic response. "It's different," I finally said. "Different from what I'm used to."

"I'm sure I'd feel the same way if I ever visited Kjora."

She laughed, and after a moment, I joined in with her. I'd let my magic die away a little as we spoke as a way of alleviating my exhaustion, and only just now realized it. The boat rocked along with the wind, moving us to the southwest. I sighed, my limbs loose with freedom.

"It's strange," I said. "Certain things are the same, and certain things are different. I can't read your alphabet, but most of the food is the same, assuming it's not a dish from – from the north." I hesitated. "And the other day, I saw a parade, all these people in costumes – we don't have anything like that in Kjora."

"Oh, the Nalendan." Asbera smiled. "Did they give you a fright?"

"A little. I felt the magic and realized they weren't dangerous." I shrugged, trying to be nonchalant.

"Oh, you poor thing. I didn't realize they were going to be parading while you were out, otherwise I would have made sure to mention them to you."

"It's fine, really."

"I've heard they're another tradition we borrowed from Jandanvar, but us Tuljans like to claim we invented their magic whenever we can." She laughed. "They're a means of protecting us from the Mists. Do you know of the Mists as far south as Kjora?"

I nodded. I couldn't bear to say anything more.

Fortunately, Asbera didn't seem so keen on talking about them, either. "There is a group of priests who live out on the plains whose entire job is to watch out for the Mists. Whenever they feel them encroaching, they call for the Nalendan to protect our village."

I shivered. I wondered if this was our fault, if Kolur had brought the Mists here.

"How often do the Nalendan cast their charm?" I asked. "I mean, how often do the priests feel–"

"Oh, pretty often. Twice a month or so." Asbera interrupted me before I could say the word *Mists*, her expression uncomfortable. But she must have seen something in my own expression, fear or something worse, because she smiled and laughed. "My father used to say the priests can't actually see anything at all, and they just call down the Nalendan to amuse themselves."

But her words did nothing to console me.

I wound up with wages of thirty-five stones after we returned from that trip – it turned out lamprey was a favorite among the Tuljans. I ate dinner with Asbera and Finnur that evening, just as we had after the first trip. No lisila, but Asbera did bake the lamprey with wild roots and strips of dried yak meat. It was more delicious than I'd expected.

After dinner, Asbera walked me up to the deck of the *Crocus*. Night was just starting to fall, streaks of gold sinking into the water. The north wind blew strong and sweet-scented, and it knocked the vines and charms around, stirring up their magic.

"I have a gift for you," Asbera said.

"Oh, that's – you don't have to do that." I shook my head. "You've given me enough already–"

"It's nothing," she said. "Just a little thing." And she pulled a stonework jar out of her dress pocket. "I used to keep meal in it, but the side cracked." She handed it to me. "It'd be perfect for saving stones."

I took the jar and turned it over in my hands. I almost wanted to cry.

"Just make sure you keep it locked up in the captain's quarters." She laughed. "I'd hate to see your savings get whisked away."

"Thank you," I said. "This was very thoughtful."

We looked at each other in the long violet shadows. It felt good to have a friend.

And so the days went by. They turned into one week, into two weeks. Our wages at the end of each fishing trip were good and steady, and with each payment, I made sure to drop a few stones into my jar. Sometimes at night, I'd lift the jar and shake it next to my ear, listening to the stones banging around. It was reassuring, a reminder that I was *doing* something to get home. Better than waiting for Kolur or anyone else to take care of my problems for me.

One afternoon, I shook out a handful of my saved stones and went into the village to find a wizard. It took a long time, in between my trouble understanding the Tuljan accent and something about the way I was asking, but eventually an old man pointed me to a tent on the outskirts of the village. I couldn't read the sign jutting out of the frozen earth, but I pulled on the bell and the man who answered wore faded, tattered blue robes beneath his coat.

"Yes?" he said, peering at me suspiciously.

"Are you a wizard?"

"Of a sort." He stepped out of the tent and studied my face closely. "How'd you get so far north, Empire girl?"

I sighed. "I'm from Kjora. Can you send messages across the islands?"

His eyes narrowed at that. "Across the islands? Why would you want to do such a thing? Surely if you're *here*, you can travel south on your own."

His words made my cheeks burn. "No," I said. "I can't. Can you send the message or not?"

"Can you pay?"

I held up my stones.

· That was all it took. The wizard was worse even than Larus, but at least he could send a messaging spell. I wrote a note to my family. I'd been wanting to do it since I left Kolur, but I didn't know what to say, if I should tell Mama the whole truth about him or not. I spent a good amount of time with the quill in one hand, staring down at the parchment while the wizard tapped his fingers and sighed impatiently.

Dear Mama and Papa, I eventually wrote, *I want you to know I'm safe. I'm just out having an adventure, like Ananna of the Nadir. You don't need to worry.*

I wasn't sure how true that last part was, but I knew I didn't want them to worry, even if they did need to.

I stood with my arms wrapped around my chest as he enchanted the parchment and turned it to sparkles of magic that floated on the air.

"How will I know they get it?" I said.

He shrugged. "You won't. Takes a long time for messages to travel across the islands."

And that was that. I hoped by the time the wizard received a reply from them, I'd be on my way home.

After that, my time aboard the *Annika* smoothed out, but I never truly felt like I belonged. I took my meals with Asbera and Finnur and hung my hammock up alongside theirs, and that was enough to quiet the whispers and stop the curious looks. It wasn't ideal, but it wasn't terrible, and that was good enough for me.

When the ocean wasn't safe or when Reynir couldn't find any worthwhile catches, we'd have a day or two off. Asbera showed me around Rilil, pointing out the different shops, the grocer and the magic-dealer, the moneylender and the ship repair. Other days I spent alone, when I needed to be with my thoughts. I walked down to the beach, following the road that had brought me here, and fed scraps to the sea birds. I said a prayer at the circle on the edge of town, listening for the voices of my ancestors.

I never heard anything.

I also never heard anything about Frida and Kolur. Asbera didn't go in much for rumors, and the rest of the crew wasn't friendly enough to share what they'd heard. Still, I wondered. If they were still in Tulja, if it had been the right thing, leaving them and coming to work for Baltasar.

One day, we had a short run out to the Brightly Sea. We took only half the crew and were back by lunchtime with a big catch of skrei, and I was grateful that Baltasar had asked me along, since it was easy work for quite a bit of pay.

I walked along the docks, a pouch of nearly fifty stones weighing down my pockets. I was in a good mood and didn't feel like eating salted fish back on the *Cornflower*. So, even though I knew it was wasteful, I walked down to the Yak's Horn, an alehouse Finnur had talked about. He said the ale was good and the food was better, and that sounded like a fine idea to me.

The Yak's Horn was located at the far end of the docks. I made my way along the damp stone path. Things were busier than usual – more boats in the water and more fishermen crowded around them. I paid careful attention to the voices, hoping to hear a southerly accent, someone who could take me back to Kjora.

And I heard one. A familiar one, shouting curses into the air.

I stopped. I was standing in front of a junk that was all carved up in the Jolali style with icons of the sea spirits. It didn't have sails yet, but the wood was freshly painted, and it was in better shape than most of the boats here. The name across the side read *Penelope II*.

"I told you, boy, I don't want the twisted, I want braided! Holds together better." Kolur stomped across the deck.

I almost walked away. I had nothing to say to him, and if he'd had the money to buy that gaudy new boat, he'd had the money to send me home back in Skalir. But before my anger could overtake me, a second figure joined him, not Frida but a young man. The spiky, elaborate icons shielded the young man at first, but as he darted back and forth, I saw his pale skin and pale hair, his graceful way of moving. He looked entirely human now, his ethereal beauty replaced by a bland, forgettable handsomeness. But I still recognized him immediately.

Isolfr.

I stared at him. He stammered out something to Kolur – "Yes, sir, I'll run to the supply shop now" – and then scurried over to the ladder. I was too bewildered to move. Kolur shouted something toward the bow of the ship, probably at Frida, and then walked out of my line of sight.

And then Isolfr dropped down to the dock, a loop of rope draped over his shoulder. He had his head down.

"What the hell are you doing?" I said.

He jumped, stopped, looked up at me. For a moment, his eyes glimmered like starlight, but then they returned to a normal, flat blue. It was my imagination, I told myself, a trick of the sunlight.

"Well?" I said.

"Please, miss," he said, "I'm going to the repair shop."

I scowled at him, not having the patience to deal with his tricks. But then he winked.

"The repair shop," he said again, and scrambled off.

I sighed. I did not want to get involved with him again. I wanted to eat my lunch and go back to the *Cornflower* and shake my jar of stones and think about home.

But I was also angry, angry that he had foisted upon me the warning about Lord Foxfollow and then disappeared, that he had transformed himself into a blind spot for Kolur and Frida and then wheedled his way aboard this new version of the *Penelope*.

So I followed after him. I figured it was the only way I'd get answers.

I waited for him outside the repair shop, leaning up against the post of a sign I still couldn't read. The repair shop was all aboveground, and every now and then, the wind would blow the curtain door aside and I'd see him studying the different loops of rope. When he came back outside, he lifted one hand in a wave.

"What in sea and sky is going on?" I said.

"I can explain." He smiled. "You're hungry, yes? Would you like to get something to eat?"

"No." I didn't like that he knew I was hungry. "I want you to explain what the hell you're doing." I leaned close to him, lowering my voice. "You wouldn't let me tell Kolur who you were, and now you're *working* for him?"

"Well, you ran off." Isolfr turned and headed down the path, over to an empty space where the shops ended. He tossed the rope to the ground and gestured for me to join to him. I did, stupid me wanting my answers, and he cast a spell that washed over us both like a sudden wind.

"What was *that*?"

"So no one can hear us." Isolfr sat down on the rope. "So yes, I'm working for Kolur, but he doesn't quite *know* that. He thinks I'm a Tuljan boy named Pjetur."

"You're insane," I said. "Why are you doing this to us? To him?" I pointed to the docks, in the direction of the *Penelope II*. "How'd he even afford that ship, anyway? Was it you? Do you have money? Could you have sent me home?"

"He didn't buy it with money." Isolfr ran his hands over the rope. "He got the boat in exchange for a spell he and Frida performed – Jandanvari magic, very dangerous." Isolfr looked up at me. "And the boat wasn't seaworthy. Still isn't. That's why we're still here, doing repairs."

"Doing repairs to go on a fool's errand, is that it? And now you're helping him? You aren't even human. Why do you *care*?"

Isolfr drew his knees up to his chest. "I'm helping him because you won't," he said quietly.

"Because I *won't*?" Anger flushed in my cheeks. "I tried! But I had no idea what to do. You just gave me all these warnings and then – then *Gillean* was on deck and he was *dead*–"

"That was Lord Foxfollow," Isolfr said. "He found out. I had to go into hiding."

I wanted to hit him. "I'm lucky Kolur turned out to have magic. All you did was tell me what was coming and give me no way to fight it, and then you wouldn't even let me warn Kolur."

Isolfr's cheeks colored, twin spots of pink like on a doll. "I admit that clouding his memory may not have been the best course of action."

"They why did you do it?" I glowered at him. "Why are you *still* doing it?"

The color on Isolfr's cheek deepened. "You wouldn't understand."

"I think I have a right to know." I crossed my arms over my chest. "You're the reason I'm stranded here, after all. If you hadn't gotten involved–"

"You and Kolur and Frida would be dead," he interrupted. "Lord Foxfollow would have hunted you down."

"He only found us because we gave Gillean a funeral." I threw my hands in the air. "And we only had to give Gillean a funeral because his body dropped on our boat. Don't try and lay the blame on me, Isolfr. Don't you dare."

Isolfr shrank back. The magic of his spell shimmered around us, sweet and bright like honeycomb candy. "He would have found you anyway," he said. "Maybe you would have gotten all the way to Jandanvar first. But he would have killed you eventually."

There was an intensity in his voice I didn't expect. It shuddered through me and left me cold. But I wasn't going to back down.

"I still wouldn't say that anything you've done has helped us." I peered at him, trying to find some clue in those washed-out human features. "Why are you keeping Frida's and Kolur's minds clouded? At least tell me that much." I paused. "I have a right to know."

Isolfr looked down at his hands. "You're right," he said.

I preened, hearing that. But it wasn't enough to quell my anger with him.

"Well?" I said.

"I'm getting to it." He looked up at me. "It's Frida. She's terrifying. When she was training in Jandanvar, she called down one of my brothers and she – she *bound* him to leach out his strength for her spell. My sister had to save him. He almost died."

"Can you even die?" I snapped. But Isolfr's eyes widened and I felt a pang of guilt. "Sorry," I said. "That wasn't—"

"Yes, I can die," he said. "Just not like you."

"What are you?"

He ignored my question. "Kolur was helping her. If either he or Frida saw me in my true form, they'd know what I am. They'd – recognize me. And I – I didn't want that."

"You're scared of them." It was a strange thought, and an unsettling one. A month ago, I would have found it laughable that anyone could be scared of Kolur, but now I wasn't so sure. He'd pretended to be a fisherman when he could have been a wizard. Maybe there was some wicked explanation. I shivered.

Isolfr looked away. The magic around us rippled and flickered. For a moment, I thought it was going to disappear completely.

"I was sent to warn them." He spoke down into the grass. "To give them aid. But I couldn't do it." His shoulders hitched, and I felt a twinge of pity for him that turned to irritation quickly enough.

"Who sent you?"

"My superiors. Their names are cloaked, so there's no point in me even saying them." He almost sounded miserable. "I don't know why they sent me. I told them what Frida and Kolur had done—"

"They wouldn't have hurt you," I said. "If you really are trying to help."

"I am!" He leapt to his feet and grabbed the rope. "And anyway, I'm working with them now, aren't I?"

"In disguise! You could have just done that from the beginning."

Once again, I'd said something he didn't want to hear, so he ignored me.

"This is pointless. I hope Kolur makes you empty their chamber pots." I stalked away from him and straight into the spell. At first I thought it was going to hold me in place, but the air yielded when I passed through. My ears rang, and my skin prickled. When I turned around, Isolfr was gone. No, not gone, just invisible. The way I'd been a few seconds previous.

"Don't come looking for me!" I shouted into the empty field. Then I stormed back down to the road. Isolfr didn't follow me, thank the gods. It figured that not only did I have to get saddled with some magical do-gooder, I had to get saddled with a cowardly, incompetent one.

The wind picked up, northerly and sweet-smelling. I shivered and drew my coat closer around my chest. And for a moment, I worried. Not about Isolfr – he wasn't human; he could take care of himself. But Kolur. Kolur and Frida too, both sailing into the trap of Lord Foxfollow with only Isolfr to help them.

I shook my head. No. Kolur had lied to me. About where he was taking me, about his past. His business wasn't mine any longer. Lord Foxfollow cared not for me; I didn't want to steal away his bride. All I had to think about was earning enough money to get home.

The wind continued to blow, and I continued to shiver beneath my coat.

CHAPTER TEN

I hoped that would be the end of it. I hoped Isolfr would slink back to the *Penelope II* and do whatever weaselly things he could to keep Kolur and Frida out of trouble. Meanwhile, I'd continue to sail out with the *Annika* and we'd all go our separate ways. That's what I hoped life would be like.

And for a while, it was.

The jar in my captain's quarters grew heavier with stones, even though I had to dump out a handful to pay Rudolph the rent for my little moored *Cornflower*. I drew down the winds as the *Annika* sailed up and down the Tuljan coat, I ate meals with Asbera and Finnur, I fetched water from the well and bought food from the grocer.

It should have been peaceful, if not satisfying. But it wasn't. Something always niggled at the back of my head, a note of discomfort that made me toss and turn at night as the waves slapped against the walls of the boat. Whenever I was in town, I found myself looking over my shoulder, watching for the Mists.

I wanted to blame my encounter with Isolfr, thinking he must have planted ideas in my head. But deep down, I knew that wasn't it.

After a particularly long trip aboard the *Annika*, I went over to the *Crocus* for the usual dinner with Asbera and Finnur. I climbed over the railing, like always, but this time I saw something that made my heart pound: They had switched out the twisted-up vine charms, swapping the old for the new, and added at least twice as many as before. The charms hung from the masts like sails, dropping small oval leaves across the deck.

Seeing them stirred up a whisper of fear.

"Hanna! I thought I heard your feet on the ceiling." Asbera's head appeared in the hatch. "Dinner's almost ready." She stopped and set her hands on the deck and stared at me. "What's wrong?"

"You changed the vines," I said.

Her expression flickered. "Yes," she said. "I brought in some new charms. For protection."

"Were you robbed?" The question sounded naive, even to me.

Asbera shook her head. She shifted her weight like she was uncomfortable. "It's nothing, Hanna, it really isn't. You just have to be careful this far north."

"We know what the Mists are in Kjora."

"I know you do." She smiled. "Nothing's happened, you understand. It's just – a need for precaution."

I went down to dinner feeling uneasy.

The next day, I went into Rilil for the first time in nearly a week, and I saw that the charms hanging above the shop doors had gotten bigger too, plumped out with gray moss and dried flowers and wrapped in red ribbons. Tuljan characters were scratched in the soil and stained with red dye. I didn't have to read them to know that they were protection spells.

Compared to the elaborate earth-magic charms of the Tuljans, my bracelet from the Skalirin magic shop seemed paltry and weak, but I knew it was better than nothing. To calm myself at night, I practiced the protective wind charms I knew, standing up on the stern of the *Cornflower*, facing out to sea. I called the south wind, and its magic washed over the boat, settling in all the nooks and crannies. I hoped it would bring me the protection I needed.

One evening, everything still bright with the late spring sun, I went for a walk along the docks, my hands tucked tight into my pockets to protect against the chill. I stopped when I spotted the *Penelope II* against the horizon, her Jolali carvings cast in silhouette against the white sky. At that point, I turned around and went back home.

I'd just wanted to know if Kolur had finished the repairs or not. I'd just wanted to know if she was still in port.

The *Annika* crew wasn't an exception to all this new paranoia, either. They took to muttering prayers whenever we left the docks and before we returned, whispering to themselves in a thicker-than-usual Tuljan dialect, the words guttural and unfamiliar. Finnur, seeing me listen in one morning, grabbed me by the hand and said the prayer over me, flashing a bright smile when he finished. "Now you're just like the rest of us," he said. It was from him that I learned the words were a prayer at all – an ancient one to guard against the Mists.

And then there were the Nalendan.

We saw them one morning as we dragged the night's catch to the market. The jangling, pounding music drifted down the street, and everyone in the crew stopped and set their loads down, even Baltasar. I followed their lead and rested my package of ling at my feet and stood straight and unmoving. The music set me on edge, even if it was a protection spell.

The costumed men approached, chanting the same song as before. Magic shimmered around them. The shopkeeper across the way tossed flowers and the man dressed as a pine tree bowed to her, the pines needles of his costume shining in the light.

Magic settled around us like a blanket.

The costumed men passed, and the air sighed with relief. The crew gathered up their packages, but the high spirits from our successful catch had disappeared. Asbera was frowning.

"What's wrong?" I whispered to her as we made our way down the street.

"The Nalendan," she said. "They were just here, remember? And to see them again, so soon–" She shook her head. "No matter. We should be grateful for the catch, don't you think?"

I nodded, although her words kept me on edge. We didn't speak the rest of the way to the market.

The costumed men disappeared around a curve in the road, but I could still hear their music on the wind.

A week later, Asbera and Finnur and I went out for drinks. We'd gotten back from a four-day trip and had the next few days off, so it seemed a fine idea to go down to the mead hall for a round or two. I knew we hoped the drinks would help dull the fear that had been cutting through Rilil lately. Not that any of us admitted that out loud.

The mead hall was crowded when we arrived, the lighting dim and smoky. I looked over the mass of faces, scanning for Kolur. I was about as keen on seeing him again as I was on seeing Isolfr. But in the dark light, it was too difficult to make anyone out. All the men looked the same, with their long hair and their thick northern beards.

"In the back," Finnur said to me. "There's always a place there."

We pushed through the crowd to a table in the corner. Asbera ordered ale for all three of us. "I'm looking forward to the next few days," she said when the serving girl had left. "Some of my herbs need tending to." She paused. "Maybe you'd like some, Hanna?"

I looked down at the table and twisted my bracelet around my wrist. The herbs, like the pieces of vine, were enchanted to protect the *Crocus* from the Mists. Everyone was protecting themselves from the Mists, but not a single damn person would admit to it outright. That probably explained why the mead hall was so crowded tonight. All that fear.

"I don't want to be a bother." I'd learned not to bring up the Mists myself. It worked out better that way, to keep my head down. "I'm sure you need them."

"I can spare a few." She smiled, and Finnur looked at her and then looked at me and grinned.

"Yeah, it's a right jungle on deck," he said. "Just like Jokja. You ever hear the stories about Jokja?"

"My mother sailed there," I said. "Her captain was friends with the queen's consort."

Asbera's eyes lit up. "Really? I hear the Jokja royalty is *grand*, that the palace is made entirely out of jewels. Is that true?"

Off to my side, Finnur scoffed, but I shook my head. "Not really. But Mama said you could feel the jungle's magic if you went too close."

Asbera's eyes glittered. Our drinks arrived, and the serving girl slammed them down on the table without saying a word. Finnur lifted his up in the air and said, "To two days of freedom."

"Freedom!" Asbera and I called out, laughing. We clicked our drinks together, ale sloshing over the sides, and drank. I didn't feel free. Every day away from the boat was a day I wasn't earning money to return back home.

"Hanna?"

The voice came from behind me. It was soft and silvery like moonlight. My stomach dropped out at the bottom.

"Who's this?" Asbera grinned. "Should we know him?"

"I'm Pjetur." Isolfr sat down in the seat beside me. I didn't bother to correct him; something told me Asbera and Finnur wouldn't hear me if I did. "I work for Hanna's old captain."

"Ah," Finnur said. "So you can shed some light on Hanna's mysterious past."

Asbera smacked him on the arm.

"Afraid not. I know as little as you do."

I ignored him and scanned the faces of the mead hall again. This time I did find Kolur, sitting over in the corner with Frida. He was staring at me, scowling, but when he saw me looking, he lifted one hand in greeting.

I turned away from him.

"Kolur asked me to check on you," Isolfr said. "He wants to make sure you're all right, that you have everything you need."

"Is that so?" I stared down at the foam of my ale, looking for patterns the way you do in tea leaves and coffee dregs. I didn't see anything.

"Yes. Things have been–" Isolfr stopped when he saw Asbera and Finnur staring at him with unease. "Stormy."

"Been clear skies for me." I took a long drink of ale. "And they'll be clearer once Kolur leaves."

"Is that true?" Finnur asked. "About Kolur bringing–"

Asbera looked at him sharply, and he didn't finish his question. But I knew he was asking if Kolur brought the Mists here.

"Yes," I said. "That's why I left him."

"You poor dear," Asbera said. "No wonder you want to get away."

"You can't lay the blame entirely on Kolur." Isolfr looked shyly over at Asbera. "Hanna has a tendency to exaggerate."

I glared at him.

Asbera laughed. "Not from what I've seen."

"Not from what he's seen, either." I turned to Isolfr. "Are you finished here? *Pjetur*?"

He recoiled a little at the snap in my voice, but he did answer with "I am." He didn't move away from the table, though, only stared at me with his flat pale eyes. "You could do a great deal of good aboard the *Penelope II*, and if nothing else, it would be a free place to sleep." He paused. "I'm sorry I didn't help you enough before."

"Not interested," I said. "Like fishing better."

Isolfr granted me one last hopeless look. Then he stood and gave a weird, formal bow to Asbera and Finnur both before scuttling to Kolur's ship.

"My," said Asbera. "I bet that's an interesting story."

I swirled my ale around. "It's not."

"Prettiest fisherman I've ever seen," said Finnur.

Asbera laughed. "I was thinking the same thing. You sure you don't want to go back to the *Penelope II*? Might be worth the–" Her voice hitched. "The danger."

I knocked back a swig of ale. "Hardly." I didn't want to talk about this, didn't want to talk about Isolfr, or Pjetur, or his unsettling beauty. They hadn't even seen him in the moonlight and the ocean, the way I had. They'd only seen this watered-down version of him, his beauty faded into handsome blandness.

"You sure about that?" Finnur said. "I feel like Asbera's about to go in your place."

Asbera shrieked and shoved him, a blush creeping along her cheeks.

"She likes her fishermen pretty," Finnur said, and Asbera grew redder and redder. I watched them laugh and flirt with each other, and I didn't bother to correct Finnur. Isolfr wasn't a fisherman. Isolfr wasn't even human.

Hard to fall in love with something like that.

We wound up staying late at the mead hall, later than most of the folks there. We certainly stayed later than Kolur and Frida and Isolfr – I saw them gather up their things and leave while Finnur was in the middle of a dirty joke. When they walked away, I was finally able to relax.

By the time we left, I'd drunk much more mead than I was used to. The candles lighting the hall were as bright and golden as summer suns, and Finnur and Asbera seemed to glow, especially when they looked at each other. It was nice, all that warmth drawing us together. Stumbling out into the cold, empty street was a shock.

"Everyone's gone hooome!" Finnur sang out, throwing his hands wide. Asbera and I laughed at him, and our voices echoed up into the night air.

"Look at the stars," Asbera said, leaning back. She grabbed my arm and pointed. "Look!"

I looked. Like the mead hall candles, they were brighter than I expected, a brilliant spiral of light spilling across the black sky. For a moment, Asbera and I stood very still, clutching at each other's arms and looking up at the stars. Our breath crystallized on the air in great white puffs.

"Beautiful," I finally said.

"You act like you've never seen stars before," Finnur shouted, and he smacked me on the back, startling me out of my daze. I looked over at him and grinned. He had his arms slung around both our shoulders. "Asbera and Hanna," he slurred. "Never seen the stars."

Asbera tickled his ribcage, and he crumpled into laughter that sounded hollow in the empty street. Even after he stopped laughing, I could hear it still, bouncing off the music.

Music.

Finnur's laughter – and music.

Jangling, pounding music.

"Shhhh," I hissed. They were all wrapped up in each other's arms. "Do you hear that?"

"No," Finnur said, but Asbera tilted her head like she was listening.

"Yeah," she said. "I hear it." She pulled away from Finnur. "The Nalendan."

The name sent a chill down my spine.

"Protecting us from the – you know." Her face was pale in the starlight. "They never march this late, do they, Finnur?"

"We don't usually have this much to worry about." Finnur's voice was throaty, bitter. He must have had a lot to drink, if he was acknowledging the threat outright. I shivered. "It was your captain who brought them here, wasn't it?"

"Shush," said Asbera. "No human can control the Mists. You know that."

We pressed together, swaying in the middle of the road. A pinpoint of blue light appeared in the distance. The music rose and fell with the wind.

Coldness prickled at the back of my throat.

"Maybe we aren't supposed to be here," I said.

"Nonsense," said Asbera. "We just need to find some snowflowers to throw at them." She pulled away from Finnur and me and stumbled over to the grocer's across from the mead hall. It was closed for the night, the curtain pinned shut, no light spilling out around it. She rang the bell.

"They're closed." Finnur chased after her. The light at the end of the road grew bigger, wreathed in a shimmering halo of magic.

"I really don't think we're supposed to be here," I whispered.

I glanced over at Finnur and Asbera and found them kissing each other, like they'd forgotten where we were. "Hey!" I shouted. "Pay attention! We need to go home."

They pulled apart and both turned to me, their faces pale in the moonlight. "Don't be silly," said Asbera. "It's good luck to see the Nalendan."

It didn't feel like good luck, being out here alone in the dark. I looked back at the light. The Nalendan grew closer. Their singing was stronger, louder. I ran over to Finnur and Asbera and we stood in a line, waiting. My heart pounded in my chest. My thoughts were dizzy with drink. I didn't feel like I was part of this world.

My bracelet. I'd forgotten I was wearing my bracelet.

I touched it and the vines were cold. My heart skipped a beat. *No,* I told myself. *Of course they're cold, it's cold out here.*

The singing was louder now, louder than it ought to be. Finnur and Asbera both grinned wildly, like children waiting for gifts on midsummer. I pressed closer to them, still touching my bracelet. The wind lifted, rustled my hair. It blew in from the north and smelled of flowers. It was so soft against my skin it almost felt like protective magic.

For a split second I felt that presence I had known when I was aboard the *Penelope.* But then it was gone.

"Here they coooome," Finnur said, under his breath.

In the dark, all I could see were shadows: the silhouette of a man-sized pine, the shaggy hulk of a yak's-head mask, the twist of goat's horns, the straw-man shaped like star. I trembled. I held my breath. Closer. Closer.

The music buzzed. It didn't sound right. I told myself it sounded that way because of the drink, that the ale had made me paranoid. I gripped my bracelet tighter, and it was so cold that it seared into my fingers.

"Something's *wrong,*" I whispered. Finnur and Asbera didn't hear me; they stood transfixed, staring at the costumed men. "The music – that isn't right–"

"It's the Tuljan dialect," Asbera said, but her voice was slurred, and she sounded distant, not part of herself.

"No, that isn't it." The wind blew harder and amplified the singing. Clarified it. The words were sharp and unfamiliar. "I don't think that's the ancient language at all."

But Finnur and Asbera weren't paying any attention to me. They moved forward, toward the costumed men, drawn on some invisible wire.

"Stop!" I shrieked. "This isn't supposed to happen." I grabbed at both of their arms, yanking them back.

The costumed men halted. They'd never done that before. Their singing died away and their heads turned, in unison, and they bore down on the three of us.

A tree, a goat, a straw man, a yak. I felt suddenly diminished.

Asbera and Finnur pulled away from my grip and moved toward the costumed men. The tree smiled, his teeth bright in the moonlight.

"No!" I screamed, and I tackled Asbera and dragged her to the ground.

"What are you doing?" she asked, spitting out muddy snow. Her voice didn't sound so curiously flat. "What's wrong with you–?"

She stopped. Finnur was almost to the costumed men. The goat lifted his great shaggy arms as if to envelop him.

"This isn't right," Asbera said.

"I've been saying that!" I scrambled to my feet. The goat drew Finnur into an embrace. His eyes glittered behind his mask. Gray. His eyes were gray.

All of them, their eyes – they were all gray.

The Mists.

The air slammed out of me.

"No," Asbera whispered, low and fluttery. "No no no no."

The yak stepped forward. The mask was carved from wood and painted in dull brownish-gray. The mouth was fixed in a permanent snarl.

"Friend of Kolur." Its mouth didn't move as it spoke. Asbera let out a strangled squawk and grabbed my hand. The goat pulled Finnur closer, wrapping its furred arm around Finnur's neck. Finnur was so pale, his skin looked like snow.

"Stop it!" I shouted. "Let him go!"

"*Friends* of Kolur," the monster said.

"No!" I cried. "Just me. They've never met him. Please, let Finnur go."

All the stories about the Mists flooded through my head. You couldn't outsmart them; you couldn't undo their magic. And that was terrifying, because dressed in the costume of the Nalendan, they had undone Tuljan magic. They had turned the protection spell into a weapon.

"Let him go!" I shrieked.

The straw man hissed.

I didn't stop to let myself think, because thinking only reminded me of all the horrors I could face. I just launched myself forward and grabbed Finnur's hand and tried to wrench him free from the goat. Asbera screamed behind me, but then she was at my side, pulling too. Finnur stared numbly at both of us.

The costumed men didn't do anything to stop us, although they didn't let go of Finnur either. The goat didn't struggle, just held him tight, and the other three stood in a circle, watching.

"Curious," said the straw man with a dry, crackling hiss.

"Yes," said the tree. "Most curious."

"Come back to me, Finnur!" Asbera cried. "Please. Remember. Our little sea-house. Come on, darling–"

We pulled harder, and then, without any warning at all, the goat dropped him.

All three of us fell backward onto the cold, hard ground.

"Friend of Kolur," said the tree, and all four of the costumed men turned toward me. I froze in place while Asbera and Finnur crawled away.

"Friend of Isolfr," said the monster.

Asbera cried out, her voice strangled. I tried to twist around to look at her, but I couldn't move. I was bolted to the ground. The costumed men crowded in close.

"What do you want?" I screamed.

The wind gusted. Through the cloud of my fear, I thought I might be able to conjure the south wind, to pull out enough magic that Finnur and Asbera and I could escape. It probably wouldn't work, not against Mists magic. But I could try.

"Our lord does not appreciate what you've been doing," said the straw man.

"No," said the goat. "Not at all."

"He's sent us to make you stop," said the tree.

"You and Kolur and Isolfr," said the yak.

"I don't even sail with Kolur anymore." I concentrated hard on the wind. It was cold and damp and blew my hair straight away from my face. The costumed men's gray eyes glittered at me from behind their masks. "I haven't seen him for days. I can't help you."

Magic coursed through the wind, fine and gossamer like lace. It tingled against my skin. *Concentrate. Concentrate.*

The costumed men looked at one another.

"Of course you can help us," said the goat.

"Friend of Kolur," said the tree.

"Friend of Isolfr," said the yak.

I started to cry. The wind pummeled against my body, and my hair blew straight out behind me–

And then my hair tumbled into my face.

The wind had shifted. I could taste the south on it, mangos and warmth and the distant brightness of spice. With the southerly wind, the magic didn't feel like lace; it felt like sunlight, like ocean water, like air. It was everywhere, and all I had to do was reach out and harvest it.

I squeezed my eyes shut. The magic flowed through me, changing inside my bloodstream. I whispered an incantation in the old tongue, and I told myself it would work, it would have to work–

The paralysis lifted.

My eyes flew open, and I jumped to my feet. The wind swirled around us, looping around the costumed men like a rope. I stumbled away from them, gasping with the effort. Asbera and Finnur lay tangled up against each other, their eyes closed.

The tree broke free of my chains.

"Friend of Kolur. You cannot stop us."

I strengthened the magic, and the wind knocked him away. He landed on his back, shedding pine needles in the moonlight. I knelt beside Asbera and Finnur and sent the magic flowing through them. Their veins glowed golden beneath their skin.

"Wake up," I whispered in the ancient tongue. "Wake up, wake up, wake up."

Asbera's eyes opened first. She stared at me like I was a wild animal.

"Hanna!" she gasped.

"You must move." I said this in the ancient tongue, too. Asbera's eyes widened and her arms jerked and the wind dragged her body up until she was standing. Then it dragged Finnur up. His eyes fluttered.

"Run!" I screamed at them, still in the ancient tongue. "Run! Run home!"

The costumed men wailed over the roaring of the wind. I couldn't tell which direction it blew; it seemed to come from everywhere, north and south, east and west. Asbera and Finnur raced away, their movements jerky and awkward and not entirely their own.

I whirled around to face the costumed men. The thread of magic had tightened around them. I stared; I hadn't tightened it. I'd been tending to Finnur and Asbera, and doing so had sapped me of my strength.

The rioting wind howled and howled, drowning out the cries from the costumed men. It howled so much that it became a voice, sharp and shining and cold like ice. I wasn't sure if I imagined it or not.

It spoke the ancient tongue.

Run, it said. *Run. Run away.*

And I did.

CHAPTER ELEVEN

Somehow, I made it back to the boarding-boats. The wind faded the farther I got from the costumed men, and by the time I was back on the docks, it was a gentle breeze, strong enough to rock the boarding-boat sign back and forth on its post but nothing more. I leaned up against the signpost. My legs trembled and my lungs burned and every muscle in my body ached. I prayed to all the gods and ancestors I knew that the costumed men – the *Mists* men – wouldn't come for me. I had no more strength left to fight them.

"Hanna?"

Asbera's voice trembled from out of the thick night. It sounded small and afraid. She stood at the end of the dock, a magic-cast lantern hanging from one hand. "Hanna – what happened–"

She moved toward me, although her steps were slow and unsteady. She must have been weak, too. The lantern swayed, the blue light gliding across the docks. As she drew closer, I saw the streaks of tears on her face.

"Finnur?" I asked.

"He's alive." She hung the lantern from a hook on the sign. For a moment, we stared at each other. Then she flung her arms around my shoulders and buried her face in my neck. "Oh, thank you, Hanna, we would've – I don't even want to think what would have happened if you hadn't been there."

I hugged back as best I could. My thoughts were clouded with exhaustion.

Asbera pulled away and smiled through her tears. "You were so brave. I can't believe they – that was the Mists, wasn't it? They *desecrated* the Nalendan." She looked ill. "How is that even possible?"

"I don't know." I stood there, wobbling in place.

"We have to tell the priests," Asbera babbled. "We have to warn them. I just don't know how this could have happened."

"They were trying to find me." I stared blankly ahead. "The Mists. It's my fault you were hurt."

"We weren't hurt." Asbera grabbed my hand. "We weren't hurt, because you saved us."

I shook my head. Asbera pulled me into a hug, almost knocking me off balance, and I could smell the smoky-sweet scent of magic on her, and the sharp tang of old fear.

"Thank you," she said when she let me go.

It felt wrong, taking her thanks. Humans weren't able to defeat Mists magic; everyone knew that. And certainly not humans like *me*, some fisherman's apprentice who could control the winds for ships and not much else. Someone must have helped me.

Kolur. Kolur had dragged us away from the Mists before. And that fierce northern wind – Frida, maybe, helping him.

"You can stay with us tonight," Asbera said. "I wouldn't feel comfortable letting you go back to the *Cornflower* alone."

I nodded, feeling numb. Asbera rowed us back to the *Crocus*, and the slap of the oars against the water kept time with the beat of my heart. She took me down below, past the rustling plants and dried-out vines. Finnur was stretched out on a cot beside the hearth, liquid bubbling in a cauldron on the fire. It released peppery-scented steam into the air, and the magic tingled across my skin like an ointment.

Asbera knelt beside him and pushed his hair off his forehead. Her eyes shimmered.

"Is he going to be all right?" I asked.

She didn't answer right away, just kept stroking his hair and staring down at him. "Yes. We got away just in time." She stood up and wiped at her eyes. "Can I get you something to drink? Or eat? You must be exhausted, all that magic–"

I nodded. Yes. Food. Food was necessary to rebuild your strength. I sat down at the table and watched Finnur as Asbera rummaged around in the storage barrels. He shifted, stirred, rolled over in his sleep. Seeing that movement gave me a rush of relief.

For the first time since we'd left the mead hall, my heart began to slow.

That night, I slept on a hammock in the corner of the *Crocus* hearthroom and woke to find Asbera feeding breakfast to Finnur.

"He's doing so much better," she said when I knelt down at her side.

"Thank you," Finnur added. His voice was scratchy and thin. "That was – well, I don't want to go through it again." He started to cough, and Asbera dropped his breakfast to the side and tilted a cup of water to his lips. "I'm fine," he said, batting her hand away. He did look better. There was more color in his skin, and his eyes were no longer glassy and blank.

"Would you like something to eat?" Asbera asked, turning to me.

"Thank you, and thank you for letting me sleep here, but I need to go–"

"Don't be ridiculous," Asbera said, and Finnur coughed in protest.

"It's fine, really," I said. "I need to speak with – with someone. My old captain. I'll be back aboard the *Cornflower,* so–"

"This is no time to be alone," Asbera said.

"I agree," Finnur said.

I forced myself to stay patient. I really was grateful that I didn't have to spend the night by myself. But I needed to speak with Kolur. He'd likely saved me last night, and Mama and Papa had taught me well enough that I knew I should thank him. But I also knew the only reason the Mists were still here was because the *Penelope II* hadn't moved on yet. I wanted to know what sort of repairs they were doing and how long those repairs would take.

Asbera sighed, her brow creased with concern. "At least stay for breakfast," she said. "Make sure you have all your strength."

I hesitated. As anxious as I was to get to the *Penelope II*, I had to admit that Finnur's breakfast porridge, flecked with sweet flowers and dried ice-berries, looked nourishing and warm.

"Fine," I said. "But just breakfast."

Asbera scooped me up a bowl of porridge. I ate it mostly in silence, trying hard not to think of last night. When I finished, Asbera walked me up to the deck.

"Come back straight away," she said. "And take a bit of protection vine. It's good luck."

It was more than good luck, even I knew that, but in the morning's bright glare, Asbera wasn't willing to talk about the threat of the Mists outright.

So I snapped off a bit of vine. The magic shuddered through me at the moment of breakage, a magic far more powerful than any in my bracelet.

"Thank you," I told her. "I won't be gone long."

"Wait." She put one hand on my arm. "We have to report what happened to the priests. If the Nalendan can be violated–" She covered her heart like the thought pained her. "When you come back, we can make the trip together."

"Of course," I said. "I won't be gone long."

And with that, I was on my way to the *Penelope II*.

The sun was out, and the air was cold and brittle. People milled around on the docks, hawking cheap, weak-looking protection charms along with the usual salted cod and fishing supplies. I shivered every time I passed one of the charm merchants.

As I walked, I thought about Kolur. That was powerful magic, to stop the Mists the way he did. I wondered what other secrets he'd kept from me and Mama and the rest of the village.

The *Penelope II* was moored in its usual place. The gangplank was down, so I climbed aboard as if we were back on Kjora. I peeked my head over the railing but didn't see anyone.

"Hello!" I shouted. "Kolur? I need to speak with you."

No answer but the rushing sea. I hoisted myself up on deck. The *Penelope II* was bigger, a proper frigate, with three masts instead of two, and a wider deck. It wasn't the sort of boat you used just for fishing.

"Kolur!" I shouted. "It's Hanna! I really need to—"

"Yeah, yeah, I heard you, girl."

Kolur's voice came from behind me, as gruff as ever. I whirled around and found him climbing out of the hatchway with a loop of rope draped over his left shoulder.

"What do you want? We're still heading north, so I don't got a job for you."

"All I wanted was to thank you for last night." I rushed over to him and helped pull him on deck. "I would never have gotten away—"

"The hell are you talking about?" Kolur dropped the rope on the deck. "I spent last night patching the hull. Took me hours, too. That good-for-nothing Pjetur fell asleep at sundown and couldn't be roused. Sleeps like a man damned, he does." Kolur kicked at the rope, and squinted up at the masts. "Really don't feel like climbing up there this morning."

"You don't have to do this." I crossed my arms over my chest. "You already told me you were some great wizard. You don't have to pretend anymore."

"Ain't pretending." He looked over at me, frowning. "Did something happen to you?"

I felt cold. "Yes! I was attacked by the Mists. And I called up my magic but it wasn't enough, just me. Someone was helping–"

Kolur looked as confused as I felt. Not to mention horrified. "The Mists *attacked* you?" he said. "Sea and sky, girl, and you got *away?*"

"That's what I'm trying to tell you! Someone helped me." That cold feeling grew stronger. "It wasn't you. Frida, it must have been Frida–"

"Frida was helping me," Kolur said. "Patching the hull." He studied me, his eyes sharp and keen. "This some trick? To get back at me?"

That cold, creeping feeling turned my whole body to ice. "Not a trick," I said softly. "Someone helped me. It wasn't you. It wasn't Frida–"

Isolfr? Not that he'd done much to help me in all this time.

Kolur was still staring at me. "If you really did get attacked by the Mists," he said, "you need to talk to the Tuljan priests."

"When the Mists attacked," I said, "they called me friend of Kolur."

Kolur paused. Then he rubbed his forehead. "Shit. I'm sorry, girl. These repairs are taking longer than I expected, but they shouldn't be coming after you now that you're not a part of my crew. You really do need to go to the priests, tell 'em what happened. They'll get you protected."

I felt numb. The priests' magic had failed so spectacularly last night – not just failed, but been desecrated, like Asbera said. Corrupted.

"Thanks," I mumbled, and I turned and stumbled off the boat.

Kolur called out my name, but I ignored him.

Asbera and I walked to the temple as soon as I got back to the boarding-boats. We wrapped our arms in vines and carried moss in our pockets, Tuljan charms to keep the Mists away. Finnur was too weak to hike to the base of the mountain, so he stayed behind with Benedict and Harald, two friends from the *Annika*.

I was nervous and on edge. We took a long way through Rilil so as to avoid the place where the Mists had attacked us, walking with the yak herders back to the field of tents, the yaks grunting and shuffling over the hard soil.

"When we arrive at the temple," Asbera said as we left the edge of the village, "let me speak to the priests. They'll recognize my dialect more easily. The priests have all the worst traits of us Tuljans, and they can be terribly distrustful of foreigners."

I nodded, grateful that I wouldn't have to say anything. I didn't have much practice dealing with the holy.

"I do hope they'll be able to help us," Asbera said after a pause.

"I'm sure they will," I told her, although I had my doubts. The Mists had used the Tuljans' own charms against them–what else could the priests possibly do?

We threaded through the field of tents. Children clumped together when they saw us coming, their eyes big and curious.

"You don't see fisherfolk so much, living out here," Asbera said softly. "I remember the first time I saw Finnur. I wasn't sure he was even human."

I smiled politely, but I thought of Isolfr.

It took the better part of a day to weave through the tents. The mountain loomed in the distance, its peak shrouded with thin white clouds. We took our lunch in the grass, crouching down and eating the salted fish and crackers that Asbera had prepared. The cold, biting wind whipped my hair into my face as I ate. I would have given anything for a glass of mulled wine, but we wouldn't be back in the village until nightfall.

After lunch, we continued to walk. We had run out of things to say – and we'd had little to say in the beginning, truth be told, as I fretted over the mystery of my aid last night. I assumed that Asbera was worried about Finnur.

Our thoughts were our true companions that trip.

The tents became more sporadic in the afternoon, and soon they disappeared completely, giving way to an ocean of yellow grass. The mountain didn't seem any closer.

"It just keeps pulling away from us!" I cried. "We're as far away as when we started."

"No, we're making progress." Asbera frowned up at the mountain. "It just always looks closer than it is."

We walked. My legs ached, and my lips cracked from the cold wind. I was ready to give up, to turn around and march back to the village and huddle up on the *Cornflower* with every protection charm I could buy or cast. But then I saw a curl of white smoke in the distance, drifting up from the rocks of the mountain.

"There." Asbera sounded relieved. "The temple."

"All I see are rocks."

"It's built into the mountain's base. You have to look *close*." She pointed, and I followed the arrow of her finger. I couldn't see anything. And then, with a blink, I could: a stone building jutting out of the ground, the smoke twisting around it like a wraith.

"From here, it's not much longer," Asbera said.

We waded through the grass. Now that I had seen the temple, I couldn't imagine ever not seeing it, and as we approached, the carvings in the stone grew more elaborate. Figures rose out of the rock, the faces of gods and ancestors I didn't recognize. The same moss that Asbera and I carried in our pockets grew in hollowed-out stones that created a path leading to the temple entrance. Candles flickered among the rocks, the flames golden with magic and ever burning.

Asbera stopped a few paces from the start of the path.

"There are certain rituals," she said. "Simple ones. Just watch me and you'll be fine."

"Understood," I said. There was a temple in Kjora,

in the capital city, but I'd never been there. I'd no idea if it was like this one or not. It certainly wasn't built into a mountain.

Asbera stepped forward. She stooped and picked up two candles and handed one to me. It was cool to the touch, and no wax dripped down its side.

"Remember," Asbera whispered to me. "Stay silent. I'll speak."

I nodded. She stepped in front of me and we proceeded in single file through the entrance of the temple. It was dark on the other side of the doorway, darker than it ought to be with the wan sun still shining outside. Our candles cast small spheres of golden light, and I barely made out Asbera's outline ahead of me. She moved slowly, one hand outstretched to the cave's wall. I wasn't sure if that was a ritual or not, but I touched the wall just to be sure. It was cold and wet, the rock slimy beneath my fingers.

I couldn't say how long we walked in the dark. The moments seemed to stretch out and out until I could no longer count them. The only things that kept me from turning around were the sight of Asbera ahead and the sound of her shuffling footsteps.

A light appeared in the distance.

It was bluish white, like a star, not the eerie golden light of our candles. Asbera let out a breath. "We're here," she whispered. "Stay alert."

I nodded before remembering that she couldn't see me. "Yes, I will."

We edged forward. The bluish light grew brighter and brighter until it became a doorway, towering several heads above us and carved with the same faces as the exterior. The air smelled of burning cedar.

Asbera stopped in the doorway and spoke, her Tuljan dialect more exaggerated than usual. I gathered she was asking permission for us to enter.

When she finished speaking, the silence rang in my ears.

"Yes, Asbera Corra and the Kjoran Hanna Euli. You may enter."

The voice boomed like an echo. Asbera bowed her head as she walked through the entranceway, and I did the same, keeping my gaze on the back of her feet. She stopped. I stopped. I lifted my head just enough to see that she had lifted hers.

The room was enormous and carved out of rock that glittered and shone in the light of the lanterns drifting through the air, like leaves caught on a pond. Three priests stood in a row before us, wearing the same shaggy gray furs that the Nalendan goat-man wore. At least they didn't have on masks.

Hanna set her candle down in a grooved indentation in a nearby rock, and I shuffled up beside her to do the same. She bowed.

"Priest-lords of Tulja," she said, "we bring distressing news."

Her accent wasn't as strong now. The priests exchanged glances.

"Of what, child of Tulja?" asked the priest in the middle.

Asbera hesitated. She smoothed her hands along the fabric of her skirt.

"The Mists," she said. "The Mists perverted the magic of the Nalendan and attacked us two nights ago. They took on the form of the Nalendan and lured us into a false sense of safety by profaning the Nal ritual."

The priests turned to one another and murmured amongst themselves, too quiet for me to hear. In the blue light they looked like ghosts.

One of the priests stepped away from the others. His furs dragged along the damp cavern floor as he glided toward us. I shivered and then forced myself to stand still. Asbera kept her gaze on him.

"Yes, we know," the priest said.

"We sensed the magic crumble," said one of the others, his voice drifting out of the shadows. His accent was almost too thick for me to understand.

Asbera let out a muffled cry of fear.

"Don't worry, child of Tulja," said the priest closest to us. "We drove them out for the time being." He set one hand on her shoulder, although he looked uncomfortable with the gesture. "When they return, we'll be prepared."

Asbera nodded. "Thank you, priest-lords of Tulja." She bowed and reached out for her candle. But the priest covered her hand, stopping her.

"No. You mustn't leave yet."

Asbera froze, and a sharp blade of fear plunged into my belly.

"This one," the priest said, turning his gaze on me. I gasped at the sight of his eyes, for they had no whites, only a matte silvery blue surrounding a tiny dot of black pupil. "This one helped you escape."

Asbera blinked, looking confused. "Yes," she said. "Yes, she saved my life, and the life of my husband, Finnur Corra."

The priest smiled. It was not a warm smile.

"No," he said. "Not this one. The north wind." He pointed up at the ceiling and without thinking, I looked up. I saw nothing but pointed columns winding down from the rocks. "The north wind saved you. This one only helped."

Behind him, the other two priests murmured.

Asbera kept her back straight. I got the sense it would not be proper for her to turn around.

"Your friend is the reason they are here." The priest was speaking directly to me now, his cold metal eyes taking me in. "Your friend from Jandanvar."

I froze, too afraid to move.

"He seeks to destroy their schemes, and they shall stop him however they can."

The weight of the priest's gaze made my skin crawl.

"I'm – sorry?" I said.

"However, the north wind would destroy us all." With that, the priest whirled around and glided back to the others. They murmured to one another. Asbera glanced over at me, her face frightened and pale. She mouthed one word: *What?*

I shook my head. I knew then I would have to tell her all that I knew about Kolur, although I didn't understand what Kolur's choices had to do with me. I no longer served aboard the *Penelope*. I was just a fisherwoman saving money for the journey home. Even Isolfr had finally offered his aid to Kolur directly, more or less.

I had so many questions but I was too afraid of the priests to ask them.

"Go in peace, child of Tulja," the priest said. "You have nothing to fear. Our magic will protect you."

For a moment, I expected Asbera to protest, to demand an explanation. We had walked all this way for nothing.

Although he had mentioned the north wind – a presence on the north wind. I had felt it, too. Maybe he was just referring to Frida – maybe that was the real reason why Isolfr was frightened of her.

Asbera picked up her candle and gestured for me to do the same. She bowed deeply in the direction of the priests, holding the candle level with her forehead, before leaving the chamber. I trailed behind her. Our candles guttered in the dark, and the movements cast long, eerie shadows along the wall. I thought I saw the shape of goats and trees and yaks.

When we finally stepped out of the cave, the sky was purple with twilight. Both candles were extinguished at once.

"What were they saying?" Asbera looked at me. "Someone helped you? You know someone from Jandanvar?"

I took a deep breath and set my candle down on a nearby rock. Asbera cursed and shook her head and snatched it up. "We have to drop them in the urn."

"Oh. Sorry."

"What was all that about?"

"I didn't understand all of it." We walked away from the cave, and when we passed an urn carved out of the rocks, Asbera tossed both our candles in. I never heard them hit the bottom. "Kolur, my old captain, trained as a wizard in Jandanvar. He's trying to win back the love of the Jandanvari queen. That's why I left him. I thought it was stupid, and I just want to go home." Tears edged at my eyes. "I don't have any ties to the Mists, I swear. They're trying to stop Kolur, and I'm entangled in it now–"

I collapsed on an outcropping of rocks, ignoring the patches of ice and frozen mud. My tears stung hot against my cheeks. "I didn't even know what he was doing until we landed in Tulja. And now I'm stranded here, and the Mists are attacking, and I don't know what to do. I keep feeling something in the north wind, and I don't know why. My magic comes from the *south*–"

"Oh, sweetheart." Asbera sat beside me and wrapped her arm around my shoulder and pulled me in for a hug. I wept out all my frustrations.

"It's not your fault," she said after a few moments had passed.

"I know, but it just–" I shook my head. "I don't know why all this is happening to me."

"Dumb luck." Asbera smiled. I wiped the last remaining tears away from my eyes. "And it was dumb luck that you happened to run into Finnur when Baltasar had been saying for weeks he was sick of Reynir messing up the winds. Dumb luck that we became friends."

I smiled at that. I knew we were friends, but it was another thing to hear her say it out loud.

"The priests will keep us safe," Asbera said. "They always have before. And sooner or later, this Kolur is going to leave for Jandanvar, right?"

"He says the repairs are taking longer than he expected."

"But all repairs end eventually. See? Soon everything will go back to normal." She grinned. "Maybe you'll even marry some Tuljan fisherman and stay here with us."

I laughed. "Maybe."

Asbera stood up and pulled me to my feet. The sun was liquid gold on the edge of the horizon.

"Time flows differently inside the temple," Asbera said. "How would you like to spend the night with the yak herders? I used to be one of them. I'm sure they'll extend their hospitality."

I didn't like the thought of walking through the night, and I suspected Asbera felt the same, even if she wouldn't say it directly.

"Yes," I said. "I think that would be lovely."

CHAPTER TWELVE

I was too accustomed to southerly ways, as well as life aboard a fishing boat, to appreciate spending the night in one of those round tents the way Asbera clearly did. I had some trouble sleeping that night, curled up on my bed of yakskin, listening to the wind howling outside. The north wind. I knew it because I felt flickers of that presence as the wind pressed against the white fabric of the tent. I shivered but I wasn't afraid – that presence had helped me against the Mists.

The next day, Asbera and I returned to Rilil without trouble, and the bright morning was still and cold.

Finnur healed from his exhaustion within a few days' time, although he didn't go out with us on the *Annika's* next run. "Lazing his life away," Asbera told me as we drew up the sails together. She laughed, but I could tell she worried about him. Still, he was waiting for us when we returned three days later, stretched out on the deck of the *Crocus* in a patch of lemony sunlight, braiding vines together to make more charms.

The *Annika* went on two more short trips, leaving in the morning and returning in full dark of the same day. Finnur was well enough to sail on the second trip, and when he climbed aboard, the crew shouted boisterously for him. Even Baltasar looked pleased, and he slapped Finnur on the back as Finnur picked up a coil of rope and shouted, "Back to work!"

There were no more attacks from the Mists.

I didn't let my guard down, though. In those first few weeks after the attack, I wore my bracelet everywhere, even to bed, and the dried vines grew so brittle and worn that they finally frayed and fell apart. I was lucky it happened while I was aboard the *Cornflower* and I was able to find the bracelet lying unceremoniously on the middle of the deck. I repaired it with a bit of red yarn from the magic shop, murmuring Kjoran protection charms while the south wind swirled around me. When I slipped the bracelet back on, its magic was stronger than it had been before, and it pulsed with my heartbeat.

The magic around the village began to change after our visit to the priests – a gradual fortification that made the air taste of metal and incense smoke, like the air in the priests' temples. This new magic crackled against my own, particularly when I returned from sea and was weak from using it so much during the trip.

More charms appeared around the village, not just vines and moss, but also tiny figurines carved from mountain stone. They materialized in windows and at crossroads, always watchful. I didn't like them, because they bore the same shapes as the costumed men: a yak, a goat, a straw-man, a pine tree. Everywhere I went I felt a jolt of fear, seeing one of them lurking out of the corner of my eye.

It didn't help that I'd learned that the boats leaving Tulja rarely sailed as far south as Kjora. My jar of stones was almost half full, and I carted it down to the dock master, who lived and worked from a moored junk at the edge of the bay. He was kindly enough, his face wizened and bearded, and his eyes crinkled with a smile when I set the jar on his desk.

"I want to book passage to Kjora," I told him. "How much will it cost? These are all the stones I have saved up."

The dock master picked up my jar and gave a good hard shake. "You've saved quite a bit, Empire girl. I heard about you. Working aboard the *Annika*, yes?"

I shifted in my seat, impatient. "Yes. Is it enough to get me home? I'm from Kjora, not the Empire. And of course I'm willing to work while I'm on board the ship, too."

The dock master set the jar back down. "If you're willing to work, you wouldn't need to pay for anything." Another smile. "But you'll have a good spot of trouble finding a boat that'll take you as far as Kjora. I'm sorry, my dear."

My lungs felt hollow. I thought of all those eerie figurines watching me from the shadows of Rilil. There was even one in the dock master's office, sitting next to a window covered by a scrap of hide. A yak-man.

But even I knew this wasn't the fault of the costumed men. It wasn't even the fault of the Mists.

"You save a bit more, you might be able to buy a boat." The dock master shrugged. "Don't know about a crew, though."

"How much more?"

The dock master hesitated. He looked down at his hands. "Quite a bit more, in truth. A lug or junk capable of that sort of journey – at least three thousand stones."

I stared at him. Three thousand stones. I hadn't counted the stones in my jar, but I doubted I'd earned three thousand stones in all the time I'd been working for Baltasar.

"I'm sorry, Empire child," the dock master said, not unkindly. But his words still struck me hard in the heart.

"I'm not from the Empire." I grabbed my jar and stalked out of his boat. Out on the dock, the air was clean and crisp, and the wind was blowing from the north. I drew my thoughts into myself. I had a feeling that presence would be there, lurking, and I didn't want to sense it right now.

I held my jar tight to my chest and went back to the *Cornflower*. It had been such a push and pull to save *these* stones, eating nothing but salted fish even on my days off, taking on every day-trip out to sea that Baltasar would let me. And even then, I still had to pull stones from the jar to pay Rudolf another thirty so I could stay on the *Cornflower*.

By the time I made it back, my cheeks were streaked with tears. I stood next to the railing and gazed over the deck. The empty masts looked like dead trees. The whole thing felt like a prison. It wasn't home. No matter how kind Asbera and Finnur were, it would never be home.

And then I spotted a figurine of a straw-man.

It was set next to a piece of vine that Asbera had given me. I stared at it for a few moments, my heart pounding. My tears all evaporated with my fear.

"The Mists?" I whispered.

I crept closer, holding the stone-jar tight against my chest, squeezing it for support. When I was a few paces away, my head thrummed with magic. Good magic. Protective magic.

Tuljan magic.

I still wanted to throw it into the ocean, but I knew better than to disrespect a protective totem. So I let it be, and I went down below, where I set my jar back in its usual place and tried not to think about home.

That evening, when I went to the *Crocus* for dinner, I learned that Rudolf had installed figurines on all the boarding-boats – Asbera and Finnur had discovered a miniature goat on their deck.

"It's true magic," Asbera told me as she poured another glass of ale.

"I know," I said. "I can feel it."

She smiled. "I told you the priests would help."

Still, I had my doubts.

That was the last day when anything new happened. The twin emotions of disappointment and fear braided together into a sense of numbness that highlighted the drudgery of my routine. I'd been used to routines back on Kjora – the constant cycle of chores and tending to Henrik and sailing out to sea with Kolur – but here on Tulja, the repetition was endless and dull. Every few days,

I went out with the *Annika* and received payment that I then spent on food and boarding and patching my coat and stockings. Despite having a new goal, vague and ill defined – *buy my own boat* – I felt like I saved less money than before. One morning, I pulled on my left boot, and my big toe peeked through the leather. I stared at that toe for a long time. It didn't feel like it belonged to me.

And then I counted out stones from my jar, my heart heavy. I couldn't go without boots, not if I'd any intention of living as a fisherwoman.

In all those weeks, I didn't allow myself to think on Kolur and Frida and Isolfr. They were still in Tulja – I saw the *Penelope II* whenever we sailed in and out of harbor, her carvings distinct and strange against the dull Tuljan boats. According to the rumors swirling around the docks, most folk didn't think they'd ever get through all the repairs.

I doubted that, though. I knew from experience how driven Kolur was when he wanted something. He'd kidnapped me away from Kjora just because his fish bones told him to go north.

On and on life went, until one day, while I sat up on the deck of the *Cornflower* mending sails for the *Annika*, I heard a bell.

It tinkled just off the starboard side, down by the water. I set the sail aside and walked over to the railing and looked down.

Isolfr.

He was in his human disguise, his Pjetur disguise, all bundled up like the cold affected him. He sat in the dinghy, one oar lying across his lap. He chimed the dinghy's bell again, then called, "Hanna!"

His voice was bright and sparkling like starlight. It set all my nerves on edge.

"What the hell are you doing here?"

"I need to speak with you."

I stared down at him, and he squinted up at me.

"You could have just climbed aboard," I snapped. "It's not like I pulled the gangplank up."

"I thought I needed your permission."

I sighed. He sounded so sweet and sincere, like he didn't fully understand the ways of humans. Probably he didn't.

"What do you need to talk to me about?" I asked.

He hesitated. That got my guard up. I pressed my hands tight against the railing and leaned out far over the water. The wind blowing off it was cold as death. "Well?" I said. "What is—"

"We're leaving."

All my words came up short. I pressed away from the railing. The sun seemed too bright and too cold all once.

"Fine," I said. My voice was weak but I knew the wind carried it. "You can come up."

I turned away from the railing without bothering to check if he'd heard. I knew that he had. He wasn't human. He didn't have a human's weaknesses.

A few moments later, his icy blond hair appeared beside the railing. I gathered up the half-mended sails like they were a protection shield. He looked like a flash of moonlight off the surface of the ocean.

We stared at each other.

"I'm sorry you were attacked," he said. "I never meant–"

"So you admit it's your fault."

"What? No, of course not–"

"Then don't say you're sorry, and don't say you *never meant* anything." I grabbed my mending needle and shoved it into the sail fabric. It was satisfying, feeling that give against the needle's sharpness. A good outlet for my anger.

"Hanna." I heard footsteps and when I looked up, he was kneeling beside me, staring at me with his huge, imploring eyes. "Are you sure you won't come with us?"

My arm froze mid-stitch. The air went still.

"The Mists attacked me," I said slowly. "Because of Kolur."

Isolfr opened his mouth to speak, but I interrupted him.

"They told me that," I said. "They called me 'Friend of Kolur.'" Isolfr didn't look like himself, with his dull skin and human features and his brow knotted up with worry. "When you sail for the north, they'll follow you and leave me be."

My blood pounded in my ears. I turned back to my mending, but I couldn't concentrate, not with him crouched there beside me.

"Just go away," I muttered, not looking up. "Just leave me alone."

"I will." He touched my arm, lightly, with the tips of his fingers. Magic buzzed between us and I cried out like I'd been stung, even though it didn't exactly hurt.

"But I just – we're leaving tomorrow, while you'll be out on your fishing trip–"

I looked up at him. "How the hell do you know that? About me being out fishing?"

"I hear people talking. I wanted to give you one last chance to come with us."

I glared at him. But he didn't turn away. In fact, he looked desperate.

"Your magic is so much stronger than you realize," he said. "So much stronger than *I* realized–"

"It's still not as strong as Frida's," I snapped. "Ask her."

His shivered. "You know I can't."

"I know you're a coward. She isn't going to hurt you, whatever the hell you are. At least not if the Mists are on their way."

He looked at me for a moment, and I could tell he knew I was right. But when he spoke, all he said was, "You would be such a help. Please."

He touched my arm again and leaned in close. Magic crackled. "It's going to be dangerous, what we're doing," he said. "And there's the fate of the whole world–"

"Oh, shut up!" I yanked away from him. "The fate of the whole world? Did Kolur tell you that? You've got a lot to learn about the world, if you think him winning back some queen puts the world in danger."

Isolfr frowned. "It's not just about the Jandanvari queen. I haven't explained it properly."

"Well, don't bother. I'm not going. I just want to get back home to Kjora and convince Mama to send me off to the capital to study to become a witch. Can you do that?"

He hesitated for a moment before shaking his head.

"Then I'm staying here." I turned away from him, but I could still feel the prickle of his eyes on me, the lingering spark of our shared magic. "Please leave."

When I finally looked up, Isolfr was gone.

Our fishing trip out to the eastern side of Tulja was uneventful. The winds were in our favor, and there wasn't much for me to do beside tighten the ropes and prep the nets. It gave me a lot of time to think, mostly on Isolfr. I wished I hadn't lost my temper and sent him away. Now that he was gone, now that the *Penelope II* was likely cutting her way through the dark seas, it was easy to see that he might have been willing to answer my questions. Maybe.

But I hadn't wanted to go with them. That I knew for certain. It was unfair that Kolur was on his way to Jandanvar and his queen and I would need another three jars of stones to make it back to Kjora.

I tried to focus my attention on the *Annika*.

With the trip such an easy one, it wasn't long before the crew were all sitting around the deck, throwing dice. Baltasar didn't even complain about it from his place at the helm.

We were after capelins. They were a rarity this time of year, and Reynir seeing them when he threw the bones could mean a big payload for the rest of us, even though we had to do a day's sailing to get out to the patch of sea where the bones had spotted them. By the time we arrived, the stars had come out and the air was cold and windy. The crew was in a mood, too, after a day of easy sailing. Some of them had been drinking like pirates.

"Drop the nets!" Baltasar shouted from the helm. "We're here!"

We all shambled into action. It took the crew longer than usual to toss the nets over the side of the boat. They landed with a *slap*, and the ocean churned around us. Fish scales glinted in the moonlight.

"I remember the last time we got a load of capelin," Asbera said as we watched the starboard. "The yak herders use the oil for tanning, so they're willing to pay for it. Do you remember that haul, Finnur?"

He nodded, his eyes on the water. "Felt like enough to retire."

I laughed. "I doubt that."

He looked up at me. "Said it *felt* like it. Not that it was."

The nets filled quickly, which put us all in good spirits. As irritating as Reynir was, his bones rarely steered us wrong. Asbera and I worked together to drag our net on deck. Capelins spilled across our feet, like the stars themselves had fallen from the sky.

"It's gonna be a good trip," Asbera said.

I cast the preservation charm. All around us, the rest of the crew was doing the same, dragging the nets aboard and whooping and hollering when they saw what they'd caught. We dropped our own net back into the water. The *Annika* rocked against the waves.

"Wind's up!" Baltasar shouted. "Hanna, tend to the sails!"

Asbera nodded at me, a cue that she could watch the nets herself, with Finnur's help. The wind was shifting in an odd pattern, and it was hard even for me to tell which direction it blew from. I gathered up my strength, dragging the magic out of the air and into myself.

The wind swirled around us. The boat lurched, swung off to the port side.

"Hanna!" Baltasar shouted. "Tend to the sails!"

"I'm trying!" I pressed down the sudden surge of panic and tried to concentrate. The wind whistled in my ears and blew harder and harder. My hair whipped into my face. I had the magic fine, but this wind wasn't minding me.

The boat swung again, the bow plowing into an incoming wave. Freezing water crashed over the deck. All the heat globes blinked out. The magic-cast lanterns swung wildly from the masts, throwing disjointed shadows over everything.

"For the love of the ancestors!" Baltasar shouted. "Get ahold of the winds!"

"I'm trying!" And I was. I concentrated so hard that white spots appeared at the edge of my vision, that the magic stung as it crept through my blood. But the wind went through me like water sifting through fingers.

It wasn't – *right*.

The crew shouted around me, no longer joyful from the catch but full-on spooked. Benedict and Zakaria were already turning the sails, trying to catch the wind without enchantment. My knees buckled. Magic burned at my brain. I stumbled backward and would have fallen if strong arms hadn't caught me. Finnur.

"Something's wrong." His voice sounded far away. "It's a storm. It's–"

He was still talking, but I couldn't hear him. I twisted around to look at him. His mouth moved.

"I can't hear you!" I said. "What's going on?"

Another wave crashed over the side and knocked me flat on my back. The water was so cold, I thought I'd died. I blinked up at the sky, dazed. I heard shouting again, frantic, terrified voices.

"–na! Are you okay?"

Asbera this time. She helped me to my feet. The *Annika* swung in a wide arc, throwing off a spray of white-capped seawater.

"I'm sorry," I sputtered. "I couldn't – the wind–"

"That's because it's not wind," she said. "It's a denala."

I froze. A denala. I'd heard of such things, stories from Kolur and some of the sailors he'd drink with in the evenings, but I'd never seen one myself. They were storms of magic.

Papa had told me once they were tied to the Mists.

"No," I whispered.

"We need you to ignite more heat globes before we all freeze." Asbera dragged me a few paces across the deck before the boat tilted and we went sliding, slamming up against the masts. "This water's dangerous," she gasped out.

But I knew if this was a true denala, we'd have more to fear than just freezing.

It was already happening: When the water slid back across the boat, the surface shone like a mirror. The preservation spell that held our catches of capelin turned to saltwater, and the fish woke up again, their eyes shining like moonlight, and swam in circles through the air.

Screams of horror erupted on the deck. I knew I couldn't light any heat globes.

"Get 'em overboard!" Baltasar shouted, his voice roaring over the wind. "Before they contaminate the rest of the boat!"

I scrambled over to the nearest grouping of fish.

"Hanna!" Asbera shouted.

"You heard the captain!" I gestured for her to join me.

"Finnur!" she cried. "I have to get to Finnur!"

Sea and sky. In the panic I'd almost forgotten him – the magic-sickness would affect him the most if he was tainted with it, since he'd been struck the worst by our encounter with the Mists.

"Go!" I shouted. "I'll take care of this!"

Saltwater splashed across my face and into my mouth; I spat it out, afraid of tainting myself. Then I turned to the fish, bracing myself against the rocking of the boat. Reynir and Harald stood nearby, although they did nothing to throw the fish overboard. Of course. No one wanted to touch the globe of water they swam in.

"You," said Harald. The boat swung out again, almost flinging us all into the seething ocean. "You've got magic."

"No," I shouted back. "We can't use magic here."

"She's right," Reynir shouted over the storm. "Any magic will just make things worse."

"I ain't touching that," said Harald.

I looked at that globe of water floating a handswidth above the deck, a serene spot of calm in the midst of the storm raging around us. The denala's eye. Except there were three eyes to this storm, all hovering around the boat.

I didn't want to touch it either, but Baltasar was right; the longer we kept it aboard, the more harm it could do. So I took a deep breath and raced forward and shoved it with my gloved hands. It only moved a little, the way the preservation spells will do. "Help me!" I screamed.

Reynir and Harald hesitated. I shoved it again, and it edged closer to the side of the boat.

"I'll never get it off without your help."

The *Annika* tilted. Another wall of water crashed over us. I screamed at the cold and I was certain that my skin tingled, magic-sickness making its way through me.

I shoved the globe again. It slammed up against the side of the boat, and the water exploded everywhere and the fish slammed down on the deck, flopping and gasping. I shrieked and stumbled backward, trying to whisk that enchanted water off me. It steamed on my clothes with a sweet medicinal scent, and my head was suddenly crowded with strange images, castles in the mist and women with gray eyes.

I shrugged out of my jacket and tossed it overboard. My head cleared.

"You okay?" Reynir asked.

"No thanks to you." I whirled away from him, back toward the interior of the deck.

The *Annika* was in a shambles.

The deck gleamed silver. The masts had grown knobby

and twisted, like trees, and the sails were tattered silk dresses snapping and fluttering in the freezing, choking winds. All results of the magic-sickness, the way too much magic will change things.

The crew stood in clumps, staring up at the sky. I followed their gaze.

Clouds swirled overhead like a cyclone.

"Down below!" Baltasar bellowed. "Everyone get down below!"

There was a pause, as if we'd all forgotten how to move.

And then the boat lifted up high on the crest of the wave, tall enough it seemed we'd be sucked into the spiral of clouds. Everyone erupted into movement. We raced to the hatch, shouting and shoving. I slid down the ladder and landed with a smack on the damp floor. Water dripped through the rafters. Seimur slid down and landed on top of me.

"Get out of the way, Empire girl!" he shouted.

I wormed out from under him.

"Get to the hold," someone shouted from the darkness. Seimur disappeared down the corridor. I followed, weaving back and forth to avoid the dripping water.

A light appeared at the end of the corridor, flickering and orange. Candleflame. Good.

The hold was crowded with crewmen. A handful of candles were dotted across the darkness. For all the shouting and cursing up on deck and in the corridor, the hold was hushed and silent. In the fluttering candlelight, I found Asbera sitting in the corner, next to a barrel of drinking water. Finnur leaned up against her, his face pale.

"Hanna!" she whispered, as if she didn't want to break the silence. "You're all right."

I nodded and slid into place beside her. Finnur stirred. He looked worn out.

"Where's your coat?" Asbera asked.

I shook my head. "Water got on it." I drew my legs up close. For the first time since the storm had hit, I realized how cold I was. My teeth chattered and my bones vibrated. The candle guttering next to Asbera did not give off enough heat.

The boat lifted, tilted. Everyone in the hold let out a long, terrified gasp. Hands snatched out to grab the candles–

We slammed back down, hard.

Voices filled up the darkness, whispered prayers and Tuljan lullabies. I squeezed myself tighter, trying to draw warmth out of myself. The walls rippled beneath my back and revulsion rose up in my throat but I fought it down, because our choices now were to stay aboard and face the magic-sickness, or jump into the ocean and freeze.

I closed my eyes and told myself I wasn't going to die.

CHAPTER THIRTEEN

Sunlight.

Pale and thin but certainly there, wavering through the cracks in the ceiling. The candles had burned out in the night and men were sleeping, sprawled out in piles on the floor of the hold. I sat up and stretched. Every muscle in my body ached. At least the boat was still a boat and the walls were still walls. And none of the sleeping crew seemed affected by the magic-sickness.

I stood up, my legs wobbling, and braced myself against the wall. I realized the entire crew wasn't down here – only about five men. Asbera and Finnur were gone.

Panic seized me, cold and violent. But then I heard voices coming from up above.

I picked my way over the sleeping crewmen and climbed up on deck. The sun was blinding; I hadn't seen it that bright since we'd left Kjora. It bounced off the water's surface, flinging light all over the boat. The air was calm and sharp with cold.

The *Annika* might still be above water, but she'd been half destroyed in the denala last night. Her deck gleamed silver in places, and the sails-turned-silk-dresses had no doubt been thrown overboard. A group of crewmen stood near the helm of the ship, bundled up in cloaks and shabby furs. They spoke in low voices.

"Hello," I called out.

They turned toward me. One of them was Asbera. My lingering panic dissipated.

"Hanna!" She rushed across the deck to my side. "I tried waking you, but you wouldn't stir. I was worried."

"I'm sore," I said, as if that offered any kind of explanation. "Where are we?"

"That's what we're trying to figure out." Asbera looped her arm in mine and led me across the boat.

"Finnur?" I asked. "Is he—"

"He's fine. Resting. See?" She pointed past the helm to the stern of the boat, where Finnur was stretched out on a hammock, covered in furs. "He wanted fresh air after spending the night down below."

We joined the rest of the crew. Baltasar was there, looking drawn and worn out, like he hadn't slept at all, and Reynir and Harald. They ringed the navigation table, staring down at a map pinned with rocks.

"Hanna," Baltasar said. "Am I glad to see you're all right."

"I'm glad to see it, too." I smiled weakly at him, but he didn't return the gesture.

"Had to ditch the sails," he said. "Tainted with the sickness. We've got some old ones down below. Need patching, but they should be enough to get us home. You well enough to call the winds?"

I hesitated. "I'm – not sure," I finally answered. "And I'm not certain it's safe–"

"Oh, it's definitely not safe," Reynir said. "We'll have to wait at least a day before we do any sort of magic."

Baltasar grunted. "So we're just sitting in the water till then? Air's still as death."

"That's what I told you."

"Boys," Asbera said. "We shouldn't fight. We have to wait until nightfall to find out where we are. Not unless someone passes us by."

The rest of the crew grumbled. She was right; without the stars or a strong spell, we'd no way of locating ourselves. Standing around the navigation map was just wishful thinking.

"I hope we haven't crossed over."

Everyone stopped talking. It was Finnur who had spoken, although he sounded gruff and unlike himself. Everyone turned to him. He'd sat up in the hammock, and he swayed side to side with the motion of the *Annika*.

"We haven't," Baltasar said.

I hoped he was right. In that maelstrom of magic, it was entirely possible that the *Annika* could have been dragged out of the true world and into the Mists. But the ocean sparkling around us didn't seem like the Mists. This cold, sharp air didn't seem like the Mists, either. It felt like home.

"Don't mind him; he's still recovering from the magic-sickness." Asbera bustled over to him and pressed her hand to his forehead. He closed his eyes at her touch and leaned back in the hammock and murmured something I couldn't hear.

"Leave them." Baltasar sidled up beside me. "They've still got the panic from last night. Come, let's see about repairing those old sails. It's something to do while we wait."

I nodded, feeling numb, but I still followed him down below.

The rest of the day was spent largely in silence. Crewmen drifted up from down below in ones or twos, and Baltasar set them to work whenever they appeared on deck. By lunchtime, everyone was awake and accounted for, and to all our great relief, no human had been touched by the magic-sickness.

Together, we repaired and hung the old sails. We cleaned up the wreckage from the storm as best we could – Zakaria was the only one brave enough to touch the shiny mirrored patches on the deck, and although he stayed unharmed, the rest of us left them alone, sweeping and mopping around them instead. Benedict, Finnur, and Asbera counted our food stores and reported back that they had largely survived the storm as well. We had about four days' worth of food and water, more if we rationed.

Baltasar nodded grimly. "Depends on where we are, doesn't it?"

And we all knew that no wages were waiting for us when we returned to Tulja, even if we did get back within a few days' time. Nobody spoke about it much that first day, but it was heavy on my thoughts, and I imagined it was the same for the rest of the crew.

Eventually, the sun sank into the horizon – the west, I hoped. We all gathered on deck to watch the stars come out.

The day had been clear, but as night fell, clouds drifted across the sky, long dark streaks that blotted out the moonlight. I cursed beneath my breath, and for the thousandth time that day, I wondered why this had happened, and why it had happened to us. A denala on the same day that Kolur was to leave for the north?

Fear gnawed at my insides.

"It figures," Finnur said as we crowded around the ship's bow, "we'd get a cloudy night."

"It's not so cloudy," Asbera said, and she was right. Pricks of light appeared against the black sky. I held my breath as I tilted my head back, my body shaking, afraid of what I might see.

Beside me, Asbera let out a long sigh.

The Jolix Lion stretched out in the northeastern corner, languorous and bored as always. Nora's Pot was in its usual place as well, cooking up that healing balm Nora used to save Petra. Although I couldn't see all of the constellations in the patchy sky, I saw enough to know we were in our world.

"We're still here." Asbera drew me up in an embrace. "We haven't crossed over."

Relief rippled across the boat as the crewmen spotted the usual constellations. I dropped my head all the way back until I was able to see the Ice Star, burning bright and brilliant like a flame. It always rested near the top of the sky; I'd heard that if you looked at it from Jandanvar, it would lie directly overhead. It wasn't directly overhead now. Another relief.

Baltasar had already pulled out the sextant and was peering through it at the horizon. "At least two days' north," he barked. The crew muttered to itself. Then, "Reynir! Throw the damn bones."

"You sure?" Reynir asked.

The Ice Star was enough to tell us how far north or south we'd gone, but it wasn't enough to give our exact location. It was risky to throw the bones when the boat had been transformed with the magic-sickness only last night – maybe not dangerous in and of itself, it was such a weak magic, but the reading might not be accurate.

"Yes, I'm sure." Baltasar tossed the sextant aside. "I want to know where the hell we are."

Reynir sighed and shuffled forward, pulling his sack of fish bones from around his neck. He glanced around the deck and then moved over to the stern, away from the silvered patches. Everyone followed him, and we moved into a circle around where he knelt on the deck.

"Give me some room," he said.

We all shuffled back a pace or two. Reynir grunted. He dumped the bones in his palm and shook them like dice.

Everyone held their breath again.

"Stand back," he said again, more harshly this time. We stumbled backward. Asbera clutched at Finnur's hand, their knuckles turning white. I rubbed at my bracelet.

The bones clattered across the deck.

I stared at them, trying to read the symbols – it was nonsense, all nonsense. I didn't recognize any of the configurations. I wanted to weep. But Reynir leaned back on his heels and made a *hmm* sound. The crew stirred, voices rising up out of the darkness.

"It's Anfinn's Rocks!" Zakaria called out. "Look, it's exactly like the map."

"I see it," Reynir snapped, although I suspected he hadn't.

The crew jostled forward. I'd never heard of Anfinn's Rocks, but the arrangement did look something like an archipelago, islands trailing off into the sea.

Baltasar knelt beside the spray of bones. "Someone get me the damn map!" he shouted.

A flurry of activity. The navigation map drifted down from overhead. Baltasar spread it out on the deck.

"Give us some light," Reynir said, and a candle was produced, the wax burned down low. Harald handed it to Baltasar, who set it between the map and the stones. I stood up on my tiptoes, trying to see. So did everyone else.

Baltasar leaned forward. His eyes flicked back and forth between the map and the bones.

"Identical." He glanced at Reynir. "What do you think, fortuneer?"

"It looks the same, but that doesn't mean much."

Baltasar nodded and then clambered to his feet. "You heard him. Light up the ship, men! Look for signs of Anfinn's Rocks. We've got to confirm."

"With what?" someone called out. "Ain't gonna be able to see far enough with candles."

Reynir rubbed his forehead. "Magic-cast lanterns ought to be safe, after this long."

Baltasar looked at me. "What do you say, girl? Think it's safe to cast the lanterns?"

I fumbled for a moment, surprised that Baltasar was asking for my opinion. Reynir seemed surprised, too, and a little angry about it. "Yes, it should be safe. As long as we don't light too many."

"You heard 'em. Light the lanterns!"

Lanterns shimmered on across the boat. The sudden surge of magic made me dizzy, and I swooned for a moment. Maybe this had been a mistake.

Finnur caught me. "Did the same thing to me," he said. "It'll pass."

"Do we want to be close to Anfinn's Rocks?" I asked. My head was still fuzzy.

"Oh, yes," said Asbera. "It'll only be two days' sail from there to get back to Tulja, and it's an easy voyage."

I nodded. Lanterns swung around us. Zakaria brought one over to Asbera, and she set it onto a nearby hook and slid it over the side of the boat. A circle of light appeared on the water, bobbing with the waves.

Even with the lanterns lit, I couldn't see much beyond the confines of the boat. But then Seimur shouted, "Land in the distance! Port side!"

I turned around. Seimur hung over the railing with the lantern, pointing off in the distance. It took me a moment to see the outline of something jagged and dark against the stars, like a distant mountain.

Baltasar stomped over to Seimur. "Too far away to tell," he grunted. Then he turned around to speak to the crew.

"We'll wait till sunup," he shouted. "We've waited this long; a few more hours won't kill us."

Reynir ran over to him and whispered something in his ear. Baltasar nodded.

"You gotta choose between the lanterns and the heat spheres," he added. "We don't want any surprises. Better to light a fire if you're cold, anyway."

Asbera pulled in her lanterns and muttered the familiar incantation. The lantern's glow faded into darkness. "Don't want to make things worse for you," she said to Finnur.

"So that's it, then?" He sighed. "We've got to hang around for another night?"

"It's not so bad," Asbera said. "We should be home in a couple of days, like Baltasar said."

Finnur shrugged. I didn't blame him for seeming doubtful. He was still weak, deep down inside him, from the Mists attack, and now he was trapped aboard a ship half transformed from the magic-sickness. There was no guarantee we were anywhere close to the Anfinn's Rocks.

Reynir and Zakaria dragged the brazier up on deck and broke up an empty water barrel for the firewood. The brazier was supposed to be for cooking, I was told, but no one ever used it anymore, since the *Annika* didn't take the long voyages she used to. It was nice to have a spot of warmth to gather round, and nicer still to know that warmth wasn't bringing even more magic aboard our boat.

I sat with Asbera and Finnur as the crew took to telling stories, mostly old Tuljan folktales. A few of them I recognized, although they were different from the stories I knew in small ways – here a character was a yak herder, on Kjora he was a blacksmith. But the basic idea was the same. A story of the north. Mama'd told me this once, that all the island stories were the same when you got down to it, that to her Empire ears they were all northern and she couldn't tell them apart. She was teasing, I think, but I thought of her now, hearing those similarities. And my heart about broke.

No one noticed when I slipped away from the fire. I pressed against the boat's railing and closed my eyes against the wind. We were moored without our sails, and the *Annika* bobbed up and down with the motion of the waves and didn't do much else. I looked down at the dark water, sparkling with the reflection of stars.

Something moved beneath the surface.

I gasped and jerked back, although my first thought was of Isolfr, not the Mists. I'd seen him the same way, hadn't I, all those months ago? A flash of movement beneath the waves.

"Isolfr?" I kept my voice low, surprised by how hopeful I felt. It would have been a relief, in a strange way, to see him now. A bit like how the stars reminded me that we hadn't crossed over.

The shimmer came closer to the surface. "Isolfr," I said, a little louder now. "Is that you?"

But the water went dark.

I sighed and pulled away from the railing.

The next day was cloudy and gray, the sky threatening sea-snow. The crew gathered along the port side of the boat, where we had the clearest view of the land in the distance. It was dark and rocky and not particularly welcoming. But the crew was thrilled to see it.

"That's Anfinn's Rocks for certain," said Harald. "I ain't gonna forget that coastline any time soon."

Baltasar blustered up to us and peered through his view glass. I'd no way of knowing if the land was Anfinn's Rocks or not, and so I watched him and looked for some sign that we'd be on our way home soon. I didn't trust Harald's assessment.

Baltasar slid his view glass shut. "It's the Rocks," he said, with the gravelly authority of a sea captain. "We're on the northern side. Have to sail around, but it won't be too much trouble."

The crew cheered and slapped one another on the backs. Finnur dragged me and Asbera both into a hug.

"Nice to have everything turn out, huh?" he said. "Didn't get blown too far off course, and now we're on our way home."

"Yeah, yeah," said Asbera, laughing. She kissed him.

I smiled, but I wasn't so sure everything had turned out. Why had we sailed into a denala in the first place? Such things only happened when powerful wizards were casting powerful spells. The rest of the crew seemed to agree that it must have been someone on Anfinn's Rocks, especially now that we'd confirmed our location – apparently, Tuljan priests trained there – but I wasn't so certain.

"Hanna, ready the sails," Baltasar shouted. "Asbera, Reynir and Zakaria, grab the ropes in case there's a problem with the magic. We're heading home."

More cheering, but I couldn't shake the cold, creeping feeling that something was wrong.

I walked among the masts and held out my hands and felt for the magic on the wind. It blew in from the southeast, with a sweetness to it that reminded me of summer sunshine. Perfectly safe.

I repeated that to myself as I shifted the winds in our favor. *Perfectly safe, everything is perfectly safe.*

It was a simple matter to call the necessary winds to drive the *Annika* southward, and I didn't have to expend much energy holding the spell. The denala had made the magic more malleable, like soft clay, and this far from the storm, the threat of magic-sickness was no longer a concern.

For the first time in days, we sailed forward.

The crew's good spirits lingered, even when the clouds thickened and snow fell across the ocean. I spotted Benedict and Harald tipping their heads back and trying to catch flakes on their tongues. Enough of it fell that it started piling up on deck.

"Clear it off," Baltasar shouted from the helm. "Before it freezes."

The crew took care of the snow largely by shaping it into balls and throwing them at each other. Even though I was managing the winds, I joined in, flinging a clump of snow at Finnur's head. He roared with laughter and came chasing after me. I kept expecting Baltasar to shout at us to quit, but he seemed as amused as anyone else. Pretty soon, the *Annika* was the scene of a great snow fight. The winds carried us home, and we just kept flinging snowballs at one another.

And then something changed.

I was back at the stern of the ship, reaching behind some of the crates we stored there to get to a pile of fresh snow, when I felt the wind snap, like it had broken in two. I stood straight up, the snow forgotten. All around me, the crew were shrieking and laughing, but there was a buzzing whine in my head that made it sound like screaming.

I grabbed onto the railing and squeezed my eyes shut, feeling for the wind. But I couldn't grasp it. It squirmed around me, slippery and just out of reach.

"You okay, Empire girl?" It was Harald. I opened my eyes and looked at him, pink-cheeked and grinning. He had hoisted up a snowball and was aiming it at me, but he didn't throw it.

His grin melted away.

"What is it? What's wrong? Should I get Reynir?"

Something moved out of the corner of my eye. I looked out at the water, but all I saw were the coruscating waves.

"Hanna?" Harald stepped closer to me. I was trembling. Something was wrong with the magic. It twisted away from me, vibrating as if it spoke–

Voices–

They communicate on veins of magic.

"Something's wrong," I said.

Harald's eyes widened.

And then something shot out of the ocean and grabbed Harald and pulled him overboard. It happened so quickly that all I saw was shining silvery water and the bright, bright red of blood.

Screaming.

Harald was screaming.

He slammed back up over the railing, his body limp. Blood splattered across my face and it was hot and wet and I screamed and stumbled backward into someone's arms – the thing that had grabbed Harald?

No.

Baltasar.

The ship was silent save for Harald's screaming. His body swung back and forth, dripping blood. I realized that Baltasar had one arm around my chest, his hand clutching a knife.

"What the hell is that?" he whispered.

"I can't see," I gasped. And I couldn't – I couldn't see what it was. It looked like the ocean had grown claws.

They can blend in with their surroundings.

Harald dropped out of sight.

There was a splash.

The screaming stopped.

That sudden silence hurt my ears.

"Harald!" Baltasar shouted. He shoved me away. "Get away, girl." Then, louder, "Have you all gone stupid? We need weapons! Get down below and grab the pistols!"

"What happened?" someone shouted. "What happened to Harald?"

I kept stumbling back and back until I was standing among the masts. The sails fluttered and snapped. My face was wet. When I went to dry it off, my fingers came back red.

I choked back vomit.

"He's dead." Baltasar stomped back to the helm. I didn't understand how he could be so calm. "Something dragged him into the water."

All the voices of the crew started up at once.

"What–"

"How could–"

"I didn't even–"

"Get the weapons!" Baltasar jerked the wheel away from Reynir and shoved him in the direction of the lower deck. "Put a fucking protection spell on this boat and get the *damned weapons*!"

"Hanna." Asbera's voice sound far away, and when she grabbed my hand, it was like she grabbed it through fabric. The magic chattered and vibrated. It was close. *They* were close. *They* had taken Harald, and they were still here. "Hanna, we have to arm ourselves. Come on."

She tried to pull me toward the hatch, but the flood of crewmen heading in that direction made me dizzy. I shook my head. "You go," I said. "I need the air."

She frowned but she did as I said, letting go of my hand and disappearing down below. I leaned against one of the masts and took a deep breath. Harald's blood was sticky on my face. I kept hearing his screams on the air.

I closed my eyes and tried to shut everything out. Voices drifted up from down below as the crew dug out whatever weapons Baltasar kept aboard the boat – it couldn't be many. We weren't a warship, just a fishing vessel. We could hardly defend ourselves against pirates, much less what monsters waited in the depths.

And then the magic shifted again, melting into the air, growing slippery and hard to grasp. And I heard something. Not voices, not screaming. Something else. Like water bubbling in a pot.

I stared into the darkness beyond the boat. At first, I thought I was the only one who heard it, but all around me, the crew stopped in place, looking out toward the water. The sound grew louder. Our fear strung the air out as tight as a wire.

The crew's terrified whispers picked up. I slid forward, moving on a thread of magic, my eyes on the railing. The sound was everywhere.

The ocean had learned how to breathe.

I came to the railing and looked down.

The water churned, wild with froth and still pink with Harald's blood. I shrieked and stumbled backward into Baltasar. He dragged me to the center of the boat.

"Stay away from the edge!" he shouted. "How do you think Harald got killed?"

"I know how Harald got killed!" I screamed, but Baltasar was gone, his feet pounding over to the other side of the boat. The rest of the crew clumped around the masts. I whirled around and found Asbera and Finnur pressed close to each other. Asbera's eyes were wide and determined, and she clutched an old-fashioned roughhewn sword in one hand. Finnur had a dagger, a small silver blade.

"I got you this," Asbera said, drawing a knife out of her belt.

"I don't know how to use anything." My voice shook. "I'll just use my magic."

Something thumped against the side of the boat.

Finnur dragged me behind him. Asbera shoved the knife at me and lifted her sword over her head in a fighting stance.

Another thump.

"Stay quiet," Baltasar hissed.

Through the haze of my fear, I concentrated on the wind. It was still blowing us south, back toward home. I reached in deep. I didn't have much experience with magical weapons beyond protection spells, and there was already a protection spell on the *Annika,* one more advanced than any I could cast.

I tightened my grip on the knife. It was small and felt unsteady in my hands.

Another thump. Another.

"Ready your weapons," Baltasar whispered.

I wondered how many of the crew actually knew how to fight. I wondered if it even mattered.

The thumping grew louder. More persistent.

It was joined by a scratching like dead leaves against rocks.

The crew pulled closer together.

The wind's magic flowed through me, even though I had no idea what I would do with it.

A face appeared over the railing.

For half a second, I thought it was Isolfr, and I had no idea if I should be terrified or relieved. But then the sails snapped out of the way and the thin afternoon sun shone across the face, and I saw it wasn't Isolfr at all. He had at least tried to look human.

There was nothing human about this face.

It was long and narrow, with a pointed snout and sharp teeth that glowed against the gray light. It scrabbled on deck, flinging off water, its body thin and low to the ground. It moved like a snake, even though it walked on four legs, each of its feet ending in a spray of huge, curved white claws.

It was the color of water, and mist curled around its body, creating a trail that led back to the ocean.

The magic whooshed out of me. I wasn't a witch. I was just a fisherman's apprentice. And I was going to die.

A pistol popped, and the creature slammed up against the side of the railing. Liquid light oozed out across the deck.

"We can kill them," Asbera gasped. She hoisted her sword higher. "We can kill–"

The creature lifted its head and jumped back on its feet. It threw back its head and let out a shrill, rattling cry. I slapped my hands over my ears. My knife clattered to the deck. The crew shrieked and fumbled with their weapons. Pistol shots echoed across the boat, smoke drifting up along the sails.

More creatures appeared over the railing.

The crew dispersed. Most of them scrambled up into the masts. Benedict ran screaming down below. Baltasar shouted for order, but we weren't soldiers, and we weren't going to listen. I would have been running for the masts too, if it hadn't been for Finnur's hand on my arm.

"Stay," he said, his voice hard. "We need your magic."

The creatures spilled over the railing. There were too many to count. They wriggled across the deck, their claws clicking against the wood. One after another after another. Like insects.

Baltasar fired his pistol into the onslaught. White blood splattered the wood. Zakaria and Seimur fired from up in the masts. With each shot, the magic reverberated and I got a taste like rot on my tongue.

The creatures squirmed closer.

Finnur and Asbera and I stumbled back.

"Climb up!" Asbera shouted. She swung her sword and sliced one of the creatures in half, and it rolled away into the shadows. The magic roiled. I knew it was drawing itself back together. "Get to Reynir."

Yes. Reynir. He'd know what magic to use. I crawled up the masts, my body slick with panicky sweat. One of the crew grabbed me and pulled me up to the crosstree before firing back into the churn of creatures. From here, I could see Asbera and Finnur and Baltasar cutting their way through the swarm. Thick gray mist curled over the railings, wrapping around the deck like ghosts. And that blood, that blood like light – it was everywhere.

"Hanna!" Reynir swung down beside me. "Please tell me you can feel it. The magic?"

I nodded and blinked back tears.

"We won't get rid of them, but we should at least be able to protect the boat and send them back to the ocean."

I nodded again.

"If you can't do this, you better tell me."

My heart pounded. I'd beat back the Mists when we were attacked in the village (*with help, you had help*) and the winds were even stronger here, especially so high above the deck.

"I can do it," I said. I almost believed it.

"Take my hand." Reynir grabbed mine. "Pull out the magic. You'll have to cut through the Mists first. You use the wind, right?"

"Yes." I couldn't look away from what was happening on deck. The mist was thicker now, thick enough that Asbera and Finnur were silhouettes in the dim light.

"I use the ocean. That should be enough to expel them. Concentrate!"

I squeezed my eyes shut. It was easier when I couldn't see the monsters snarling and snapping down below, even though I could still hear the pistol shots and the creatures' horrible screeching. The wind roared against my ears. Slowly, it shifted, until it blew in from the south, until it was *my* wind. The boat tilted and turned and I tightened my grip on the masts. It was hard to find clean magic, though, magic that hadn't been corrupted by the Mists, and as I searched, my chest constricted and my throat swelled up.

"Keep – looking–" Reynir sounded strangled. "Just – keep–"

The wind. I shut him out, I shut out the screams down below, and I focused on the wind. It was the wind of my father and mother both: my father's birthright and my mother's ancestors. And for that reason, it was mine. It did not belong to the Mists. Its *magic* didn't belong to the Mists.

And then, there, beneath that cold, thick Mists enchantment, I found it, a glimmer of power, warm like the sun.

"I've got it!" I screamed.

Reynir squeezed my hand more tightly and began to chant in the old language. Through his strange dialect, I recognized the spell. It was a plea for protection.

I joined in, and our words blended together even if we didn't speak them the same. The wind flowed around me and flowed through me, and the magic lit up my blood and became a part of me.

My eyes flew open.

For a moment, I didn't see the world as it was, mist and blood and violence and terror. I saw only the magic. It suffused everything with light: the boat, the creatures, the rest of the crew. And I was aflame.

"–protect us all," Reynir and I shouted at once, our voices ringing out in unison. And there was a sudden, sharp intake, a sudden, sharp stillness–

And then a blast of light.

It knocked me back. Reynir's hand slipped away from mine, and for a moment, I was falling, serenely, through the open air. I stared up at the cloudy sky through the forest of sails. I didn't realize what was happening.

My arm burned.

I'd stopped, midair, and was dangling from the bottom crosstree. Seimur had caught me. His face was strained. I grabbed hold of the sail rope.

"I got it!" I said. "You can let go."

He did, leaning back with a sigh of relief. I swung out on the rope, arcing out over the deck. All the creatures were gone from the *Annika*, but I could see them out in the ocean, frothing up the water. One of them launched itself at the boat, but there was a shudder of magic and it slammed backward.

I swung back to the mast and climbed down. The deck was splattered with light and streaked with smears of red blood. Human blood.

"Asbera!" I shouted. "Finnur!"

"Hanna!" Asbera's voice was a beacon. I stumbled toward it, exhausted from the spell-casting, my thoughts thick and unclear. "Hanna, I need your help!"

Her words were slurred. My feet slipped over the spilled blood. Light flung up and clung to my trouser legs. I ignored it. Asbera was over by the starboard side of the ship, hunched over a dark lump. No, not a dark lump – Finnur. And he wasn't moving.

"What happened?" I shouted. I slid over beside her and fell to my knees. Finnur's eyes were open, his mouth twisted open in an expression of horror and surprise. He was bleeding from his shoulder, blood soaking through his coat.

"He's still alive." Asbera's face shone with tears, and her voice shook. "I can feel his heart beating." She pressed her hand against his chest and closed her eyes. "I can feel it."

I put two fingers on the side of Finnur's neck. His pulse fluttered against them, faint but steady. I lay a finger underneath his nose and felt him breathing.

"If he's still alive," I said, "we can save him." I had no idea if this was true but I had to say something. Asbera looked up at me, her eyes blinking back tears.

"How?" she said.

"We'll come up with something." I pressed my hand against his wound. "We need to stop the blood. Could you get me some water?"

Asbera nodded and bounded away. Finnur had dropped his knife beside him when he fell, and I picked it up and used it to cut away his clothes. By then, Asbera had returned with a bucket of drinking water. Baltasar was with her, carrying an Empire-style sword covered in glowing blood.

"What's wrong with him?" he asked.

"I don't know." I pulled off my scarf and dipped it in the water bucket, then wiped away Finnur's blood. His wound was small, a cluster of sharp punctures arranged in a circle.

"He was bitten," I said.

Asbera knelt beside me. She cupped Finnur's face in one hand.

I looked over at Baltasar, hoping for guidance. But his face was set in stone.

"Can you cure him?" he asked.

I listened to Asbera sniffling beside me.

I shook my head.

"Well, then, we'll have to make good time back to Tulja," he said, and he walked away.

CHAPTER FOURTEEN

We moved Finnur to the captain's quarters, laying him out on a hard, wobbly cot. Reynir dug up some dried herbs that I pressed against Finnur's wound before dressing it with scraps of fabric. "If there's any poison from the magic," Reynir told me, "the herbs should suck it out." But he didn't sound too convinced.

Asbera sat with Finnur through the night, not sleeping. I didn't sleep, either, just paced back and forth across the cabin, going through all the spells I knew, trying to find one that could help. The winds aren't much for healing – it's sailors' magic, explorers' magic. Sea magic could heal, but Reynir told me it was impossible to get to the water with those Mists monsters trailing behind the boat.

"I wish I knew what that they were doing here," he told me. We were sitting up on deck, next to the brazier. The rest of the crew was sleeping, and I'd told Asbera that's what I was going to do, too. But I went up on deck instead and found Reynir staring into the flames. I don't know why I sat down beside him. I guess the terror of those monsters was enough for me to set aside our differences.

"The Mists always have some purpose when they come through," he muttered. "They don't do it just for kicks. But what could they possibly want from us?"

I drew my legs in close to my chest. The wood crackled and threw off sparks of yellow light that reflected in the glowing bloodstains that still splashed across the *Annika*.

"I think I know who sent them," I said.

Reynir looked over at me, suspicious. "What?"

I frowned and rubbed my hands together.

"What do you mean, you know who sent them?"

"My old captain." I looked at the flames. "He did something to anger a lord of the Mists. Foxfollow."

"But your captain's not on the boat."

"Does it matter? The Mists already attacked me once. I should have seen it coming." The thought made me queasy with guilt. I stood up. The monsters shrieked out in the water. At least none of them broke through the magic. "Now Finnur is going to die."

"We're sailing as fast as we can." Reynir pointed up at the sails. "You're seeing to that, aren't you? More impressive than I expected."

I looked up. The sails were stiff from the north wind. I wasn't controlling it at all; the direction had shifted not long after the battle with the creatures. But I could see how Reynir might think I had, because it blew so strong and sure and unwavering. I didn't feel like correcting him.

"I just wish there was something more I could do to help."

"If I can't help, you certainly can't," Reynir said. "But the priests can do something. We'll be there soon."

Even his insult sounded empty. I thought of the priests in their stuffy cave. I couldn't imagine them saving Finnur. This was Mists magic, and they couldn't even keep Mists magic out of their own town. Out of their own rituals.

Isolfr, a voice whispered in my head. *Isolfr will be able to save him.*

I scowled. No. Isolfr could barely save himself. And besides, he would be gone by the time we returned, him and Kolur and Frida, all of them.

I had to find a way to save Finnur on my own. He'd gotten me this job aboard the *Annika*; he'd helped me find a place to live. Saving his life was the least I could do.

I walked back to the captain's quarters. Asbera knelt at Finnur's side, clutching his stiff hand in her own. I sat down beside her. Finnur's expression hadn't changed; his eyes were still open, his face still terrified.

"If we weren't at sea," Asbera said softly, "we'd could at least gather the moon moss and prepare the healing draught." She closed her eyes and took a deep breath. "But there's *nothing–*"

I didn't tell her there was something. The sea. We had the sea. But we couldn't get to it, not with those creatures following alongside us as we sailed home–

Home. Sea and sky, we were leading them back to Tulja.

I looked down at Finnur. In truth, he was more important to me than Tulja. Let Baltasar worry about bringing the creatures to dry land. Let the priests use their magic to keep them at bay. I just wanted Finnur to live.

"Are you sure there's no moon moss on board?" I asked.

Asbera sighed, ran one hand through Finnur's hair. "It's not something we typically keep on boats."

I frowned. Then I slid off my bracelet and placed it on Finnur's heart. Asbera looked up at me in surprise.

"I bought it in a magic shop in Skalir," I said. "It's brought me some luck." Not enough, but I didn't think I needed to add that. "It could only help."

She nodded, her face blank. I stood up. "I'm going to see if I can find anything. I don't know much about earth magic, but if there's anything that I think will be useful, I'll bring it to you."

She nodded again. Then she wiped at her eyes and said, "Thank you."

I made my way to the storage room. I didn't think I would find anything, but I couldn't stand the thought of sitting around, watching Finnur not move. Reynir had gone looking for supplies, but his focus was on ocean magic. Asbera had been too distraught to look for herself.

One of the few things I did know about earth-magic was that it could be eked out of ordinary materials – cooking spices and flowers from a vegetable garden. Surely we had some of that on board.

The galley was empty, although I could hear the snores of the crewmen through the wall. I didn't find much. Mostly drinking water and crackers and salted fish. I collected one of the empty fish jars, thinking the leftover salt might be useful. A line of small wooden barrels was lashed against the far wall, and I pried open their lids. Most of them were empty, but I did find a few sprigs of dried lavender in one, probably left over from a longer voyage. It crumbled when I touched it, but I was able to sweep the remains into the fish jar.

I didn't know if Asbera would be able to do anything with what I'd found, but it had to be better than nothing.

I took the fish jar back to the captain's quarters. Asbera looked up when I walked in, and I held out the jar like an offering.

"Salt," I said stupidly. "And lavender."

Asbera blinked.

"Plant magic?" I pulled the jar up close to my chest. I felt like I'd made some terrible mistake. "To help with–"

"Oh." Asbera shook her head. "That's sweet of you, but I can't – there's nothing we can do with salt and lavender."

I looked down at the jar. Worthless. Everything was worthless.

"I do appreciate the thought." She smiled, just a little. "But earth magic can be so complicated, particularly when you aren't on dry land."

"Oh. Of course. That makes sense."

"I think your bracelet's helping a little, though. Come look."

I set the jar on the floor and went to Asbera's side. The bracelet was glowing. Not enough to cast light, but enough that even someone not touched by magic could see the enchantment in it, fighting with the magic that had poisoned Finnur's blood.

"His heartbeat is stronger." Asbera laid her hand against his neck. "See?"

I felt his pulse. Stronger, yes, but not what I'd call strong.

There wasn't much more to say. I put my hands in my lap. The *Annika* rocked back and forth. Every now and then, I'd hear scratching from the creatures in the water, but our shield held firm, even if nothing else did.

The north wind continued to blow us home, great strong gusts so powerful, they could have been produced with magic. This left me with little to do the next day other than watch over Finnur so Asbera could sleep. She didn't want to – I think she was afraid he would slip away while she was gone. But she curled up in the hammock at my insistence, and a few minutes later, her breathing had grown steady and even.

The bracelet's glow was dimmer than it had been earlier. Asbera probably hadn't noticed; otherwise, I doubt she would have fallen asleep. But I could see it, and feel it, too: the bracelet had fulfilled its capacity.

The thought made my chest hurt, but I knew I shouldn't expect so much, not from a cheap trinket from a magic shop.

I knelt down beside Finnur. He skin was waxy and almost translucent, and if I looked hard enough, I saw the glow of magic in his veins. It wasn't the soft glow of the bracelet – this was harsh, violent light. Poison from the Mists.

My heart twisted. I lay my hand against the side of his neck and felt his heartbeat, faint and unsteady. I closed my eyes. Even his skin was cool to the touch, like ocean water. The bracelet had staved off the inevitable, but he was dying.

Something stronger would have to save Finnur.

The boat's rocking lulled me into exhaustion. The creatures scrabbled against the boat's hull. I thought of the warning that Isolfr had given me about Lord Foxfollow: *You need to recognize those creatures that are particular to the Mists.*

Thinking on Isolfr gave me a weird, sharp pain in my chest. I stretched in my chair, trying to shake it off. Part of me still thought he was responsible for all this, that he was the reason the Mists were after Kolur, that he'd *led* us to the Mists–

But that didn't explain Gillean.

I didn't want to think about Gillean, but I did anyway. I couldn't even think about him as he'd been in that space between worlds. Couldn't think about him alive. No, I had to think about him as he'd been in death, his face twisted up in anguish, his body stiff, silver blood everywhere.

Like Finnur, in truth.

Except Finnur wasn't dead. I hadn't been able to save

Gillean, but I still had the opportunity to save Finnur. Even if I didn't know how yet.

I played over the future in my mind, unwinding it like Mama's spool: We would arrive back at Tulja, but we wouldn't be able to approach land, not with the creatures tearing up the sea. We'd have to get rid of them first. I didn't care about Tulja, but I did care about Finnur.

And even if we did get rid of the creatures and brought Finnur on land, he'd still be at the mercy of the priests or the healers, and who knew if they had to skill to run up against Mists magic.

Hopelessness threatened to swallow me whole, like the ocean itself. I looked over at Asbera, still sleeping in the hammock. She twitched, groaning a little. Both of them had shown me so much kindness and here I was, doing nothing, *nothing* to help Finnur.

There had to be something.

I thought.

I thought.

I thought of Gillean.

Gillean – face twisted, blood shining. Gillean, standing in a room made of light, terrified.

Gillean.

I sat straight up, my heart racing. Isolfr had called Gillean from the Mists and met him in that in between place. It had been simple magic, too: a song, a gesture. And the north wind.

Wind-magic.

I looked back at Finnur. Blood rushed through my head. I was teetering on the edge of a precipice, trying to find my balance. When I thought about what I wanted to do, dizziness swept through me.

Use Isolfr's spell and call whoever's responsible.

My cheeks burned. *Call whoever's responsible.*

It was stupid. Dangerous. And on some level, I understood that. But I was too exhausted and too overwhelmed to really think on my actions. For the last day, I'd sat by and watched as Finnur slipped away from us, and all I'd done to help was lay my bracelet on his heart.

I left the captain's quarters and went up on deck. Reynir was sitting next to the fire, listening to Seimur play a tune on his flute. They were probably trying to drown out the screeching and splashing of the creatures.

Reynir stood up when he saw me. "Is something wrong?"

I shook my head. "I just need you to go down and watch Finnur for a little while. Asbera's still asleep and I – I need a rest." My voice wavered. Reynir narrowed his eyes, but he didn't comment on it.

"Of course." He nodded once. "You need your rest, too."

He walked away. The rest of the nighttime crew had their attention focused on Seimur and his melancholy flute. A sad song at a sad time.

While they were all distracted, I crept over to the stern end of the boat, taking care not to get too close to the edge. The wall of magic that Reynir and I had built was still in place, solid and potent, and I didn't worry too much about being dragged out to sea by one of those creatures. But I was aware of them, aware of their sharp teeth and the poison those teeth carried, and I knew they were aware of me, too.

The wind was cold and icy and rattled through the sails. I knelt down on the cold deck. Closed my eyes. I sang softly, barely above a whisper, afraid one of the crew would hear me and come asking questions.

No one did.

I concentrated hard on the lyrics, the alien consonants of the old language clumsy on my tongue. The magic in the north wind was stronger than I expected, and stranger – more refined than wind magic should be, like a tamed lion. But I was able to catch it easily enough and intertwine it with the music.

Power shuddered through me, the start of something.

The gestures came to me like second nature: the thumping on the deck was the thumping of my heartbeat, and the arc of my hand was the arc of my breath. The wind grew colder. Dots of snow melted on my face. The screech of the creatures fell away.

I opened my eyes.

The *Annika* was gone.

I stood inside a mirror. The walls and ceiling and floor reflected me back into myself, and so I felt hollow and transparent. I'd done it. I'd come to the world between worlds.

"Whoever's responsible for the attack on Finnur of Tulja," I shouted into the cavernous space, "I call you!"

I was met with silence. I turned in place, and my reflection moved with me. With Isolfr, this place had been golden and full of light, but now I felt like I stood on the surface of the moon. Maybe I'd done something wrong.

Footsteps.

I froze, my heart pounding. I couldn't tell where the footsteps came from, and the sound of them bounced all around the room. For a moment, I was certain an army approached.

And then the footsteps silenced.

"Now, what's this, then?"

The voice was as silvery and liquid as the room itself. It didn't echo, only fell dull and flat like a heavy stone to the soil.

Slowly, I turned. I had no idea what I expected to find: a monster like the creatures surrounding the *Annika?* A beautifully inhuman boy with starlight skin? The Nalendan? But it was a man, just a man, tall and slim and dark-haired. He wore a charcoal-colored jacket cut in a style I'd never seen before. Not Empire and certainly nothing like what the men of the north wore, not even wealthy ones.

His eyes were gray.

I could only stare at him. He strode forward, swinging a wooden cane in time with his steps. Each one fell as flat as the other.

I forced myself to speak. "Are you Lord Foxfollow?"

He stopped again. Tilted his head. "Who are you?" he said.

I knew better than to tell him my real name. "A girl from Kjora."

"I don't know this Kjora." He swung his cane and settled it across the back of his shoulders. "How do you know the name Lord Foxfollow?"

"It was given to me by a friend." I felt like I couldn't catch enough breath, much less speak. My words were miracles. My heartbeat pounded in every part of my body.

"A friend?" The man smiled, slow and easy and unsettling. "Not a friend from your world, I wouldn't think. Was this the same friend who taught you to flatten realities?"

"What?" His question caught me off guard. "Flatten realities?"

"Yes. All of this." He gestured and drew in the room with his arms. "How could a little *human* girl like you call me here?"

I drew myself up, gathering all my courage. "I guess little human girls aren't as weak as you think."

The man laughed. "I suppose not. Tell me, are you the one who beat back my operatives in the human village?"

"Your what?" I frowned. "You mean the costumed men?"

The man waved his hand dismissively. "Yes, yes, they took the form of that silly human magic. Their defeat was no real trouble for me, at any rate. I was merely curious. I sincerely doubt you're the one who *actually* defeated them."

I didn't say anything, remembering the rush of the north wind, my own stilted confusion.

"You must have had help bringing me here, then, as well."

"I didn't." I glared at him, a colossal act of bravery. "I called you on my own. I have questions for you." I took a deep breath. "You never told me if you're Lord Foxfollow or not."

A pause. The silence amplified my fears.

"Of course I'm Lord Foxfollow," he said. "That was who you called." His voice shifted into a woman's voice – my voice. "*Whoever's responsible for the attack on Finnur of Tulja!*" He grinned, rakish. "Or do you not trust your own magic?"

I wanted to falter, but I stood strong. "Why did you send those monsters after us?"

Lord Foxfollow's smile stayed fixed in place. "My deepest apologies," he said. "I never meant to send my menials after you."

"What?" I said.

Lord Foxfollow waved one hand dismissively. "It's a dull story. Now, why did you call me here?"

I looked up at him, at the lovely carved planes of his face. He smiled at me and his gray eyes glittered. "Come, my dear," he said. "You went to all this trouble to bring me to this space. And you claim you did it all on your own, too." He strode over to me and trailed his fingers down the side of my cheek. His touch was cold and damp, like ocean spray or winter humidity. Or mist.

I shivered and pulled away from him.

"My friend." I tried to choose my words carefully. "His name is Finnur Corra. He was bitten by one of your mons– by one of your menials, and he's fallen into a coma. I need you to help me." I lifted my chin defiantly, but I felt like I was caught in a web. A silvery, gossamer, glittering gray spider's web.

There was a long silence.

And then Lord Foxfollow roared with laughter.

"Oh, my dear, my dear, you collapsed realities to try and save your friend? That's sweet, it really is."

"So you'll help him?"

"Look at me," he said.

I did as he asked without thinking. In the shining light of that reflective space, his skin was suffused with a pale, moonlight glow. His eyes roiled like storm clouds. The silvery web tightened, and I looked at his mouth to get away from his eyes.

"I'm afraid I can't do anything to help your friend." I saw his answer more than I heard it, the words rising off his lips. "I could, of course, my powers are... quite impressive. But I simply don't feel the need to waste them on a human, particularly when it's a human's fault he's hurt."

"What?" My legs and arms burned, and I realized that tears were dripping down my cheeks. "What are you talking about?"

"My dear, my dear." Lord Foxfollow smiled and wrapped his arm around my shoulder. I wanted to get away, but I couldn't move. He pointed his cane at the mirror across from us. Our reflections were a pair of smeared blurs, distorted by mist. "Why talk when I can show you? I can recreate the past much more easily than you can remember it."

The mirrors melted away and revealed the Rilil docks at night. Stars swirled overhead. The boats were tucked in their usual places. Everything was quiet and empty.

"I'll show you," Lord Foxfollow whispered, his lips pressed close to my ear. I trembled from the pain in my heart. "I'll show you... the *Penelope II.*"

The scene blurred and the jagged, uneven lines of the *Penelope II* appeared, illuminated by the soft blue light of a magic-cast lantern. Lord Foxfollow squeezed my shoulder more tightly. He smelled like cold, damp steel and men's perfume, and it made me dizzy.

"Watch close," he whispered. Even his breath was cold.

The water around the *Penelope II* began to churn in a way far, far too familiar to me. I shrieked, and Lord Foxfollow clamped one hand over my mouth. "You don't want to miss anything," he said.

The water rose up around the boat, solidifying into the gleaming, cold shapes of the monsters. They crawled aboard, one after another.

I yanked his hand away from my mouth.

"Why are you showing me this?" I sobbed. "What does this have to do with not helping Finnur? Stop. Stop it!"

Lord Foxfollow flicked his cane, and suddenly I could see aboard the ship. Frida and Kolur were crouched beside each other under the masts, firing pistols into the onslaught of monsters. Isolfr was nowhere to be seen. Of course.

"We have to send them away," Kolur shouted. His voice sounded strange, tinny and distorted. "Like we practiced back in Jandanvar."

"Send them where?" Frida shouted back.

"Does it matter?"

Everything in my body went cold.

"Ah." Lord Foxfollow's arm slipped away from me. "She understands."

"This is a trick," I whispered. "This is a lie."

Across the room, Frida climbed up the highest mast and Kolur fought his way to the bow of the boat. The wind buffeted them, knocking the boat around in the bay. Ocean water splashed over the side. I knew they were doing magic, even though I couldn't feel the ripples of it in my own body. I could see it, a swirl of wind and water and starlight.

The monsters disappeared.

Kolur collapsed across the deck.

Lord Foxfollow brandished his cane, and all I could see now was my reflection again. Lord Foxfollow smiled at me in the glass.

"He sent them to you," he said. "He's strong for a human. Much stronger than he looks."

For the first time, I noticed a hardness in Lord Foxfollow's voice, like a vein of ice running through water.

Lord Foxfollow grabbed my chin and jerked my face toward his. My whole body was numb. He tilted my gaze up until I met those flat gray eyes. I was falling into them, tumbling through them, and I knew with a shuddering certainty that Kolur had sent the monsters to me on purpose. It was punishment. Punishment for not helping him.

Lord Foxfollow's fingers dug into my face. His nails were sharp. The pain bled spots of light into my vision.

"Don't blame me," Lord Foxfollow hissed. "Blame Kolur Icebreak."

The memory of those images flickered through my thoughts, one after another. The monsters swarming the boat. Isolfr gone. The pop of pistol shots.

Send them where?

Does it matter?

He didn't do it on purpose. My certainty otherwise was a cold mist inside my head, but it didn't come from me. It came from Lord Foxfollow.

"You're a monster!" With a tremendous force of will, I pulled away from Lord Foxfollow. My feet clattered across the mirrored floor. He couldn't hurt me here, he couldn't hurt me here. "Just like your menials. A monster."

Lord Foxfollow tilted his head.

"No," he said. "I'm just different from you."

Rage bubbled up inside me. I thought of Kolur standing at the wheel of the *Penelope*, the wind blowing his hair away from his face. I thought of Asbera weeping over Finnur, and of Finnur himself, frozen and tormented because of one bite to the shoulder.

And although there was no wind in that place, I gathered up what magic rested inside of me, a residue from all the spells I'd cast, all the winds I'd called down.

I gathered it up and I wove it into a hard knot of fury and then I cast it at Lord Foxfollow, a cyclone of light.

It struck him in the chest and dissipated. Of course it didn't hurt him. Lord Foxfollow looked at me sadly.

"My dear," he said, "that was highly uncalled-for."

All my anger turned to fear.

"Begone," he said.

The mirrored room disappeared, Lord Foxfollow disappeared, and I drifted, dazed, through a cold and dark space.

He had undone my magic with a single command, and I understood then that he could have done that from the very beginning. That he was only humoring me.

The dark space brightened. Spots of light appeared overhead. I blinked at them. Stars. They were stars. I was lying flat on my back, staring at the stars.

No, not lying.

Floating.

I flailed, my heart racing. I caught a glimpse of what lay below me: dark ocean and the *Annika*, so small it looked like one of Henrik's toys.

"No." I struggled against invisible bindings. "No. Foxfollow!"

My voice carried on the wind. The wind, sweet-smelling and gentle – that wasn't Foxfollow's doing. He would have just dropped me into the maelstrom of monsters down below. No, this was the north wind, buoying me along, keeping me adrift.

I stopped struggling. The wind caressed me. It was cold, yes, but it was a comfort, too.

"Thank you," I whispered, although I wasn't sure who I spoke to.

The wind whistled in response, and then it floated me down slowly, gently, and laid me to rest in the bow of the *Annika*.

CHAPTER FIFTEEN

Lost. Everything was lost.

I sat up. The familiar creaks and moans of the *Annika* were drowned out by the shrieking of the monsters in the water. The boat rocked back and forth as the north wind blew us steadily home.

But we couldn't go home.

"Hanna!" Asbera's voice rang out in the crystal night. She ran over beside me, Reynir at her side. "What happened? Benedict said you disappeared–"

"I was trying to help Finnur," I muttered. "But I can't. I can't."

"Trying to – *How?*" Reynir threw his hands up. "By just *disappearing*? Can you take the rest of us with you? Or take *Finnur* with you, at least?"

"I didn't go somewhere that could help Finnur." I stood up, shaky after flying on the wind. The monsters thrashed against the side of the shield.

"I was worried," Asbera said. "I thought something had happened to you, too."

"Something did. But I'm fine." I stalked away from

the railing, back toward the brazier at the boat's center. Baltasar sat beside it, staring into the flames. He glanced up at me when I joined him.

"Worried about you, girl," he said.

He sounded exactly like Kolur. I looked down at him, at the firelight bouncing off his skin, and felt like crying. What if Lord Foxfollow hadn't been lying? What if Kolur had sent the monsters to me on purpose?

I shook my head. "I just wanted to help. But I didn't find anything." I sat down in front of the brazier and stuck out my hands to warm them.

Reynir and Asbera walked over to the fire, although they hung back, sticking to the shadows.

"Isn't anyone watching Finnur?" I asked.

"Scimur is." Asbera frowned. "I was – we were worried. What were you trying to do?"

I took a deep, shuddery breath. The night howled with sound, clawing and shrieking, and so I focused my attention on the crackle of the wood inside the brazier.

"Find the person who hurt Finnur."

Baltasar gave a bitter laugh. "Did you?"

"He's of no use." I closed my eyes against the tears. "What are you going to do when we get back to Tulja?"

Silence. When I glanced over at Baltasar, he was staring into the flames.

"Well?"

"Been trying not to think about it," he said. "Enough to worry about."

Behind him, Asbera gasped. "No," she said, and stumbled over beside us. She knelt beside Baltasar and grabbed his hand, her eyes big and imploring. "No, you can't – we have to go home. Finnur's dying."

"I know he is." Baltasar wouldn't meet her in the eye. "Told Reynir to come up with something."

Asbera and I both looked over at Reynir at the mention of his name, but he was looking down at the deck.

"I don't have anything yet," he said in a cold voice. "But perhaps Hanna can find a way, if she can meet with our attacker in some realm in the sky." His eyes glittered in the firelight. "I'd prefer not to see my home destroyed and my family murdered."

"Oh, stop it," Asbera said. "That doesn't help."

"You aren't helping. You're the reason we're going home in the first place. I told Baltasar we should sail in circles until we found a way to get rid of them."

Asbera's eyes flashed with anger.

"Enough!" Baltasar roared.

Magic flooded across the deck of the ship, bright and hot and smelling of the south wind. I jumped and drew into myself, searching for my own magic. Asbera grabbed for my hand. Baltasar hoisted up his pistol.

The enchantment faded away, twinkling on the air. One of the monsters had almost broken through our shield.

"They're getting stronger," Reynir said in a flat voice.

I scanned across the magic, sucking down breath, trying to steady myself. Over on the starboard side, the shield was marred by a thin line of light, illuminated by the stars.

A crack.

"Whatever you did," Reynir said, "it made them worse."

"Maybe you made it worse," Asbera said. "You're the one being cruel."

I slumped back down in front of the brazier. Baltasar didn't say anything, but he didn't put his pistol away, either. One of the monsters let out a long, echoing howl that sank down into the marrow of my bones. I imagined that howl sliding over the empty ocean and disappearing into the cracks between worlds. I imagined Lord Foxfollow whispering spells to his monstrous little pets, giving them the strength to break through our stupid human magic.

"He's right," I said. "It is my fault."

"Hanna—"

Asbera reached out one hand toward me, but I stood up and glided out of her reach. The shields hummed, but the churning on the other side was louder and more urgent.

I'd called Lord Foxfollow to me; I'd shot him with my magic. And all I'd done was give him reason to send his monsters after us in earnest.

Morning dawned, the sun a pale white disc hanging high in the sky. I felt like I'd only just fallen asleep, and I had; the nights were getting shorter. This far north, soon they'd be gone completely.

I had slept down in the crew's quarters, curled up in a hammock so that no one would speak with me. When I woke, I went up to check on Finnur. Asbera was sitting with him, a plate of salted fish in her lap. Untouched. Finnur was still pale, still cold, still breathing.

"Baltasar says we'll be home by this time tomorrow." Asbera didn't look at me. "But we still don't know what to do about the monsters." Her voice cracked, and she took a deep breath and straightened her spine. "He's right; we can't go back to Tulja, not until they're gone." Her hands trembled as she pushed Finnur's hair aside.

I felt empty. Finnur looked like a corpse, his skin was so pale, so bloodless. Once again, I thought of the vision that Lord Foxfollow had shown me – Kolur and Frida gathering up the strength of their magic and sending the monsters straight to us. I shivered. Why would Kolur do such a thing?

He wouldn't.

The voice whispering to me wasn't my own. It sounded like the wind. I went very still, straining to hear it.

He wouldn't hurt you on purpose.

Asbera kept stroking Finnur's hair. Her cheeks glimmered with tears.

He wouldn't hurt me.

Foxfollow would.

It was an accident. Foxfollow showed me something that had truly happened, but he had been trying to frighten me, to make me feel abandoned. Except the voice on the wind was right – Kolur wouldn't have hurt me on purpose.

He didn't know where he was sending the monsters. But he had sent them away.

And I had seen it.

I bolted out of the cabin, into the bright wash of sunlight. A handful of the crew tended to the sails, and Baltasar stood up at the wheel. The shield shimmered in the sun.

Everything was quiet except for the monsters' screeching.

The sound was horrific, like listening to an animal die, and louder than it had been even last night. I walked over to the masts. Zakaria looked up at me and nodded. He had shoved rolls of fabric into his ears. All of the crew had. I didn't want to do the same, though. I thought I should listen. There might be something in the screams that could help.

There was still no need for me to call the winds – that was the only good thing about this trip, that the winds had been on our side all this time. Or maybe it wasn't the winds themselves. Maybe it was that presence in the wind. I couldn't feel it, exactly, but I'd heard its voice down below.

I looked over at the port railing, at the shield. Off in the distance, the ocean was steely and calm. It was only around the boat that the water thrashed.

I walked closer. Slow, careful, cautious steps.

"What are you doing?" Zakaria shouted. I ignored him. "Don't get too close!"

The air was thicker around the railing. The shield sparked out at me, touching the magic in my blood. I took another step closer.

A monster leapt out of the water and slammed into the shield. Magic flared. Ocean water landed at my feet.

The monster slid away.

"Told you not to get too close." Zakaria was at my side now. He pulled the roll of fabric out of his ears. "They've been doing that all day."

"Where's Reynir?"

"Up in the masts, strengthening the shield." Zakaria pointed. "Could probably use your help, you know."

I squinted up into the sunlight. Reynir was a burst of enchantment amongst the sails, a silhouette wreathed in a halo.

"No," I said. "I need *his* help."

I left Zakaria. Reynir was fully enveloped in his magic, his eyes closed, a stretch of rope knotted around his arm. I waited until he finished, standing there amidst the cries and shrieks of the monsters.

It didn't take long. Eventually, his light faded, and he sagged against the rope, his chest rising and falling. I climbed up the masts.

"Hanna?" he said, squinting at me. "Is that you? The real you? You know how it is with magic–"

"Yeah, it's the real me."

"What are you doing here?" He leaned against the mast and unwound his arm from the rope. "Has something happened with Finnur?"

"No, he's the same." I leaned forward. "Reynir, I need your help. Probably Asbera's, too."

He looked at me with his tired eyes. "For what?"

"To get rid of the monsters."

A pause. The wind whistled around us. It smelled sweet, like honey, nothing like the cold steely scent of the Mists.

"Have you known how to do this the entire time?" His voice was low and accusing.

"No! Well, not exactly. I learned something when I went to the in-between place."

"I knew it."

"I didn't realize I'd learned it until just now. I thought I'd been betrayed, but it was – a trick. Kolur, my old captain, he's the reason they're here in the first place. But not–" I stopped and took a deep breath and told him what Lord Foxfollow had showed me.

"How do you know it's not a trick?" Reynir said.

I glared at him. "I don't, all right? But we have to do something. The monsters are just getting stronger, and if we circle around trying to figure out something else, not only will Finnur die but the rest of us will too, because those monsters are going to break through the shields."

Reynir looked at me. The boat rocked back and forth, and the monsters' screeching bore into my brain.

"Do you know how your captain did it?" Reynir asked. "Sent them away?"

I took a deep breath. "Not exactly–"

Reynir sighed.

"Will you let me finish? No, I don't know how he did it exactly, but I do know it's possible, and I know that Kolur's a sea-wizard, like you, and Frida, who was with him, she's a wind-witch, like me–" I trailed off. *Isolfr.* But he wouldn't have done anything outright, not if he was still refusing to reveal who he was. "And we'll have Asbera, who can work a bit of earth magic. When you get down to it, magic's just strength of will, right? So together, we ought to be able to throw the monsters someplace else, out at the open sea–"

"So they can attack some other poor ship the way they attacked us?"

"We'll have to throw them farther. The Green Glass Sea, in the south. My mother told me those waters are laced with magic, dangerous magic, and that should be enough to destroy the monsters."

I stopped, breathing hard. Reynir watched me. He looked worn out: dark circles under his eyes, lank hair. But I imagined I looked the same way.

"Have you spoken to Asbera?" he asked.

I shook my head. Reynir sighed. "This isn't going to work."

"We have to at least try."

"We don't even know what to do."

"I saw them do it from a distance. I can figure it out. *Please*, Reynir. Please. Even if you don't care about Finnur, the whole boat's in danger–"

"I care about Finnur," he snapped. "Fine. But I'm not taking the blame when you make things worse."

"Thank you," I said, ignoring his slight. Fighting with him wouldn't do any good right now.

I climbed back down and Reynir slowly followed, wiped out from repairing the shield. We walked into the captain's quarters together.

It was quiet in there, the walls shutting out most of the monsters' wails. Dark, too, since Asbera had drawn the curtains over the windows. Asbera was curled up in the hammock, her eyes closed. I doubted she was sleeping. Not if there was no one else to watch over Finnur.

We crept in. I looked to Finnur, the way I always did. No change. Asbera's plate of fish sat beside his cot, half eaten.

"Hanna." Asbera's voice drifted through the shadows. "You're back."

"I need to talk to you." I knelt down beside her. "Me and Reynir, we may need your help for something–"

She frowned and sat up. She looked even more worn-down than Reynir did. She looked like she'd died and been reanimated.

"What?" she said, voice barely a whisper.

"I think I know how to get rid of the monsters," I said.

"What?"

"I – I saw it. In the in-between place. Kolur did it."

"Your old captain?"

I nodded. "I couldn't see all of what he did, but I saw enough. Enough that I think Reynir and I can do it ourselves. But I want your help, your extra magic, just in case."

Asbera looked over at Finnur. Tears streaked down her cheeks.

Finnur didn't move.

"Of course I'll help you," she said. "Why wouldn't I?"

We waited until nightfall. Magic is stronger at night, when the world is wrapped in shadow. Kolur had sent the monsters our way at night as well, and I figured we needed to do it as much like him as possible.

But waiting until night left us little time. The *Annika* would arrive at Tulja soon – already we'd begun to pass the tiny rocky islands that marked the edge of Tuljan waters.

Baltasar cleared the deck for us. All the crew were told to wait down below, and he waited with them, at my request. Without the crew, the deck was even eerier. The shield cast a yellowish glow over everything, and the monsters shrieked and howled like they knew what was coming. Every now and then, one of them flung itself at the shield, and magic would scatter across the deck like flaring embers from a fire.

"Is everyone ready?" I asked. I'd already explained what I'd seen in the in-between place. It wasn't much to go on, but it gave us a sense of where to stand and what to do.

They both nodded. I took a deep breath.

And then we took our positions.

Reynir stood up at the bow of the ship, where the ocean splashed up around him. Asbera was at his side. Her magic wasn't as strong as his, but she could supplement it.

I climbed to the top of the main mast, just as Frida had done, and faced north, into the wind. I didn't call the south winds, not when we were so close to home and with Finnur's life so close to ending – I didn't want the *Annika* to blow off course. The north wind had been sweet to me these last few weeks, and that presence seemed to like me well enough. I should be able to use its strength.

The wind blew hard, rough and cold against my face, and I closed my eyes so it wouldn't draw out tears. Besides, wind-magic works best when you go by feel.

"North wind," I whispered. "I call upon you, cold brother of the south. Drive us forward. Bring the ocean to our feet."

The wind lulled.

My heart lurched inside my chest. "No, no, no," I whispered. "No, please, north wind, I need your–"

And then the wind gusted so strongly that it knocked me backward. I grabbed hold of the rope to keep from falling, and my eyes flew open and I could see the stars, swirling overhead, beautiful.

The north wind had saved my life once again.

"Thank you," I whispered.

The wind flattened out the sails, and the *Annika* plowed forward, dipping into the black, icy ocean. The monsters howled their protest. I held on tighter to the rope and concentrated on pulling the magic from the wind into myself, so I could transform it and unite with Asbera and Reynir.

I didn't dare look at anything but the stars. I didn't dare break my concentration. The wind poured over me and poured through me, and it was transformed into a beam of energy, cold and strong.

"Come on, Reynir," I whispered. "Come on, come on."

The wind blew harder. I tightened my grip on the rope. The magic drained out of me like blood, but I held on, and for a moment I thought I saw Isolfr's face–

A force blasted across the ship and slammed into me. Magic. It was wild and tumultuous like the sea, and it left me damp, my hair curling at the ends. That magic twisted together with my magic, sea and wind. Just like in Kolur's spell.

As our power combined, I saw glimpses of Asbera's face alongside Reynir, and I could feel the two different strains of their strength.

The magic flowed between all three of us, an arc of power. Everything fell away but the rushing of enchantment, which roared like the ocean, like the wind. I couldn't let myself think consciously anymore, and so I let the magic think for me. Think *through* me. Together, we sent it running over the sides of the ship, a waterfall of light that caught the monsters like a spider's web. They howled and thrashed. But they were trapped.

We had to act fast, before the Mists became aware of what we were doing. "To the Green Glass Sea," I whispered, and my voice was Asbera's voice, and Reynir's voice. "To the Green Glass Sea. To the Green Glass Sea. To the green glass sea. To the green glass sea to the green glass sea to the—"

The air cracked with a great thundering tension. Our magic drew tight like a coil.

"Release!" I screamed, and the wind tasted like saltwater.

Distantly, through the rush and roar of enchantment, I heard Reynir's voice shout, "Release," and then Asbera's, layered on top of each other like we were singing a melody.

A pause, long enough that I could feel the texture of the magic all around me, damp and cold and strong and shimmering like starlight.

The monsters let out one last howling screech, all in unison.

And then the magic transformed into an explosion of light brighter than the sun. I screamed and shut my eyes, but the dazzle stayed, burned against my eyelids. In the flash, I saw bright green waters, far away in a warm part of the world, stirred up by a denala. The storm rained monsters into the sea.

And, thank the ancestors, there were no ships on the open ocean to witness it.

Then even that image was swallowed up by the brightness.

The boat rocked. I leaned into the rope and took deep breaths as the magic subsided, pulling back like the tide. The wind died down, and the sea quieted. My eyes fluttered open. There seemed to be more stars than when we began.

I had forgotten what silence sounded like.

"Hanna." The voice drifted in on the wind. It wasn't Asbera's and it wasn't Reynir's. For a moment I thought it was Finnur, but no, the accent was wrong. "Hanna, I'm so glad–"

"We did it!" Asbera's head poked up on the mast. "They're gone. Those awful creatures are gone!" She climbed up on the mast beside me. I straightened up and untangled my arm from the rope. It had seared a red line into my flesh.

"I saw it," I said, feeling dazed. "The Green Glass Sea. Did you–"

"Yes," She pulled me into a hug. "I saw it, too. They're gone. *Gone.*" When she pulled away, her eyes shone with tears. "We'll be able to disembark," she whispered. "We'll be able to save him."

I nodded. Everything felt fuzzy. Distorted. Had I really seen Isolfr's face in the swirl of magic? That didn't make sense. Had he been following the *Annika* after all?

But I didn't have time to think on those questions. Asbera pulled me down the mast. After the brightness of the magic-burst, the darkness was too dark, and we both stumbled through the shadows. I banged my knee against the unlit brazier and gave a sharp cry of pain. It echoed in the silence of the open ocean, a comfort.

No more monster cries.

A faint blue light appeared on the deck, bobbing along through the darkness.

I thought of the Mists, disguised as the costumed men.

Then voices rose up, chattering and relieved. The crew. I slumped against Asbera in relief.

"Did you see that?" Reynir bounded up to us, a magic-cast lantern swinging from one hand. "That light? Oh, and the Green Glass Sea – never thought I'd live to see the Green Glass Sea."

Asbera laughed, although it was too strained, too frenetic, to be mirthful. I smiled. Truthfully, I never thought I'd see the Green Glass Sea, either.

The crew crowded around us, stomping their feet

and cheering. Baltasar slapped Reynir on the back. "You sure they're gone?"

Reynir looked to me. "You can't be sure about anything with magic," I said. "But everything played out the way I saw it."

Baltasar nodded, satisfied. "Well, then. Let's see if we can't make this boat go any faster, eh, boys?"

The crew cheered again, and there was a mad scramble to pick up the ropes and angle the sails to best catch the wind.

Which was still gusting in from the north.

Asbera slipped away from the crowd, moving through the liquid light of the magic-cast lanterns, toward the captain's quarters. I followed her.

Finnur was still frozen in place. Asbera hung the lantern on the hook above the bed, and as the light slid over him, I almost thought he moved.

"How's he doing?" I asked.

"The same." Asbera lifted up my bracelet and laid her hand on his heart. "Part of me thought – well, I thought that when we cast the spell–"

Her voice trailed away. I walked over to her and wrapped my arm around her shoulders. Finnur screamed silently up at the ceiling.

Asbera laid the bracelet back on his chest.

"It's not long now," I told her. "We'll be there by dawn."

"You'll help me, won't you? Take him to the priests?"

"Of course." Even though I didn't know if the priests would be of any help. Kolur knew how to beat back the Mists – but he would have sailed away to the north.

I gave Asbera a hug, squeezing her tight, and listened to the waves crashing up against the sides of the *Annika*. The crew and the winds had us going fast, like we were driving straight into the dawn itself.

Asbera and I stood side by side in our embrace, waiting for the sun.

CHAPTER SIXTEEN

Benedict spotted land just as the sun peeked above the horizon. I was asleep when the call went out, and the clanging of bells wove through my dreams, which were of starlight and the wind. I opened my eyes to find the crew scrambling up on deck.

"Land!" Benedict shouted. "We're home!"

My heart leapt at the word *home*, even though Tulja wasn't home, not really, not for me. But it was home for Finnur. There had to be someone here who could bring him back to life.

I ran up on deck and found the crew preparing to make port, so I grabbed a rope and started tying down the sails. We worked largely in silence, the gray dawn lighting our way. Asbera wasn't on deck, but the captain's quarters glowed with the light from a magic-cast lantern.

"How's Finnur?" I asked Reynir when he joined me at the masts.

"Still alive." Reynir nodded. "I watched over him last night." He hesitated. "Asbera insists there's no change, but I took his pulse and it was weaker than it was yesterday."

I kept winding the rope around my wrist. "At least we're back," I said after a time.

Reynir grunted in response.

The *Annika* sailed through the still, calm waters of the bay, missing one of her crew and nursing another, but not trailing any monsters to land. As the docks appeared in the dim light, I checked over the side of the railing, afraid one of the monsters had found its way back to us. But there were only the dark waters.

"Listen up," Baltasar shouted from the helm as we approached the docks. "Gather round."

We did as he asked. The wind pushed us gently toward the shore.

"I know you're all relieved to be home," Baltasar said, his rough hands gripping the ship's wheel. "But first thing we need to do is to send word to the priests. Finnur's our priority, but you need to tell them about Harald as well. Reynir, I'm putting you in charge of that. Compose the message yourself. Benedict and Seimur, I'm asking you to rent a pair of yaks and take the message in person. You know how the priests can be."

There was a stilted pause at Baltasar's blasphemy. He pulled a couple of stones out of his pocket and tossed them down to Benedict and Seimur. "For the yaks," he said.

They nodded.

"The rest of you can clear the boat. But stay close – head over to the Yak's Horn if you want. Don't know what the priests'll need to get Finnur better. May be sending you out on errands."

The crew muttered their agreement.

The *Annika* slowed as she sailed into the docks proper. I stayed up on deck to help with the wind, standing by the railing so that the crew could scramble up and around the masts. The light peeked over the horizon, illuminating the boats lined up in the bay. There were five of them, more than I expected. Fishing vessels, mostly.

Including one lined with spiky, Jolali-style icons.

I gasped and clutched the railing so that I could lean out over the water. The *Penelope II*. She was still docked at Tulja. They hadn't left after all. Lord Foxfollow's attack must have left them weak.

I whirled around. "Baltasar!" I shouted. "Baltasar, I may be able to help Finnur, faster than the priests."

He had all his concentration focused on bringing us to the docks, like a good captain, and he didn't look at me when he answered. "What are you on about, girl?"

"I know someone who might be able to help. I thought he'd be gone by the time we arrived, but his boat's still here."

"And who's that?" Baltasar adjusted the line of the boat as we moved closer to land. "Your old captain?"

My blood vibrated in my body. Finnur; we'd be able to save Finnur.

"He's a powerful wizard," I said. "It's worth a try, and he can come faster than the priests—"

"Right you are on that. Go fetch him when we get to land. I'm willing to try anything."

I nodded and turned back to the starboard side. The *Penelope II* gleamed in the encroaching dawn as the *Annika* settled into her customary place at the docks.

When the crew were dropping anchor, I raced into the captain's quarters, grinning with the good news about the *Penelope II*.

Asbera sat at Finnur's side, laying damp cloths on his forehead. My grin vanished.

"What's wrong?" I slid into place beside her. Finnur's expression was the same, still that frozen terror, but his skin was pale and tinted blue. Horror crawled over me. "Sea and sky, is he–"

"Not yet." She tucked a cloth around his throat. "His temperature has risen. I'm not a healer, but it feels too hot–"

I immediately laid the back of my hand against his cheek. His skin burned.

"Maybe it's a good thing," I babbled. "Maybe it means he's coming back around."

Asbera shook her head, her hair falling into her eyes. "It took too long," she whispered, and draped another cloth, this time across his chest. "I know you got us here as fast as you could, but the priests will take at least a day–"

"We may not need the priests." I grabbed her hand and squeezed it. She looked over at me, confused. "The *Penelope II* is still here. Kolur might able to help. I know he's familiar with Mists magic."

She didn't say anything, but a light came back into her eyes. A glitter of hope.

"You should open up the windows," I said. "Maybe the cold air will help bring the fever down. The wind's still blowing out of the north."

She nodded. "Thank you," she whispered.

"I won't be long," I said. "I promise."

I raced along the docks, my hair streaming out behind me. A few fishermen stood scattered around their boats, and old Muni with his fish stand was already set up in the usual place. They all stared at me as I ran past, but I didn't care. I was only focused on getting to the *Penelope II*.

Her masts poked up against the horizon, dark against the pink dawn. Her sails were down. I breathed with relief – she wasn't going anywhere yet. But I didn't slow. My feet pounded against the old saltwater-soaked boards, and I sucked in cold salty air until my lungs burned. When I finally came to the *Penelope II*, I stumbled to a stop and I leaned over, trying to catch my breath. Everything was quiet here except for my panting. Even the ocean seemed to have fallen silent.

The gangplank was down, so I climbed aboard. No one was on deck, but I could smell the residue of magic, like burnt salt. A scrap of woven blue fabric had been nailed to the boards beside the ship's wheel. A Kjoran protection charm – I'd grown so used to the Tuljan ones that the sight of it startled me. I wondered how new it was.

"Hello!" I shouted. "Hello, is anyone here?" I walked across the deck, my voice lifting with the wind. "It's Hanna. Please! I have an emergency!"

No answer. I turned slowly in place. The waves sloshed out in the bay. A cold fear gripped at me. Maybe they weren't here at all. Maybe Lord Foxfollow had killed them, or dragged them away to the Mists. Or done worse, somehow.

"Hello!" I screamed again, panic turning my voice ragged. I ran to the hatch and flung it open. The underbelly of the boat was lit with a faint blue glow. A lantern. I scrambled down, taking deep breaths every time my foot touched the rung of a ladder. "Kolur!" I shouted when I made it down. "Frida! Anyone?"

The *Penelope II* was not laid out like the original *Penelope*, and the corridors twisted off in strange narrow angles. It must have been the Jolali style, but the confusing layout just made me frustrated. I could hear the ocean everywhere, but nothing else, no human voices, nothing. "Kolur!" I screamed. My voice echoed like I stood inside a cavern, not a boat. Another side effect of the magic that had been done here.

"Be quiet."

Frida. I recognized her voice.

I whirled around. I couldn't see anything but blue-lit darkness. "I can't see you," I said, lowering my voice. "I need to speak with Kolur."

"He's resting." Frida ducked through a low-hanging doorway. She was dressed in sleeping clothes. "What are you doing here?" She looked at me. "You shouldn't come with us, if that's what you're thinking. It's too dangerous. Stay here until you can find passage home."

Her voice was sharp-edged and it made me shiver. *Too dangerous*. At least they were being honest now.

"It's not that." I shook my head. "I need Kolur's help. The magic he did a few nights ago, when Lord Foxfollow attacked – it hurt one of my friends."

Frida froze. "How do you know that name?" she hissed. "Lord Foxfollow."

"I know everything that's been happening." I jerked away from her. "Plus, I *talked* to him. He showed me what Kolur did, sending the monsters into the open sea. He sent them straight to the *Annika*."

Frida's hand went to her mouth. "No," she said softly. "No, we didn't mean–"

"I know you didn't." I slumped down. "But one of those monsters bit my friend and put him into a magic-sleep and I have to know if Kolur can help him. Please? They sent for the village priests, but it's almost a day's journey for them to leave their cave and I don't think Finnur – that's my friend – I don't think he has enough time. So will you please let me talk to Kolur?"

The words spilled out in a tumble, and when I finished, I had to steady myself against the wall and catch my breath. Frida looked away from me, her hand still covering her mouth.

"What?" I asked breathlessly. "What's wrong?"

The lanterns threw liquid light across us both. I wanted to scream. Finnur was dying, and Frida wouldn't help me.

"Kolur can't go to your friend," she said softly.

"What? Why not?"

"Magic-sickness." Frida looked back at me. "Parts of him changed – he can't leave the ocean, not for the time being. Pjetur and I wove a spell to reverse the effects, but it will be at least a week's time before he's able to breathe air again."

The world fell away. I heard a rushing in my ears like the air was pouring out of my body. I hadn't seen *that* in the vision Lord Foxfollow gave me. Only the magic.

I pressed up against the wall, my whole body shaking, Sea and sky, we were lucky the magic-sickness hadn't infected us on board the *Annika*.

"I'm so sorry," Frida said. "I am."

"You can heal him," I said. "You're powerful, I've seen it–"

She stared at me sadly. "I've never had the ability to heal," she said. "I wouldn't feel comfortable, not against Mist magic. I'd likely cause more harm than good."

Panic hammered through my thoughts. "What if we put Finnur in the ocean?" My voice echoed around the strange corridors of the *Penelope II*. "We could put him in a rowboat and Kolur could look at him that way–"

Frida shook her head.

"Why not?" My voice trembled. I didn't want to cry in front of her, but I was afraid I was going to anyway. "Please, I swore to his wife–"

"He's too weak to work magic," Frida said. "Yes, he could look at your friend, but he couldn't do anything about it. Not in his current state. It would destroy him, turn him into saltwater."

I couldn't hold back my tears any longer. I stalked away from Frida and ran through the corridors, choking back my sobs even as tears streaked down my face.

"Hanna!" she called out, but I ignored her. I stumbled through the murky shadows until I came to the square of sunlight illuminating the ladder leading back up on deck. Finnur was going to die. Kolur couldn't help him, and the priests would never get there in time.

The burden of my responsibility hung like a weight around my neck.

I climbed back onto the deck of the *Penelope II*. The sun had risen completely, lemony and bright like the summer sun back home. I felt like it was mocking me.

"Hanna, don't go yet."

I stopped. I almost recognized the voice. It was more human than I remembered.

Isolfr dropped down from the masts, landing softly on his feet like a cat. The sunlight refracted through my tears, and in that liquid haze, he shone the way he had when I first saw him.

"I was just leaving," I said, trying to hold my head high. I turned away from him.

"Wait."

There was an urgency in his voice that I didn't expect. I stopped, staring off at the dock in the distance. The wind blew my hair into my eyes. I was blinded.

"My friend's going to die," I said. "I can't stay."

"What?" Isolfr walked over to stand beside me. I thought he was going to put his hand on my shoulder, but he didn't. "Why? What happened?"

"Don't you know?" I snapped. "Don't you know everything?"

Isolfr looked down at his feet. His cheeks reddened. "Not in this body." He lifted his eyes, peering at me through his lashes. "But I heard you yelling, and so I know that it must be serious."

I hesitated. The wind blew harder, gusting in from the west. I thought I smelled summer on it, the fresh scent of berries and wildflowers.

And then I told Isolfr everything. I was desperate.

He stared at me as I spoke, not once looking away. His eyes were the same color as ice. They were the only part of him that didn't seem human.

"I can help," he said. "Take me to him. But we have to move quickly."

I stared at Isolfr, taking in those blandly handsome features, those unsettling eyes. It made sense, in a way. Isolfr was not human, and Finnur had been struck down by inhuman magic.

"You don't trust me," Isolfr said.

"Why should I?" I snapped. "I won't put my friend in any more danger–"

"I want to help him!" Isolfr shouted. "I want to help you."

I'd never heard him raise his voice before, and I took a step back, shocked.

Isolfr seemed to shrink down inside himself, back to the soft Isolfr I knew from our time at sea. "I'm not from the Mists," he said.

"You've certainly told me that enough times," I snapped. "Not that you'll say where you *are* from–"

"I'm from this world," Isolfr said. "From the north."

"Jandanvar?"

He hesitated, and that was how I knew. Somehow, he came from Jandanvar.

"I know what to do to help your friend," he said.

The wind gusted again.

I nodded.

"Show me the way." He ran toward the gangplank. I followed, too scared to let myself get hopeful.

"We kept him on board the *Annika*," I said. "It's moored at the usual place – the seventh dock."

"All right, yes. I know where that is."

We ran. I focused on the line of Isolfr's back ahead of me. Then the *Annika* rose up against the docks. With the masts empty, she looked haunted.

Zakaria and Reynir were standing guard next to the ladder. They looked up at us as Isolfr and I skittered to a stop.

"Who the hell is this?" Reynir asked, jabbing his thumb at Isolfr. "Baltasar said you were going to get your old captain."

"He couldn't come. This is – Pjetur. He can help."

Reynir narrowed his eyes at me.

"We don't have time for this! Move!" I shoved Reynir aside, and he let out a surprised cry of protest that made Zakaria laugh. But neither of them tried to stop me.

I let Isolfr climb up the ladder first. *Please don't betray us*, I thought. *Please please please*.

The deck was empty except for Baltasar. He sat over

by the ship's wheel, smoking a pipe and staring off into the distance. He glanced at us when we scrambled on board.

"This is Pjetur," I said before he could ask any questions. "He's not my captain, but I know he can help." *I hope he can help.*

"Where is he?" Isolfr stopped in the center of the boat and sniffed at the air. "He's far gone. I need to see him *now*."

"Captain's quarters." Baltasar blew out a ring of smoke. "Sure hope you can help him, boy."

Isolfr nodded. The way the sun shone on him, he didn't look human at all but like some manifestation of the spirit world, a creature of light and magic.

A creature of wind.

I went very still, thinking of the north wind, the whistling, whispering voice, the way it had cradled me down from the stars–

No. It couldn't be.

Isolfr disappeared into the captain's quarters. Baltasar studied me through the haze of his pipe smoke.

"What is he?" Baltasar asked.

I decided not to lie. "I don't know."

Baltasar turned back to the sea. "You better get in there. He might need your help."

My entire body felt shaky and indistinct, and the world didn't seem real. But I nodded and walked over to the captain's quarters with careful, quick steps. Cold, brittle magic was already seeping out through the walls. It wasn't human magic. But it didn't belong to the Mists, either.

The door swung open when my hand passed by it.

The scene inside the room was a quiet one, not the wild display of enchantment that I'd half expected. Asbera stood pressed up against the far corner, her arms wrapped around her torso. Finnur's shirt was peeled away from his chest, which gleamed pale and weak in the lantern light. I slid over beside Asbera.

"It's that boy," she said, her voice flat. "The one at the mead hall. I don't remember his name."

"He didn't give you a real one." I hesitated. Isolfr was tracing patterns on Finnur's chest with his fingers, runes that I didn't recognize. They glowed in the darkness. "His real name is Isolfr."

"He's not human."

"No, I don't think so."

But Asbera didn't seem to be talking to me, not really. "He's kjirini."

"What?"

Asbera blinked. Isolfr ignored both of us, all his concentration focused on painting those runes on Finnur's body, working with light and magic.

"It's a Jandanvari word." She looked at me. "I don't know how to translate it, not exactly. Sometimes they use it to mean wind, but a particular kind that sweeps in from the north."

I went very still.

"It also means magic," Asbera said. "But a certain ki–"

And then Isolfr began to sing.

Asbera cried out and grabbed my arm. She never finished what she was going to say.

Isolfr's voice was not a human one, and he did not sing a human song. The notes were low and whistling and mournful, *somehow just like the wind,* and it filled up the room with a presence strange and eerie and – familiar.

A word that means wind.

The north wind.

And so, I finally understood completely: Isolfr was the presence in the north wind; the presence in the north wind was Isolfr.

I didn't know how and I didn't know why, but I *knew.*

Magic materialized on the air and dotted across my arm like snow. Asbera pressed closer to me. I wrapped my arm around her. We pressed close together.

Isolfr's voice grew louder. The music seeped into me and drew out my emotions: loneliness and fear. Homesickness. A yearning for something beyond home, for something larger than just me. Tears streaked down my cheeks. When I looked at Asbera, she was weeping, too.

Across the room, Isolfr flickered. In one second he was Pjetur, a dull and handsome human boy, and in another he was Isolfr, shining like the moon, sharp-eyed, elven, too delicate to be real. He shifted back and forth between the two. The song grew louder and louder.

And then Isolfr's hand slid into the skin of Finnur's chest.

Asbera shrieked and moved to lunge forward, but I caught her and held her tight. This was not evil sorcery. I could sense it deep inside me, a hard echo inside my bones. It was the magic of the north wind, the magic that brought me home from the in-between world, the magic that drove the Mists away outside the mead hall. He was helping.

Isolfr's hand disappeared completely.

He shut his eyes and flickered once, and then remained Isolfr, his skin glowing with foreign light. The song shifted, abruptly, into something faster and more howling. It didn't even sound like music anymore, just the shriek of wind in a storm. The enchantment in the room thickened. The walls rippled like sails. I squeezed Asbera tighter.

He was using wind-magic, but not any that I'd ever seen.

And then, with a gasp and a cry, Finnur sat up.

Asbera screamed and tried to lunge forward again, but I stopped her. I didn't want her interfering with Isolfr's spell – his hand was still tucked inside Finnur's chest, and the magic still vibrated around us.

Finnur's twisted expression hadn't changed, and even though he sat up now, he was as still and waxy as before. The light in Isolfr's skin pulsed. His song fell away, and the silence was like the silence in the eye of a hurricane. He stared at Finnur straight on.

Asbera whimpered.

Isolfr took a deep breath. He seemed to suck in all the air in the room. The lanterns flickered. The walls flapped and snapped, no longer wood but fabric. Asbera grabbed my arm so hard that her nails dug into my skin. But I didn't move. I could only watch Isolfr, transfixed by this strange wind magic.

With his free hand, Isolfr opened Finnur's mouth.
And kissed him.

But it wasn't just a kiss; I could hear the air passing between them, a roaring rush like being caught in a wind tunnel. The air in the room grew thin and weak. It was hard for me to breathe.

Isolfr snapped his head back and yanked his hand, completely unbloodied, out of Finnur's chest.

There was a long, terrible pause. Asbera sobbed.

And then Finnur blinked.

"Finnur!" Asbera ripped away from me. I didn't stop her this time. Finnur looked over at her, dazed. Then he smiled. It was a smile to light up the darkness.

Asbera threw her arms around him. "I thought you were going to die," she said, sobbing into his hair. "I thought I'd lost you forever."

"I thought of you," he whispered. "While I was trapped. Sometimes I saw your face–"

Asbera kissed him.

Isolfr was lying on the floor of the cabin, stretched out, pale. He looked like Pjetur. I knelt beside him. He dropped his head to the side and blinked up at me.

"Is he alive?" he asked.

I nodded. "And awake."

Isolfr smiled and turned his gaze back to the ceiling. "That was more difficult than I expected. The poisons had gone in deep."

I hesitated. Asbera was still weeping behind me, but I could hear the happiness in her tears. I felt that happiness myself. Finnur was alive.

Isolfr had saved him.

"We should give them some time alone," I said.

Isolfr nodded, though he didn't move. I stood up and held out my hand. When he took it, his skin was cold to the touch. I pulled him to his feet. He was lighter than I expected. There was something intangible about him. Like air, magic, wind.

He didn't let go of my hand once he was standing, and he leaned up against me for balance. I could feel him shaking.

Asbera and Finnur ignored us both; they were too wrapped up in each other to care that we were still in the cabin. So I just led Isolfr out onto the deck. The captain's quarters looked the way it always had, out here. Baltasar was gone. I wondered if the spell from the cabin had frightened him.

"Will they be safe?" I asked. "With the magic-sickness?"

Isolfr nodded. He stumbled over to the side of the boat and slumped down, his back pressed up against the railing. He took a deep breath. "It's not true magic-sickness. It'll fade in time."

"Not true magic-sickness?" I frowned. The air was warm and unmoving, like summers in Kjora. I sat down beside Isolfr. "If you don't mind me asking – what kind of magic *was* that anyway? It felt like it belonged to the wind–"

"It did." Isolfr looked at me, his eyes clear and pale and icy. "But not the sort you can do. The sort I can do."

I stared at him for a long time, trying to work things through in my head.

"Your sort can stop the Mists."

He nodded.

"It comes from the north wind, doesn't it?"

He sat very still. I didn't think he was going to answer. But then he nodded again.

"So it was you," I said. "The night the Mists attacked in the form of the Nalendan. You saved me."

"No." Isolfr gave a weak laugh. "No, I *helped* you. You were holding your own quite well, but human magic–" He shrugged. "You have a talent."

I shrugged, but I looked away from him, my cheeks burning.

"Thank you," I said, speaking to the air. The ocean glittered around us. "Thank you for everything." *Everything* was such a simple, meaningless word, but I didn't know how else to say it.

He seemed to understand.

"It was my pleasure," Isolfr said.

Two days later, we held a funeral for Harald. I thought it would be at sea, because he died in the water, but Tuljans honor their dead with fire and smoke.

There was a procession from the *Annika*, the whole crew draped in garlands made of dried flowers and summer moss. Harald's family was there, too. They were yak herders, land people. His younger brother was only ten or so, and he ran to the edge of the docks and stared out over the sparkling water.

"The first time he's ever seen the ocean, probably," Asbera said softly. "It's rare for us to come so close to the edge of the land."

Because Harald's body had been lost to the Mists, his friends carved an effigy of him instead. They scraped his features into a post of soft pine and painted in his skin and eyes and hair. The effigy was laid down on a cloth of woven yak fur and scattered with the same white flowers the Tuljans tossed at the Nalendan. Protection, Asbera explained. To draw his soul out of the underworld of the Mists.

Finnur was quiet in that time before the procession started. He hung back, sipping a cup of mulled wine to stay warm. Asbera and I helped in the preparations, me following Asbera's directions for how to drape the garlands and how to scatter the flowers. But Finnur just watched us.

"He's been like that since he woke up," Asbera said. We were lighting the candles for the procession, one after another, with natural fire and not a bit of enchantment. "He saw things, you know, while he was under." Her voice hitched. "He was in a prison, he said, wrapped up in cold gray mist. He couldn't move, but they showed him things, showed him terrible things happening to me, to our children – we don't even *have* children." Her hands were shaking. Gently, I took the lighting candle away from her.

"He's back now," I said. "I'm sure it'll take some time, but he'll get better."

Asbera looked up at me.

"He's got you," I said. "He'll be fine."

She smiled, wavering and thin. But then she asked, "Why did this happen to us?"

I paused for a moment, thinking. Then I set the candles aside and hugged her. "Bad luck," I whispered. "But Kolur will be gone soon. He'll take the Mists' interest away with him."

Asbera wiped at her eyes. "I hope so."

I hoped so, too. But at the same time, the thought of Kolur leaving almost made me sad.

The procession started. Musicians led the way, playing the clanging, droning song I associated with the costumed men, although no one wore costumes. Harald's effigy followed, carried on its pallet by three of the crewmen and Baltasar. Then his family. Then the rest of us. We carried our candles close to our chests and stayed silent as the music led the way, winding us through the village. People stepped out of their shops and threw white flowers as if we were the Nalendan. They watched us with solemn faces.

Eventually, we came to the open fields. Here, villagers stood outside their tents, all of them holding their own candles. By now, it was almost dusk and the candles glowed like stars in the purple twilight. I had never seen anything like it, all those licks of flame gathering toward us as we moved deeper into the fields.

Our procession grew as we twisted through the tents. The music never stopped, but it still wasn't enough to cover up the occasional bursts of throaty sobs.

We walked, and walked, and walked, until we came to a clearing paved over with smooth flat stones that were blackened and charred.

The music stopped.

For a long time, nothing happened. We stood in a ring around the stones, me and Asbera and Finnur all side by side. The only sounds were the wind through the grass and the muffled hush of weeping.

Then Baltasar and the crewmen set Harald's effigy on the stones. They stepped back, and Harald's mother took their place. Her whole body trembled as she knelt beside the effigy and anointed it with oil. She had covered her face with a scrap of tattered old lace, and in the flickering candlelight, she looked like a ghost.

She was the first to touch her candle to the effigy. The flame caught and trembled, and she blew out her candle and then stumbled back, into her husband's arms. Baltasar went next, and then Harald's father and brother. Then the rest of us. One at a time, villagers touched their candles to the effigy, even as it was already consumed by flames. By the time it was my turn, I could only see the fire. But Asbera whispered in my ear, "Just hold your candle to it," and I did, grazing its tiny flame against the fire's huge one.

I felt something, a tremor of magic inside me. The release of a small part of Harald's soul, from the Mists back to our world.

I stepped back into the cold night air, my face stinging with the fire's heat. I blew out my candle. That was a sort of magic, wasn't it? That transfer of a small light into a large one.

We watched the fire burn. It rose higher against the starry sky, letting off flares of sparks and a great tail of dark smoke that, to my surprise, smelled sweet, like incense. Finnur stared into the fire, the light staining his skin orange. His eyes seemed to glow. Looking at him gave me a hollow feeling, but then he reached over and took Asbera by the hand.

I knew, looking at them, that it was enough.

That night, the *Crocus* was hung with dozens of tiny floating lanterns, the deck covered in dried sea lavender. Seimur played Tuljan songs on a carved guitar while Benedict sang along, both of them perched on the empty helm so their voices carried across the deck. All of the moored boats were lit up that night. A funeral in the evening and a celebration at night. It was the Tuljan way, Asbera told me.

I sat in one of the chairs that we'd dragged up from down below and sipped a glass of honeyed mead, watching as Asbera and Finnur spun each other around in an elaborate Tuljan dance. All of the *Annika* crew was there, and most of the folk from the docks and the people who lived in their tents out on the tundra. Almost all of them were clapping and stomping time to the music as Asbera and Finnur danced. It was reassuring to watch: Finnur's skin was full of color, and he moved with a liquid grace that didn't suit someone who had, two days ago, been trapped in an eternal sleep.

Finnur tossed Asbera up in the air and caught her at the waist. Everyone erupted into cheers, and Asbera laughed and covered Finnur with kisses. The music jangled on.

Cold whispered against the back of my neck, just for a moment, and then it was gone. I glanced up and saw Frida crawling up the ladder, her hair twisted into a dark, knotted braid.

Isolfr was with her.

No one else had seen them yet. I stood, mead sloshing over the side of my cup. Frida lifted her hand in greeting. Another cheer went up and rippled into the night.

"You still haven't left," I said when Frida and Isolfr walked over to join me.

"No," Frida said. Isolfr didn't look at me, only watched the dancing, the lights shining in his eyes. "Kolur hasn't recovered." She smiled. "He can at least come out of the water for a bit at a time now. So it should be soon."

Isolfr looked over at her when she said *soon*, and then over at me. His expression was grave. "Yes," he said. "Soon."

"Don't look so sad," I told him. "You're at a party."

"I'm not sad." He smiled. "But I don't go to many parties."

Frida shifted her weight. "I'd like something to drink."

"Talk to old Muni there." I pointed up at the bow of the ship, where Muni was perched with a great towering barrel. "He's got the mead."

Frida thanked me and slipped off into the crush of people. Finnur and Asbera were still dancing, both of them spinning wildly in tandem, although now their crowd of onlookers was dancing, too. For a moment, Isolfr and I watched them in silence.

"Finnur and Asbera haven't noticed you're here yet," I said.

"I haven't let them."

I looked over at him. He looked like Pjetur, more or less, but the light of the lanterns seemed to strip his disguise away, revealing the imprint of his real features.

"Why not?" I said.

"I don't want to steal the attention away from them." Isolfr nodded. "It's their party."

I wasn't certain if I believed him, but I decided to accept his answer. After a pause, I walked back over to my chair and sat down. Isolfr followed and crouched down beside me, one hand on the armrest.

"Why aren't you dancing?" he asked.

"I don't know any of these songs." I took a drink of my mead. It had cooled in the chilly night air. "And I don't know any Tuljan dances."

"So if you were on Kjora, you'd be dancing?"

I smiled a little. "I guess."

Isolfr was looking hard at me. He squeezed the armrest. "How much longer until you're able to go home?"

Silence. The music played on, Seimur's singing growing louder and more riotous. In the flash of dancers, I spotted Frida spinning around with Reynir. She held her drink high over her head, and her mouth was open in a continuous laugh.

"What did you tell her and Kolur?" I said. "About being able to heal Finnur?"

He stared off into the darkness beyond the boat.

"Isolfr!"

He sighed. "I made them forget." He looked down at the floor. "I–I actually made all of them forget. Asbera and Finnur and everyone else in the village."

"You what?" I sat up, knocking my drink over. It spilled across the floorboards in a gleaming amber strip. "Why? Why would you do that?"

"It's easier." He kept looking down. "They think the priests healed Finnur. What does it matter?"

"You didn't make me forget."

"No." He looked up and his face was nothing like Pjetur's. I was transfixed by it, caught in a spell. I couldn't look away.

"Stop that," I said.

"Stop what?"

"Holding me in place like that. Whenever I see the real you–"

"I can't help it," he sighed. "I'm sorry. I didn't take your memory away because – because I need you, Hanna."

I closed my eyes. The music flowed around us, and so did some vague, unfamiliar magic. His magic. I wondered if he'd made us invisible to the party. If we were shades now, or spirits. Ghosts.

"Not this again," I said.

He put his hand on my arm, and I was shocked at how cold it was. Like ice water. I looked over at him.

"I'm not here because I want Kolur to win back the Jandanvari queen," Isolfr said. "I'm here because we can't let the Mists through to our world–"

"This isn't your world." I snatched my arm away from him.

"Yes, it is."

The party twinkled on without us.

"You aren't human," I said softly. "That's all I meant–"

"I'm not human, but this is still my world. My home. And I won't see it destroyed by Lord Foxfollow." Isolfr stared at me. "That's what he wants, you know. The queen of Jandanvar will bring him here, and then he can hurt everyone the way he hurt Finnur."

I trembled, remembering the horrors of the prison where Foxfollow held Finnur. I thought of Asbera weeping at Finnur's side as he screamed in silent anguish.

I thought of that happening to everyone, north and south, east and west.

"You know that I'm right."

"Why me?" I was shaking – I was cold, despite the heat globes drifting around the party. But I knew I wasn't at the party anymore. I wrapped my arms around myself, trying to keep warm. "What do you need me for? I'm no one special–"

"You have ties to the south wind," Isolfr said. "And you have a talent for magic. You're exactly who I need."

"But I'm not even a proper witch. Just a fisherman's apprentice." I glared at him. "And you wanted *Frida* in the first place–"

"And I was too much of a coward to work with her, yes. Is that what you want to hear? That every time I look at her, I remember what she did to my brother?" Isolfr's eyes shimmered, and for a moment, I was afraid he was going to cry. "I am a coward. That's why I need you. Because you're brave."

I stared at him. "I don't think you're a coward," I said.

"He's tried to do it before, you know."

"What?"

"Lord Foxfollow. He's tried to come into our world before. And he was stopped. Twice." Isolfr straightened his shoulders. His Pjetur disguise was melting away. "You're named after one of the people who stopped him."

I realized then that I couldn't hear the music anymore. The party had receded into the darkness. Isolfr and I sat on an island of shadow, and the *Crocus* and all my friends were a dot of light far in the distance. But I didn't care.

"What are you saying?" I said.

"Your mother served aboard the *Nadir*, didn't she? Surely she told you the story about how Ananna stopped the Mists from crossing over into our world."

"Yeah, I've heard the stories." I felt very cold. "Are you saying *that* was Lord Foxfollow? The lord she defeated?"

Isolfr nodded.

"So you want me to help you because Ananna and I have the same *name*?"

Isolfr scowled. "No. I want you to help me because you're talented and brave. I already told you that."

"Fine. But I'm not Ananna. She was a pirate queen when all that happened."

Isolfr leaned close in close. He smelled of honey and ice-flowers. "How well do you know the stories?"

"I know them fine."

"Then you should know she wasn't a pirate queen when she defeated Lord Foxfollow. She was your age." Isolfr leaned back.

I stared at him. "What? Are you sure about that?"

"Of course. The problem is that story usually gets entangled with her later adventures. But she was your age when she sent Lord Foxfollow back to the Mists. Now it's your turn to do the same."

I looked away from him. All around was a thick inky blackness, darker than night, and the faint glow of the party.

"All I want," I said, staring at that glow, "is to go home."

Isolfr grabbed my hand. This time, I let him. His sharp inhuman features gleamed like a star.

"I swear to you," he said, in a voice like ice and snowfall, "that I'll see you safely returned to your family. All I ask is that you sail to the north and stop Lord Foxfollow from permanently entering our world."

For a moment, I was struck dumb. Isolfr squeezed my hand tighter.

"Make sail with us," he said, and this time his voice was normal, musical, the voice I knew. "Make sail with us and join your magic with mine. It's the only way."

The only way. I looked at the party again, shrunken and bathed in light. It seemed like a wizard's trick, a toy to enchant children. I thought about the jar of stones sitting aboard the *Cornflower*. Half empty. Nowhere close to enough to buy a ship and a crew.

I thought about the chill of speaking with Lord Foxfollow in the in-between world. I thought of the torment he had visited upon Finnur.

I'd never thought of myself as brave.

I looked at Isolfr. My heartbeat rushed in my ears.

"You can't guarantee my safety," I said. "But I'll go with you anyway."

ACKNOWLEDGMENTS

As always, I would like to thank my parents and Ross Andrews for their love and support. Special thanks goes out to all my friends-who-write: Amanda Cole, Bobby Mathews, Alexandre Maki, Laura Lam, and the members of the Northwest Houston SFF Writer's Group. Writing is such a solitary activity that it's a joy to find others willing to discuss the highs and lows in intricate detail.

Furthermore, I would like to thank my agent, Stacia Decker, for reading *The Wizard's Promise* and offering excellent suggestions for improvement, as well as for her constant hard work regarding my books and my career. Thank you to my editor Amanda Rutter for agreeing to take a chance on another set of stories set in this little fantasy world I made up all those years ago. And thank you to the rest of the Angry Robot staff – Mike Underwood, Lee Harris, Marc Gascoigne, and Caroline Lambe – for the wonderful support they give their authors. And I would be remiss if I did not mention the hardworking Angry Robot interns who have been wonderful about helping with marketing connections: Leah, Vicky, and Jamie.

Finally, I would like to thank the readers, reviewers, and bloggers who helped make *The Assassin's Curse* series such a success. Thank you all!

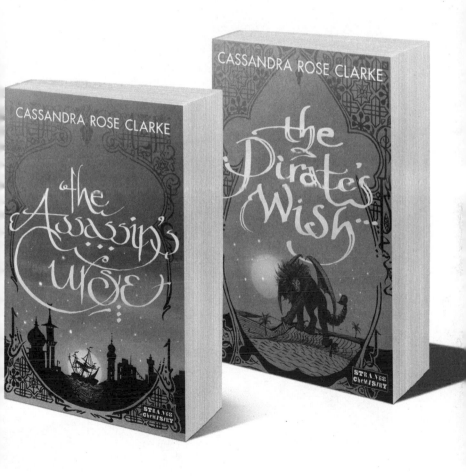

EXPERIMENTING WITH YOUR IMAGINATION

There are so many ways to cage someone...

EXPERIMENTING WITH YOUR IMAGINATION

"Utterly imaginative, Zenn Scarlett is a story
that will have you desperate for answers until
the very end."
Melissa West, author of Gravity

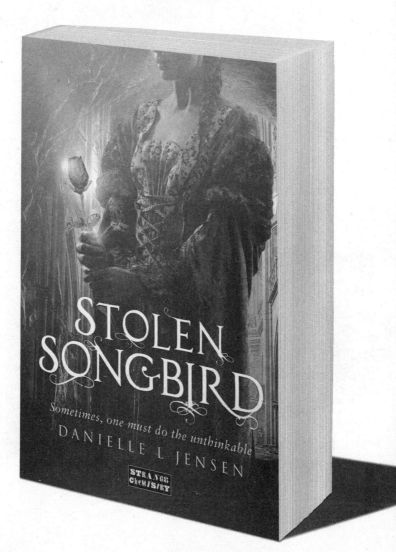